The Ghost Ships of Arizona

(Matt Drake #11)

By

David Leadbeater

Copyright 2015 by David Leadbeater

All rights reserved. No part of this publication may be reproduced, distributed, or transmitted in any form or by any means, including photocopying, recording, or other electronic or mechanical methods, without the prior written permission of the publisher/author except in the case of brief quotations embodied in critical reviews and certain other non-commercial uses permitted by copyright law.
All characters in this book are fictitious, and any resemblance to actual persons living or dead is purely coincidental.

This ebook is for your personal enjoyment only. This ebook may not be re-sold or given away to other people. If you would like to share this ebook with another person, please purchase any additional copy for each reader. If you're reading this book and did not purchase it, or it was not purchased for your use only, then please return it and purchase your own copy. Thank you for respecting the hard work of this author.

Thriller, adventure, action, mystery, suspense, archaeological, military, historical

Other Books by David Leadbeater:

The Matt Drake Series
The Bones of Odin (Matt Drake #1)
The Blood King Conspiracy (Matt Drake #2)
The Gates of hell (Matt Drake 3)
The Tomb of the Gods (Matt Drake #4)
Brothers in Arms (Matt Drake #5)
The Swords of Babylon (Matt Drake #6)
Blood Vengeance (Matt Drake #7)
Last Man Standing (Matt Drake #8)
The Plagues of Pandora (Matt Drake #9)
The Lost Kingdom (Matt Drake #10)

The Alicia Myles Series
Aztec Gold (Alicia Myles #1)
Crusader's Gold (Alicia Myles #2)

The Disavowed Series:
The Razor's Edge (Disavowed #1)
In Harm's Way (Disavowed #2)
Threat Level: Red (Disavowed #3)

The Chosen Few Series
Chosen (The Chosen Trilogy #1)
Guardians (The Chosen Tribology #2)

Short Stories
Walking with Ghosts (A short story)
A Whispering of Ghosts (A short story)

Connect with the author on Twitter: @dleadbeater2011
Visit the author's website: **www.davidleadbeater.com**

All helpful, genuine comments are welcome.
I would love to hear from you.
davidleadbeater2011@hotmail.co.uk

Dedication

This book is for everyone who adheres to Alicia's one true creed:

'One Life, Live It.'

PROLOGUE

California, 1587:

Mukat watched the strange procession uneasily, not entirely sure what he was seeing. The bizarre warlike men with their shiny helmets and jangling clothes had dispatched a small canoe from their outlandish wooden ship. Mukat had never seen a ship before, his tribe were isolated out here in the dunes, but he had heard stories from the elders who'd visited something they called *missions* before other tribes destroyed them. On first setting eyes upon this ship the Cahuilla elders had been reservedly pleased, but upon seeing vast arrays of guns and grim-faced soldiers, they had quickly changed their minds. Stories were told of the Spanish and what they had done to tribes when they first came to these lands—before attempting to establish their missions.

A decision was made.

Kill the invaders.

The ship itself, anchored in the bay, would provide a valuable cargo, they were sure. Mukat watched the scouting party rowing ashore and wondered why the invaders couldn't see the Indian canoes arrayed in their hundreds among the shallows. Was it vanity? Inexperience with the area? Was it that the Cahuilla were so wonderfully skilled? The darkening skies certainly helped. The bustle aboard the ship of war was another, more telling factor—men rushing about their jobs. Mukat wondered why they would go to such lengths. His tribe had survived, lived, loved and died happily within a small area for many, many years. They had little contact with the outside world, and fought only to protect their meagre lands. And yet, sand-covered and sparse and valueless as they were, outsiders constantly sought to visit. What did they hope to find?

Mukat readied himself as the invaders landed. He was aboard a canoe, charged with attacking the large ship whilst a smaller contingent of his brothers dealt with the scouts. Once the fighting and the shouting started they would begin, but he was hoping for more cover, more darkness to fall.

The Indians waited until the last possible moment, allowing the scouting party to disembark, then haul up their canoes and make ready. Mukat now ordered his warriors to begin rowing. Hundreds of small vessels shot out of the shallows, cloaked by the plunging night. By the time the first cry rang out they were over halfway to their goal. By the time the men on the boat gathered and acknowledged the threat they were almost aboard.

Mukat and his warriors gripped their knives between their teeth, affixed their bows to their backs and climbed the long thick ropes toward the deck of the ship. Luckily, the sailors were careless and had flung out more fixing points than just the anchor—they were clearly intending to stay here for some time, a fact already ascertained by such a huge warship carefully navigated so close to the shallows.

Perhaps they were merely repairing a broken mast. Resting after a battle at sea. Exploring for their leader, sat at rest far away in his gloried halls. Perhaps they were only curious. It did not matter. They were a threat, and whatever their original intentions were, once they set eyes on new lands and new peoples they would become more than curious. Mukat had seen it happen before.

They would become greedy.

He reached the deck of the ship first, landing with callused bare feet atop the slick planking. In a moment he adjusted. The tribesmen were no strangers to water—though they generally lived inland, Lake Cahuilla was nearby, enormous and of frequent use. Mukat saw an armed soldier headed his way, the man waving an arquebus—a handheld gun—as if it were a flag.

Mukat used bow and arrow, firing a volley far faster than any of their enemies could comprehend. His closest warriors preferred different weapons, using lances and spears, war clubs and tomahawks. They fell among the invaders too, screaming their war cries, righteously fighting for their lands. A shot smashed into the deck beside Mukat's foot, sending splinters into his flesh. He looked up, saw a sailor perched above and then climbed to his side, as agile as a squirrel. The man beat at him with the partly wooden weapon, face registering both shock and fear. Mukat withdrew a short knife and cleaved his enemy's ribs, throwing him down amidst his brethren. Standing for a moment, he surveyed the tableau, measuring the flow of battle.

Warriors swarmed up from the bobbing canoes and onto the decks. Already the wood was greasy with blood, its shine dulled by the ever-darkening skies. His brethren had no armor, but ran hard at the sailors as they fired their weapons. Many survived, screaming, falling among the attackers. Some did not, falling and writhing as they died. A knot of battle formed along the deck. Hatchets rose and fell. Clubs swung hard. Guns fired their deadly cargo. Mukat again took up his bow and fired arrow after arrow into the enemy ranks until his quiver was depleted. Other braves joined him and did the same. Another phalanx of steel-helmeted men surged around the other side of the deck. Mukat and his bowmen jumped down onto them, using knives and short-spears. Men fell, rolling and slipping. Mukat grappled an invader, tore off his helmet, and buried his tomahawk deep into his skull. The man went instantly limp. Mukat wrenched the tomahawk free, still on his knees, and swiped at the thighs of another. When the man partly collapsed, Mukat severed his hamstrings and then part of his neck.

Another surge of soldiers sent men staggering by, their loud weapons sometimes falling nearby as they passed. Mukat ignored them, fearing what he did not know, shunning the guns. The bulk of his world consisted of worries over constant subsistence, sand storms, visions visited upon the medicine man, the appearance of strangers, legends of Coyote the Trickster God, Temayawet, ruler of the land of the dead, and the temptations of Menilly, the Goddess of the Moon. It did not cover weapons beyond those he could make himself.

Mukat rose once more, his feet painful and seeping blood. Many of his brothers were injured, all of whom he recognized with fondness. A knot of fighting moved to his right, the sailors now using deadly looking blades too. Wrestlers fell overboard to continue their struggle in the waters below. Mukat visited his tomahawk and knife upon a ragged rank of the enemy, flashing the blades across stomachs and throats and faces until they were overcome.

The sailors fought hard against the aggressors, their actions and features attesting that they too were hardened men who had seen battle before. The Cahuilla were more suited to hand-to-hand combat aboard the deck, however, and they soon began to gain the upper hand. The sailors fell and some even tried to surrender, but the Cahuilla would leave none alive.

A captain then appeared above decks, shouting and gesturing and parading in some ridiculous finery until a brave stopped his unintelligible words with a well-placed arrow to the throat. The man's body collapsed over the upper deck and fell among his battling men, sending them sprawling. The Cahuilla fell upon the injured, sensing victory and reward. The ship would be theirs.

Mukat parried a sword strike, then took a hard blow to the face. His opponent was a weathered individual, dirty of face and with clumped hair, a food-heavy beard weighing down the bottom part of his head. An oddly shaped nose and caved-in cheekbone verified this man was a fighter. Mukat needed to end it quickly. It wouldn't do to win through such a hard battle and then die at the end.

A fist smashed down onto his shoulder, staggering him and making him lose his grip on the tomahawk. The ragged sword raised, lit only by the ship's lanterns. Mukat scrambled underneath the swing of the weapon and then rose up, spear in hand, thrusting its point through the man's underbelly as far as it would go. With a shudder the figure fell.

Mukat crawled through the folding legs and out the other side, to be faced with yet another foe. Weary, he raised a hand, grabbed a wrist and flung the attacker to the side. His half-naked body was cut and bruised and bloody, but he was a warrior and would never surrender so long as breath occupied his body. A sailor fell at his side, reached out for his neck and tried to throttle him. Mukat broke the wrist and jumped up. To his left and right men surged in tiny clusters, grappling, stabbing and bludgeoning. The ship rocked slightly in the small swell. On the beach the victors stood watching, their hatchets and war clubs held high. Scalps were being waved. More canoes were being readied.

Mukat ran from enemy to enemy, stabbing and breaking bones, helping his warriors where he could. The sailors backed away, suddenly rallied by one noisy individual and forming lines, one behind the other. What they had left of their guns were raised and aimed. Someone shouted and the first rank opened fire. Balls of shot screamed out of muzzles. One of the weapons exploded, killing its owner and the man at his side. Warriors fell, some dead and some wounded, their blood painting the deck.

Mukat leapt for the newly opened gap, squirreling his way among the ranks, slashing and hacking. The second rank opened fire, killing more of his brethren, but now they were all charging and closing the gap at a rapid rate. Fearless they came, even as the third rank opened fire before falling to pieces under the Cahuilla onslaught. Enraged, the warriors hacked until they were spent, the carnage around them the proof of their bravery, their manhood and their victory.

Mukat stood upright in the aftermath, basking in triumph and listening to the groans of the wounded that—on one side at least—would soon be silenced, enjoying the stiff breeze from across the sea that cooled his fiery skin. Their homelands were safe, their families and treasures secure from one more pillager. Time now to relax and reap the rewards of their sacrifices.

Mukat made a sound that called the braves together. He directed groups to the top of the ship and others inside, reminding them that lone stragglers may still remain, especially where the valuables were being stored. As he spoke the wind whipped up again and storm clouds scudded across the dark skies, torn by an approaching storm. The Cahuilla were used to predicting bad weather and Mukat suddenly knew there was something coming that not even his warriors could obstruct.

"A storm approaches," he said aloud, eyeing the swell of the sea and the rock of the boat. By the moment the wind began to whip up. "We will make this quick."

What the Cahuilla might term a valuable might be far removed from what others called the same. Mukat knew this. Clothes and material, certain foods, weapons, other raw items—these were all precious treasure to them. Gold coins and baubles not so much, although they too might have their place if the missions ever sprung back up.

His men swarmed the ship, looting what they could and dragging many items up to the deck. Some were discarded. More canoes came alongside, preparing to carry the plunder.

Even now the swells were tricky in the shallows and the errant gusts of wind were beyond dangerous. More than one canoe capsized, though the Cahuilla were all strong swimmers and swam ashore. Mukat eyed the approaching storm with fear. Had they angered the gods in some way? The demons, perhaps? Or the Trickster himself? Surely defending their lands was no reason to punish them. But then demons were fickle things.

Mukat helped drag several items to the edge of the ship where braves were ready to lower them into the waiting canoes. Still more men came running up from the depths of the vessel, gesturing wildly.

You have to see this, he understood.

He cursed the gods. The Cahuilla had taken a great victory here today, defeating soldiers who meant them harm even if they didn't initially know it. After a hard-won victory came the chance to gather the spoils of war; they could use these goods to improve their lifestyles. Now, the great approaching storm was threatening to take all that away.

Mukat cursed into the coming gales. The deeper darkness of rain clouds swarmed towards him like a fast-moving sand blizzard, seemingly reaching out with inky black fingers. Water spat at his face. The waves churned. The gods, it seemed, were indeed angry.

Dare he defy them further?

Mukat lowered his head and ran to his men. Even now, they held items of plunder in their hands, some weighed down so heavily they could barely stand. Someone told him about the great chests in the lower hold, once heavily guarded but now defenseless, and the enormous locks and straps that held them closed.

Clearly they posed the source of the ship's greatest riches. And just as clearly the Cahuilla could not open them. Not in so short a time frame.

Mukat rushed by them, dragging one man with him to lead the way. The huge ship began to rock as the storm enveloped it. Mukat knew his men would be escaping even now—they would not wait for him and rightly so. He ran past open and closed doors, bright lanterns and burning bodies. He ran past a table bigger than his entire tepee, lavishly set with goblets and golden plates and heaps of food. He ran past a groaning man who reached out two hands, beseeching him for help. This ship was such an odd place to be—even paintings hung on the walls. Sometime later he reached the hold, stopping as flickering lanterns picked out the source of all his men's interest. Seven chests sat in a row, very large, each so big they would take many men to lift and have to be removed one at a time. The obvious answer was to empty them, but Mukat now saw the cause of his men's torment.

Locks larger than any he had ever seen were attached to the sides. Mere spears and even rocks would not quickly dent them, let alone open them. In addition, two broad, solid metal straps wrapped around the circumference of each chest, imposing loops interrupted only by the addition of yet more locks.

Mukat blinked rapidly. Yes, the chests presented a great deal of trouble but it was that simple fact that told him they were worth the effort.

As the ship rolled under the onslaught of the storm he knew the answer was but a simple one.

"We leave," he said. "And later, we come back."

"Why don't we stay?" his companion asked.

Mukat eyed the dark hulk all around him. "Devil's home," he said. "Not ours." He would never be able to relax inside this unfamiliar, imposing, ghost-ridden place.

The two men turned and ran hard. Even down here they could hear the storm's fury. Mukat again considered the depth of that anger. Had the gods sent these men to *save* the

Cahuilla? Possibly from an upcoming event?

Mukat pondered as he ran, at last emerging from the nightmarish below-deck environment and into his real home—the great outdoors. The scene that greeted his eyes, however, was not at all inviting. Torrents of water lashed sideways through the air, peppering his face with little painful darts. As the ship listed toward the seaward side, great rolling waves greeted his vision, bigger than any he had ever seen. A forlorn canoe bobbed around out there, smashed from wave to wave, empty. The hellish skies pressed down as if trying to smother all life from the earth. Lightning danced from cloud to cloud, demons and devils skipping and cavorting at the top of the world.

Mukat fought his way to the ship's rail, holding onto his companion as best he could. Together they gripped the solid wood and looked toward the shore. People were gathered up the beach, beyond the reach of the foaming waters, people drenched and miserable and frightened but still determined to wait for their leader. Mukat would not disappoint them. Grabbing his companion, he stared into the man's eyes and nodded.

"We swim," he said. "We live."

Together, they climbed over the rail and fell to the raging waters below. Mukat hit first, the sudden quiet below the surface a sharp contrast to the world above. Kicking strongly, he propelled himself unerringly toward the shore. Many tribes he knew could not swim, but the Cahuilla had always been fortunate to live close to the inland sea. That was why, occasionally, they enjoyed venturing down the wide tributary that led to the great, endless sea, the place where huge ships sailed.

Today had been a mix of victories and defeat, good signs and dark omens. Today had been unpredictable in the extreme. But tomorrow would bring great fortune.

Mukat swam hard until he saw the sea bottom beginning to rise. His breath gave out just as he broke surface, into a debilitating sensory assault of stunning visions and terrible noise. Waves battered him, taking control of even his powerful body. Thunder roared down at him as if from a vast, many-toothed mouth. Lightning pierced the skies, forking down and splashing against the seas. A jagged point hit close to him, blinding his vision. Mukat threw himself toward the shore, fighting as if with a black bear or vicious coyote. The cruel creature wrapped him in liquid arms, dragging him down and then out to darker depths, but Mukat fought with all his heart and soul, still able to see the shore and safety. Tooth and nail he struggled, gradually losing his fight with the formidable beast. His strength was waning, the trial too much. He would now pay the price for leading his people into folly. Knowing that he had lost he began to relax his limbs, already accepting.

Hands and fingers gripped his arms, his clothing, even his hair. They pulled. He went with them, sucked from the very maw of the beast. His people had waded in to save him, beset by the waves and the winds but still eager to help. The Cahuilla were a family and they would prevail. Right then, he knew his people would never die, their names never be forgotten.

Mukat lay panting on the beach, men sat at his side, drenched and spent, his companion from the ship similarly worn out. The storm raged at them and did not relent that night, a spectacle to behold, a fury that would live in their minds forever. Before first light painted the horizon the mighty ship began to list, to heave and swell, and then broke from its moorings, drifting off into the eye of the storm. Mukat did not see where it went and had long since lost all desire to. The gods had spoken.

Leave it be.

Mukat would never again dare defy the gods as long as he lived.

CHAPTER ONE

Matt Drake woke and instantly wondered why he was alone. His first thought: *Mai?* was an early morning constant of late, and then he remembered...

Oh aye, she's in Japan, I think...

And the world slipped back into place. He was alone once more and even if Mai Kitano returned today, forgiven and free, a figure of pure absolution, he doubted that he could ever go back. Their time was over—of that he was sure—but he would still welcome her as an ally. They had worked that way before, many times. If Drake had changed since the death of his closest friends it was only because he could be more resolute, more caring, and less vocal about it. Promises were nothing when compared to real action.

Drake sat up in bed, eyeing the espresso machine as if it were a lifeline. The blackout curtains were useful but he could still see light bleeding around the edges, which meant the morning was marching on. He scooted over the bed and inserted a fresh pod into the machine, placed a cup under the dispenser and waited for the coffee to pour. Hot and black it was ready in seconds. He sipped at it, still reviewing his new place in the world and the events that had led him here.

If there was ever an Englishman who deserved to be called a man of action it was Matt Drake. At the same time he would hear none of it, beyond the less-than-gentle ribbing offered up by his teammates. Drake had been forced at an early age to take charge of his life and continued to adhere to that pattern—no matter which megalomaniac tried to disrupt it. At the head of it all was the loyalty he felt towards his friends.

And the agony shared by all when one of their number died.

Komodo's funeral had been surreal, an odd kind of nightmare. The one good thing about it was that it had passed without incident. Karin, inconsolable, distressed beyond measure, quantified it in a single, succinct sentence.

"If my life is the sum of those I most love then it is now over."

The team had tried to console her, but Karin had lost her parents, her brother, and her boyfriend in a matter of months. Drake knew from experience that time didn't heal the wounds caused by losing a loved one beyond an almost insignificant point. Which Karin would emerge from the ashes of the old one?

He would be there to catch and care for her no matter the depth of the fall.

As he drained the coffee and immediately made another—one was never enough from a pod machine—his thoughts turned inevitably to Alicia. The free-spirited Englishwoman had stayed true to character and charged on after the battle in Hong Kong, joining her other team in an attempt to find some long-hidden Crusader gold. This was no form of disrespect intended—or even unintended—toward Komodo or Karin or the SPEAR team, it was pure Alicia Myles and her headlong quest toward self-destruction. Drake sensed the moment approaching every day and worried for whomever was near her at the time.

And, conversely, hoped it would be him.

Hoped? he thought. *No, no. Worried . . . that was more like it. Feared. Dreaded. Was terrified of . . .*

He laughed it off, knowing inwardly that he would help Alicia in any way he could if it came down to it. Even if he had to kill her, or himself, just to save her.

Drake made an internal call on the room's telephone system. Almost immediately a gruff but well-manicured voice answered.

"Dahl residence."

Drake laughed, despite everything. "We're in a bloody hotel, you knob."

"A well-travelled, educated man's hotel room is his castle. The same way a Yorkshireman's castle is the local pub."

"Amen to that. Who needs trumpets and banquets when you can have a jukebox, a quiz and a packet of pork scratchings?"

Dahl hesitated. "Pork what? Dare I ask?"

"Probably best to let that one pass."

A moment's silence passed before Dahl spoke again. "Have you heard from Mai?"

Drake sighed. It was natural for the other team members to imagine he was at an all-time low and he saw no reason to enlighten them either way. "Not a thing, mate. She's still showing Grace around Japan. Worried about the Yakuza. Spending time with Chika and Hibiki, I guess."

"Fancy a game of table tennis?"

Drake froze and then shook his head. Did he hear that correctly? If Dahl had asked him to join him at a *Frozen* sing-along with the kids he'd have been less surprised. "Come again?"

"I noticed a table in the basement last night and two old bats. I'm sure we'll be able to rustle up a ping pong ball from somewhere."

"Okaaaay." Still wondering if "table tennis" was a code word for something a little more dangerous and clandestine he met Dahl at the entrance to the elevator three minutes later. The Swede stood large and imposing, even clad as he was in T-shirt and cargo shorts. A smile hovered at the edge of his lips.

"So what is this really?" Drake asked. "New mission?"

"No." The Swede looked upset. "It's a game of fucking table tennis. If it was a new mission I'd say so."

"You know you're gonna get your ass kicked?"

"Oh right, I forgot. Every Yorkshireman played table tennis at the local community center when he was a kid, yeah? Winner stayed on and they had to drag him away three hours later."

"That's right."

"Well, we played ping pong in Sweden too. When I was young we had a world champion."

"I do remember that anyone who played table tennis at a high enough level would never call it *ping pong*." Drake smiled.

Dahl couldn't stop his eyes widening in surprise. Drake had gotten to him and, even now, there was a friendly rivalry between the two men. When Dahl showed him to the table Drake picked up the closest bat.

"Loser has to wear an 'I love Kanye West' T-shirt for a whole day?"

"Bollocks, I could never sink that low."

"How about an 'I love Alicia Myles' T-shirt?"

Dahl cocked his head. "Did she finally get some made?"

"Yep, for her new team, but in her rush she flew off without them."

"I can live with that."

The two men faced off. Drake held up a small yellowish ball. Throwing it high into the air he readied his feet and prepared to serve . . . just as Dahl's cellphone rang.

"Wait!"

Then Drake's own phone let out a chirp. The Who's *Pinball Wizard* sang out. He let the ball fall to the floor as he plucked the device from the right-side pocket of his Levis.

"Matt Drake."

Hayden's voice, stressed, filled the room as both men hit speakerphone. "Hi guys. We need you to come in. We have a crisis down here."

Drake placed his bat on the table. "Must be Wednesday."

"Huh?"

"Nothing. What's going on?"

"Our friend Ramses has popped up big time. The myth, it seems, is actually a reality."

"I've heard that before." Dahl groaned.

"Ramses is nothing like the Blood King. Born as royalty and brainwashed whilst young. Indoctrinated into terrorism at the same time as being beyond privileged. What little we do know of him beggars belief."

"And now?"

"Well it looks like we have an early heads-up as to the staging of a giant arms bazaar, billed as the last and biggest of its kind. We're talking the kind where terrorist royalty roll up in their armor-plated Bentley Continentals, step out, order a brace of nuclear missiles, then skip off and inspect a flock of stolen fighter planes. It's happening, guys."

"When?" Drake and Dahl were already in the elevator.

"Within a month. We don't know."

Drake almost dropped the phone. "A *month?* Wow, I can't remember having the luxury of time since . . ." He paused for thought. "Since . . . well, ever."

"Ya got that right. And I said *within* a month. Could be next week, so hurry. We'll see you in ten."

Drake thought about the security they had to pass through in order to gain access to their new offices inside the Pentagon.

"Better make that thirty, love."

CHAPTER TWO

Drake entered the small room they called an office, amazed at how compact it seemed inside such an enormous building and at the same time stunned by the dazzling array of technology it offered. Hayden sat in a corner, at the head of a rectangular desk that seated eight. Before this day, Drake remembered people having to pull up extra chairs. Today, there were enough spaces around the table.

Barbs of regret stabbed at his chest. Dahl walked past, probably thinking the same thing but purposely moving forward.

He stood unmoving for a moment, then caught Karin's eye, surprised to see her. "You don't have to be here."

She nodded, her short blonde hair lying flat today. "I shouldn't be here, but this is where I want to be. I'm no good on my own."

Drake nodded. He could relate to that. A quick overview revealed the additional faces of Lauren and Smyth. He was about to question Hayden over Kinimaka when the big Hawaiian crashed through the door.

Nobody turned, nobody dove to the floor. It was Mano. It was expected. "Mahalo," he growled, trying to untangle his feet.

Hayden stared at him. "How did it go?"

Kinimaka let out a long, pent-up breath. "Kono is my sister," he said as if that explained everything. "And has been stuck in DC for too long now. It doesn't occur to her that if the Disavowed guys hadn't saved her back in LA then she would be dead. It doesn't occur to her that we're out here every day, fighting to preserve her taken-for-granted freedoms. It doesn't occur to her that DC shouldn't be compared to Hawaii." He shook his head.

Smyth grunted irritably. "A good brother-sister relationship then."

"As good as can be expected." Kinimaka carefully withdrew a chair and then fitted his bulk to it. Drake waited for something to go wrong but he and everyone else in the room was pleasantly surprised when it didn't. Even Kinimaka glanced around in shock.

Smyth wasn't done, his growl filling the space. "My sister, I wanted to choke her every day. Even looked forward to her turning sixteen, because she was a year older and said she would leave the house on her birthday. *Booyah*, I thought. *An entire year to myself.* Such joy."

Lauren looked at him. "I never heard you mention a sister before."

"She died when I was twelve." His voice dropped. "Cancer took her down very quickly. Funny how you never know how lucky you are until—"

He stopped abruptly, remembering Karin's presence in the room. "Ah, sorry."

"It's okay," Karin barely whispered. "I knew what I had."

Hayden quickly took charge of the room. "All right, guys. We have a number of things to get through this morning. First, can I ask about the stalking? Has anyone encountered anything new?"

A clever way of putting it, Drake thought. Stalking wasn't merely the imagined "art" of following a person, it was far more complex than that. Many planes of intimidation existed within that single expression—anything from moving objects around to physical confrontation. A man like Drake had never contended with a stalker, but he could well imagine the kind of hell it might put a person through.

Kinimaka spoke up. "Kono, despite her petulance, actually believes she is being stalked. I'm her big brother," he pulled a face, "and I know the kind of stunts she can pull and any other time I'd laugh and pull her hair or something, but now—"

Hayden shook her head, trying to hide a flash of amusement. "I can assign a couple of patrols to her. But I want to do it quietly. As good as Tyler Webb thinks he is, and as intimidating as he can be, I actually believe these escalating stalkings are our best way of catching him."

Dahl nodded. "He will lose control. I personally have seen no signs over at my place and neither has Johanna."

"Our place," she nodded at Mano, "has been a stalker's heaven lately. I guess we've now solved that problem. We're watching the watchers, surveilling the hidden cameras. Just hoping the asshole does it again."

"You're more self-assured than me," Smyth said. "I'd be afraid my bare ass would pop up on the Internet or something."

Hayden waved a hand matter-of-factly. "It's not like that for Webb. I'm convinced it's more about control and dominance. He is a power-hungry megalomaniac after all. He gets off on feeling he has the means and supremacy to invade any life at any time."

"Well let's hope he doesn't get off on you," Smyth grunted.

Hayden screwed her face up. "Shit, man, that's a horrible thing to put out there. Keep those thoughts to yourself."

Drake spoke up before Smyth dug in any further. "I have to say I'm so glad to see both Karin and Lauren here. Are you completely recovered?" he asked the New Yorker.

"Yeah, totally. No signs of that freakin' Pandora virus and no side effects. I'm good."

Karin smiled slightly, her eyes unreadable. Drake wondered what dark oaths they may be taking and what even darker paths they may be traveling.

"What more do you have on this Ramses character? And how do these criminal kingpins somehow convince everyone they don't really exist?"

"They use a shitload of go-betweens," Hayden said. "More station bosses than McDonald's. And they have a more complex family tree than your royal family. Or any family. The man at the top is always a mystery if he does his job properly."

"But we're talking about terrorists here."

"And they have individuals working inside their organization as clever as those who work at the CIA."

"So there will be others?" Lauren asked. "Myths or unimpeachable individuals hiding what they really do?"

"Undoubtedly," Dahl told her. "Haven't you heard of the Russian mastermind Chopa Bolokov? Or his brother—Yanksa?"

Lauren didn't even smile. "Oh, I love your English jokes."

"I'm not—"

"I know and I don't care. I thought we were talking serious shit here."

Hayden continued, "So, Ramses is trying to orchestrate the biggest event of his entirely unpleasant career. The world is a very large place and these people certainly have ways of communication we don't yet know about. They could stage something like this and, believe me, we *want* them to. We just have to be there when it happens."

A soft knock at the door brought them all around. Before Hayden could utter a word it opened and a lithe figure entered the room, sending the place into a state of shock. Drake felt his jaw hit the floor and glanced across at Dahl, wondering what they should do. Yes they were inside one of the safest buildings in the world, but this man was an enemy and working for the Pythians.

Wasn't he?

Dahl gawped back at him. It took a long moment before

anyone found their voice.

Smyth snorted loudly. "What the hell are *you* doing here, you asshole?"

"I am sorry, my friends," the figure said, moving swiftly. "But your Ramses will have to wait. I don't have long and I have a far, far bigger problem to lay upon you. No pun intended, of course. You're going to have to move and move fast if America is to survive."

Hayden audibly gulped. "S-Survive?" she stammered. "What are you talking about?"

"The return of the dark ages," came the answer. "We're all about to die. Will you hear me out?"

CHAPTER THREE

Drake peered around the lithe figure.

"Alicia with you?"

"Ah, sadly not. She is chasing Hercules, I believe. That girl cannot live a day without a man in her life. But perhaps you will see her soon, no?"

Drake shrugged. He could see from the periphery of his vision that the others had Beauregard well covered, but past memories stung almost as much as the bruises that had been inflicted. The Frenchman was one slippery character.

But there was one overbearing question...

"You do realize this is the Pentagon?" Dahl asked it first. "How..."

Beauregard allowed a self-assured smile to play across his lips. "My boss called your boss," he said. "You know how it goes."

"I had a call," Hayden said. "From Robert Price. He explained that an informant would be dropping by this morning but he never said it would be this guy."

"Wait. Wait." Drake squeezed his eyes shut. "Your *boss* called Robert Price? Don't you work for the Pythians?"

Beauregard only smiled.

The SPEAR team tensed. If the Secretary of Defense had allowed this man into their midst then perhaps he was as corrupt as had once been intimated. Drake knew that Hayden was trying to quietly investigate the new Secretary but had barely had time to breathe during the last few months. Something would give... he just wondered how bad it would be when it did.

Beauregard then sat down and spread his hands wide. "I would love to spin this out longer," he said. "The indecision on all your faces is worth my time. But sadly it is not worth the country's time, and real lives. So I will tell you this—I work for a good guy and I am in deep cover. The time is fast approaching when the Pythians will self-destruct, a fact mostly down to their leader who is about as stable as a Greek bank. You will all need a man on the inside when that happens."

Drake didn't move a muscle. "Who do you work for?"

"That is his secret to tell, not mine. But now, I am here. Will you listen?"

"What kind of question is that?" Smyth barked. "I still have the scars from our last little *chat*." The ex-soldier made a menacing move forward.

Beauregard only raised a brow. "Forget it. I got lucky." The smirk in his eyes told them he didn't believe that for a second.

Dahl also advanced. "Me and you," he said. "Right now, on the Pentagon lawn. I'll show you lucky."

Drake rubbed his face. "Just calm down will you? The man says he has information on a credible threat. Let's hear him out before we cave his fucking face in."

Beauregard nodded slightly. "That's kind of you. One of the Pythians—a mega-wealthy developer named Nicholas Bell—has been constructing a plan that could shake America to the core. It is two-pronged. On the one hand it involves the recently appropriated, Chinese created Z-boxes. On the other, and at the same time, he plans to find the ghost ships of Arizona."

Drake eyed the Frenchman for almost a minute, trying to gauge his sincerity. In the end the point was wholly moot. Beauregard was here now, talking, trying to make them listen. And *inside the Pentagon*. Drake doubted there was an ulterior motive.

What kind of madman would invent such a story and then

tell it to a Special Forces team inside the most secure building on earth?

The leader of the Pythians, Drake thought, keeping his guard high. *That's who. It's gonna be a dark day when bloody Tyler Webb finally implodes.*

Beauregard locked eyes with him. "I have information on both attacks, and it can't wait anymore. Seriously. They are imminent, yes? Imminent."

"Get the fuck on with it then," Smyth said. "So we can boot your ass outta here."

"Did you know Tyler Webb was in DC?" Beauregard asked quietly of Smyth. "Did you know that, pretty boy?"

Smyth rose fast, but it was Lauren who blocked him. Something passed between them and Smyth backed down, but the hatred emanating from his gaze was palpable.

"We suspected Webb was in the DC area," Hayden said. "Due to the intimacy and escalation of the stalkings."

"He is worse than you could ever imagine," Beauregard said. "I was security once, when he chose to visit your house, Miss Jaye. I only saw brief moments but I would be sure to burn all your underwear. And you—" he nodded at Kinimaka. "As I'm sure you know it is relatively easy to install an undetectable bug these days, especially for a man of means. Do you want the world's foremost madman knowing your location twenty-four-seven? Check everything."

Mano nodded, chewing his lip now and probably thinking of Kono. Drake maneuvered Beauregard back to the point at hand.

"You mentioned a severe lack of time?"

"Yes. Nicholas Bell—the builder—has come up with something particularly nasty. It is his turn to destroy the world, it seems. His roll of the dice. First, his fascination with the ghost ships is a long-standing one. Only recently did he figure out how they could benefit the Pythians, and then he put his plan to Webb. It is their *content* you see, pun intended, though you will not understand as yet. Bell is . . ." Beauregard paused.

Lauren leaned forward. "Torn? Hesitant?"

"I was going to say a ditherer. Wooly-headed, I believe the English might say."

"Lauren thinks he can be turned," Hayden said.

Beauregard frowned. "I haven't thought about him in such a way, but maybe. Though the timing would be critical, and soon. Your choice. But let me continue."

"I wish you would," Kinimaka said. "These ghost ships sound kinda mysterious. Not to mention scary." He smiled. "We all gonna get haunted, Frenchman?"

Beauregard didn't smile this time. "The stories run deep over in the western states. Entire ships that appear at night and vanish by day. Drowned by the sands. Creaking they pass by, their sails motionless. Such a sight would make even you shiver in your boots, I am sure. Even the Native Americans told stories of them. Legends. Sightings span hundreds of years and still persist today. Do you want to know more?"

The entire SPEAR team leaned forward.

CHAPTER FOUR

"Stories of the ghost ships began around the time of the American Civil War. We have the great Colorado River flood of 1862. The *Los Angeles Daily News* reported a sighting in 1870. The Gulf of California was once connected to what is now called the Salton Sea, once the enormous Lake Cahuilla, most of which dried up. Half-buried hulks, they saw. Some near Dos Palmas, California. Others near Yuma, Arizona. Easily viewed, they said, but when expeditions were sent out to salvage the vessels they had once again sunk beneath the drifting sands. It is believed that any ships out there might now be buried under the Salton Sea, but such beliefs, long held, are often proved wrong, especially in the modern age. Nicholas Bell, at least, believes this."

"Any idea which ships they might be?" Dahl asked.

"A good question and the answer is yes. But, alas, as fascinating as they may be, the ships are but a diversion in this room today. Webb is using them as a distraction for his fellow Pythians for two reasons. One, because he knows Bell will have to be dealt with and will thus divide his enemy's forces. And two, because he is nose-diving, crashing at an alarming rate and doesn't want them to see where he's headed. His justification for allowing Bell to search for the ships is the new fortune their treasures will bring."

Drake cleared his throat. "You mentioned that this is a two-pronged plan? And hey, what the hell happened to your French accent?"

Beauregard raised a brow but didn't look like he wanted to over-explain himself. After a moment he carried on. "I did.

Bell's plan is to salvage the ghost ships at the same time as using the Z-boxes to take down the US."

"Take down the US?" Hayden repeated. "That is a bold statement, Beauregard."

"It is. And it will only be a warning shot across the bows. A statement of intent. It will take the form of an attack upon the United States' electrical grid and will bring the deepest fear to millions. An uprising? No. Anarchy? No. But the government will have the struggles of a nation on its hands and will be hard pressed. Remember the New York blackout? The only people who enjoyed that night were very drunk."

"Or criminals," Kinimaka said.

Beauregard spread his hands wide. "You said it. Since your last escapade and the demise of Webb's lieutenant, Dudley, he has changed tactics, instead preferring to flood his ranks with dumb, violent mercenaries. This—and everything else they have going on—will put a strain on even the Pythians' finances, hence the other major reason for the ghost ship hunt. There are new Pythians now, too." Beauregard shook his head in disbelief. "A man named Julian Marsh from the UK. A woman named Zoe Sheers. And one more I do not yet know. They too have big plans and are almost as dangerous as Webb. But that man—" Beauregard paused.

"The bugger's as cracked as crazy paving?" Drake offered. "Barmy enough to bite 'is own arm off?"

Dahl waved away Beauregard's confused expression. "He's from Yorkshire."

"Well, if you mean dangerously mad then that is a poor description for Webb. I would say clinically insane enough to organize Armageddon for fun. He is trying to prove his . . ." The Frenchman struggled for words. "His *godship*. Do you understand?"

"Aye, lad." Drake nodded. "Some of us may look daft and Swedish but we're not all stupid."

"I still believe Nicholas Bell has bitten off more than he can chew," Lauren said again. "He was nice to me. He could be an ally."

Smyth made a noise like an approaching thunderstorm. Beauregard cut in. "As I mentioned, they have boosted their forces already. They will hit hard and bluntly, not caring about casualties on either side. They have two Z-boxes left and intend to use them. I'm thinking multiple, simultaneous attacks. I do not know the exact way Bell or Webb will try using the Z-boxes to attack the electrical grid but I assure you, unless stopped, they *will* do so."

"We have one Z-box," Hayden said. "And we're trying to decode it even now."

"It will not be in time, Miss Jaye. All I know is they need access to *three* US substations and the game—as they say—is already on."

Drake absorbed that. He was no expert on any kind of electrical grid but he knew country-wide substations had to number in the thousands.

"And I'm guessing you know which ones?"

"No." Beauregard looked glum. "I only know the first because that's where they're headed now, why I quickly broke cover, and why we have little to no time. It's Almaden, in San Jose, in California."

"When will they hit?" Hayden was already reaching for the phone.

"Tonight."

"But what's their goal?" Karin broke her deep silence with an intelligent question. "I would imagine that the Almaden substation is a big facility. What exactly are they looking for inside there?"

Beauregard again spread his hands. "I don't know."

"Crap." Smyth clucked. "What fuckin' good are ya?"

"I have my uses," Beauregard returned. "As others have

discovered. Perhaps this will endear me to you too."

"I'd have to fight you first," Dahl said seriously. "In proper light. Just to see what kind of style you actually employ."

"What the toff's trying to say is you're a bloody tricky twat," Drake said amiably. "And we don't take loss or defeat lightly."

"Understood. I will look forward to the day. In the meantime . . ." Beauregard rose to his feet. "Oh, and remember one thing," he added. "Tyler Webb is utterly desperate for one thing and only thing only. He calls it the Saint Germain factor and it is the *only* reason he invented the Pythians. To achieve this goal he will literally burn the world down, not caring that he might die in the process. Often I have heard him talking to himself and he says this over and over: *I don't care if I am the last man on earth.* The way he talks—he is not just waffling. He truly believes that the prospect is real."

"Which begs the question—what about the Saint Germain factor could help achieve that state?" Karin said.

Then Hayden cut in quickly. "Wheels up in ten, guys. We're headed west. Get your butts and your guns into gear. You coming with us, Beauregard?"

"If I did so I would lose everything that I have worked for."

Hayden nodded in understanding, then glanced around the rest of the team who were still staring suspiciously at the Frenchman.

"C'mon, guys. *Move it!*"

CHAPTER FIVE

Drake made ready as the Gulfstream II streaked through the clouds at forty two thousand feet, travelling around five hundred miles per hour. Endlessly modifiable and used by entities no less than NASA, the Missile Defense Agency, the CIA and John Travolta, it offered everything a frontline team like SPEAR needed. Drake made use of the weapons cache, the shower and then the onboard buffet, finally settling in his single leather seat somewhere over Kentucky. Hayden reported that both she and Kinimaka were talking to the Californian authorities over the substation threats but that all was quiet so far. Perhaps tonight wasn't the night. Or perhaps Beauregard was full of . . .

Drake heard Hayden urging vigilance and telling a clearly irate individual that they'd soon be there to take charge.

"So this electrical grid," Drake said. "I assume this isn't the first time somebody's thought to take it down. Surely there are contingencies in place."

"Sure there are," Hayden said. "But it's the Z-boxes that pose the problem. Don't you remember? They crack codes and the Pythians went to unbelievable lengths to acquire them. I guess this is a first step and I guess that they will override all contingencies."

As Hayden spoke, Drake saw Kinimaka drift away to make another call. Since the big Hawaiian gravitated over to his side of the plane the Yorkshireman heard every word.

"Mahalo, sister. How are you?"

Kinimaka listened for a moment before going ahead with what he needed to say. "Kono, the stalkings are worsening. We have people watching you but you still have to be careful. Okay? No trying to blow them off. They're around for your safety. This is serious—"

An answer stopped him short.

"I can't say when or how long. But please, change the habit of a lifetime and listen to your brother. I might not have done so well by you in the past but I'm trying to make up for that now. Okay?"

Drake tuned out, feeling a little intrusive. Hayden still concentrated their thoughts on the Z-boxes. "The Chinese developed them to be able to crack every code, every PIN, every cypher out there. Nuclear programming. Cyber warfare. Missile data. If they're in our system then we're already in deep shit. Counter programming is a good idea. A deterrent. But sooner or later somebody's going to come up with something totally off the wall . . . and mad-dog crazy. If the Z-boxes can already crack our passwords and download information then they can be used to take everything down."

"They must need some kinda access," Smyth put in. "Since substations and the like are mostly self-contained."

"Hence, an attack," Hayden said. "Now, I have another idea. Since this substation *and* the ghost ships are around California and Arizona then maybe we can split our forces? End the threat and grab a Pythian whilst we're at it. Bell, at least, is in the field according to Beau. We'll check out the substation and then separate. Yes?"

Drake's thoughts centered round their dwindling numbers and all they had lost of late. Komodo, taken whilst saving Mai's life. Mai herself feeling obligated to help Grace in Japan. Alicia, forging toward her own destruction with the Gold Team. Some fresh blood wouldn't go amiss and, as reluctant as he was to admit it, a friendly Beauregard Alain could be a significant asset.

"We're only eight strong," he said. "But if we can isolate this substation and stop the mercs I'm up for that."

"And snatching a Pythian would be a major success," Dahl said.

Yorgi spoke up fast. "I volunteer for ghost ship quest," he said thickly. "I no good with all this fighting."

"Me too," Karin said quietly. "For now."

Drake was just glad to hear her contributing. "All right. Me too. How about Hayden, Mano and the Swede take the substations?"

Dahl cocked his head. "The Swede? Really?"

"Yeah, dumbass. That's you."

"Oh, please grab my sides to stop them from splitting with laughter."

Hayden glanced around. "Pilot says we're about to land. Once grounded we have a ten minute journey to Almaden. Are we ready?"

A stream of affirmative expletives rang out.

Her cell rang again. This time her expression changed almost immediately. When she ended the call her face was dark with anger.

"The fucking facility just got hit by a huge force. There was no extra security. No extra guards. Not even local cops. Some pretentious bastard's gonna hang for this one. I know this is a big ask, guys, but we're gonna have to assault a larger force that is already attacking a fortified building. We're gonna be in one of the hardest battles of our lives."

The team didn't need to study each other, didn't need words to know this was their first real threat since Komodo lost his life.

Drake made a point of exchanging his knife for a much larger one. "Then it's a good job we're the best fucking team in the world."

The plane descended hard.

CHAPTER SIX

Mai Kitano winced as a bolt of pain radiated out from the area in which she had been shot. The wound had healed but the trauma to her body would be everlasting. Still, she had survived that dreadful night in Hong Kong, that hotel battle, the long chase across the rooftops, the alley-fight afterwards.

Some had not.

Komodo took the blow that had been meant for her. *Why would he do that? The man had a future. A girlfriend. A life.* What did she have? Nothing but a twisting gut-full of guilt and angst. Nothing but a long downward spiral. Grace was her only salvation. The young woman she had saved from the dreaded hand of the Tsugarai clan was her future, her absolution and her gift all rolled into one. Grace was already far beyond the broken, quiet figure she had saved—the girl was forward, boisterous, even offensive at times. If it had not been for the inescapable sojourn to find her parents' graves and the agony it bestowed then Mai thought she would already be as close to "normal" as she was ever going to get and fully able to make her own next decision.

Mai shielded her eyes again, now ignoring the twist in her gut. They stood together at the edge of a vast graveyard. Built on the side of a green hill the cemetery descended in steps, each one crammed full of square or rectangular gravestones, mostly gray in color, bordered by trees and dotted by tiny individual lawns. Flowers lay everywhere, adding color to the otherwise austere scene. Narrow paths ran down the center of every step. Mai couldn't help but lose herself inside a miasma of gloom as she appraised the cemetery.

No gravestone should ever need to have a teddy bear clinging to it.

Tears formed in her eyes and she led Grace downhill as fast as she could. They had already acquired a map from a groundsman and knew where Grace's parents were buried. Mai thought about them giving up when their daughter vanished. She could never imagine what it must be like for a parent to lose a child and never know...

Such morbid thoughts, she reflected, *are surely a part of why this is all happening to us. Snap out of it.*

There had to be a way to live again.

But today was always going to be drenched in sadness. The steep slope took her attention for a while, the angle making her stomach hurt yet again. Grace stepped lightly before her, concentrating on the ground. Today, the dark-haired Japanese girl was dressed in loose pants, flat shoes and a simple white blouse. Her hair was clipped back, away from her strained face. Hers was a head that had seen too much and a body that had lived too hard. The next few years should be peaceful to allow her time to catch up. Mai doubted the girl would see things the same way. Headstrong, and thinking she had already experienced the worst of the world she would crave to be out in it.

And Mai didn't really blame her.

They descended together, step after step, until the green hillside rose behind them, the summit high above. Gray headstones stretched to both sides. Mai paused to consult the map, pinpointing their destination which in fact proved to be at their very feet.

Mai stared at the gravestone. Grace looked ahead with a positive expression, determined to search on. When she started to move off Mai cleared her throat.

"We are here," she said, taking hold of Grace's hand and showing her.

Grace stared, face slipping as if she'd been struck in the face. All of a sudden the bravado vanished and what was left was a scared little girl, a child adrift, finally confronted with the reality of what had happened to her parents.

"Sit." Mai pulled her down before she collapsed. They had brought nothing with them. Neither Mai nor Grace held to any accepted ceremonies, not anymore. Mai felt almost as if her belief in decency and morality had been wiped clean. A ceremony couldn't hope to change that.

Grace knelt on the dusty path, staring at the headstones. A respectful sun beat at their backs, not too hot but simply dispensing warmth. The day was silent, inconspicuous, as the two women paid their respects to yet more who should not yet be dead.

Back at the hotel Mai gave Grace some space, giving her the use of the main apartment and shower while she retired to the bedroom. Even today, she had much to do. Sitting on the bed she stretched her back and made a call, managing a smile when Dai Hibiki answered.

"Mai? Is that you?"

"It is, my friend. I hope you are well."

Hibiki knew what was supposed to happen today and had never been one to waste time. "How is Grace?"

"She will be all right. The fight inside that one is beyond anything I have ever seen. Her will to overcome . . ." Mai paused, surprised at herself.

Hibiki's smile was obvious despite the distance. "I know of one other who might come close."

"One day again, maybe. But life drains the fight out of you, Dai. If you've done something that deprives you of all the best feelings—passion, struggle, victory, humor—how do you get past that?"

Hibiki sighed. "Are you coming to Tokyo?"

"Yes. We leave tomorrow. I will see you then."

"Okay. And Mai, before you ask—no, they haven't yet found Emiko. I know you killed her father but that girl can no longer be found. She's not trained. Not a fighter. The wolves will swallow her whole and probably already have."

Mai didn't appreciate the bluntness of his delivery but knew what Hibiki was trying to do. She ended the call before he could try anything else. Behind her, the small window looked out over a small park. Sounds of normality drifted through the barely cracked-open window—dogs barking and the groan of swing-chains. Laughter. The whooping of children. The warning shouts of adults.

Something she had been keeping from Grace now swam back to the forefront of her brain. Two days ago Hibiki had gotten word that the Yakuza had held another meeting to decide the fate of their newest nemesis—Mai Kitano. Although the original, rigged trial hadn't finished before Drake rescued her, the warriors dispatched to kill her hinted that Komodo's death may be enough, but the Yakuza figureheads had now decided that satisfaction had not actually been gained. Komodo's death was not enough.

Instead, through Hibiki, they had offered a final resolution. An ending of sorts.

They would send their best trained warrior for a showdown at a place of Mai's choosing. Only a victory would save her. Mai had instantly acquiesced to their offer, seeing a way out for her sister and Hibiki and the entire SPEAR team. The Yakuza were formidable opponents and needed to be placated. The showdown would give Mai a chance to fulfil her obligations and maybe even earn a little redemption. Life might yet return to normal.

Survival is not necessarily essential for any of that to happen.

Her mind flicked back to the night Komodo died. Yes, she

had been willing to die. Yes, she had almost accepted it. Then Komodo saved her from a death she could not have saved herself from. How did such an act change a soul? Was there more of her story yet to be written?

The warrior was coming.

Mai had yet to decide on a venue but she knew it would be Tokyo. If she died she wanted to be close to her sister and Hibiki, and far from Drake. The Englishman had to get on with his life. Their future had died the moment she killed a man called Hayashi.

The healed bullet wound throbbed. She realized that she didn't want to die. She would kill the warrior if she could.

CHAPTER SEVEN

Drake jumped out of the black SUV amidst a scene from hell. Darkness had fallen and the San Jose electrical substation stood like an alien outpost—a sparse car park led to a perfunctory wall and then what appeared to be a tangled mass of short pylons and large transformers, beyond which stood a series of small buildings. Sounds of gunfire and an explosion rocked the night even as the SPEAR team began to move, adding to the feeling that they had entered some kind of hostile extra-terrestrial movie set. Drake saw where the wall had been breached. Amassed around it were a bunch of dark-clothed figures, their camouflage completed by ski-masks. They had noticed the new team's arrival and were now training weapons upon them.

Drake ducked behind their SUV as gunfire rang out, finding himself staring up at the stars all of a sudden.

"Covering crew," Smyth said next to him.

Drake nodded. "The main gang are already inside."

"But what are they targeting?" Dahl put in.

"Haven't the foggiest," Drake said thickly. "I'll ask the first man who doesn't try to kill me."

Smyth nodded. "We ready?"

Drake shook his head at the man's enthusiasm, surveying the scene from across the vehicle's front end. Hayden and Kinimaka were out of sight and creeping around the far side of the car park. Drake waited.

Hayden rose and opened fire with her brand new Sig Sauer MPX gas-operated sub-machine gun. Drake knew from the recent round of emails that it housed the world's first fully closed and rotating bolt system, designed to enhance the safety of its user. The SPEAR team—among other frontline teams—were the first to use it in the US.

Guinea pigs almost, Drake thought. *Exactly what we need right now.*

Hayden used the front and rear flip-up sights to hone in on her target and then sprayed the gaggle of mercenaries. Kinimaka moved fast at her side. Drake watched men collapse, falling back against the shattered wall and disappearing through. As the survivors turned their sights towards Hayden, Drake rose and opened fire. The Sig felt good in his hands, smooth and well-engineered, imparting increasing confidence with every bullet that left the chamber. It took only a few moments for him to require a mag change and then he was halfway across the car park. Now in line with their aggressors he could see beyond and into the substation itself. The tidings weren't good.

Beyond the gravel path that bordered the interior he stared through the tangle of seemingly misshaped pylons. Some were listing, almost destroyed. Was this their goal then? Destroy the station's capabilities, or at least one particular transformer or grid?

Maybe. This wasn't the time.

Dahl squeezed past on the right. The Swede was totally focused, sprinting toward the next car and squeezing off bullets on semi-auto. Drake took a last look through the gap in the wall—the area was well lit. He was shocked to see the size of the mercenary contingent already converging on the main offices, a veritable swarm of unconscionable killers.

Beauregard's information had been correct. Which posed the nasty little question—who the hell was that guy working for?

Drake would never trust a double-agent. If they'd turned once they could do so again. The real reason they turned the first time was all a prospective new handler needed to explore.

The Yorkshireman played backup to Dahl for a while, running and covering and pinning the enemy down. At last they cleared the breach in the wall and met up with Hayden.

"You see how many are inside?" she asked.

"Dozens," Drake said. "I lost count."

Dahl bashed the head in of a man who suddenly rose beside them.

"Fucking zombie," Smyth growled.

Drake looked back to their transport. Inside, Karin, Lauren and Yorgi were monitoring the comms. "You guys hear anything?"

"You have major backup on the way," Lauren said, probably talking for Karin who would be collating the information. "But it's still fifteen minutes out. Maybe a few cops here in five, but that's as good as it gets. The FBI are en route too."

Drake shook his head. "These pricks will be vamoosed by then."

"Contact from inside the substation suggests they are trying to defend."

"No," Hayden said. "Tell the staff and security men to stand down and hide as best they can. This ain't worth their lives and the mercenaries are tooled up to the max. We're gonna try to slow them down."

"Understood."

Drake climbed over what was left of the wall first, much to Dahl's annoyance. The Swede quickly jumped across next and then the entire team were running carefully between pylons and junction boxes, exploring the starkly-lit alien world and trying to keep sight of the mercs ahead. Drake squinted, aware that such bright lights would leave an afterimage on his retina and impair his vision once they were clear. An explosion rang out. They saw an entire section of wall collapse and then the mercs were inside, scrambling over the rubble. Gunshots sounded, but Drake just hoped they were warning rounds and that the staff had heeded their warnings.

Another contingent of men had stayed behind, either to aid escape or deter the authorities. Drake and his team did not stop. They raced ahead, taking cover behind pylons and wincing as bullets chimed and reverberated around them, sometimes passing straight through.

To a man, they dropped to the ground.

Drake aimed for legs, taking three men down. He crawled to the next available cover. Dahl fired at his side and Smyth beside him. The ground was hard concrete, almost blinding in the artificial light. The entire place hummed as if possessed by a swarm of bees and, above, sparks flew as if neighboring pylons might be attracted to each other.

The SPEAR team fell among the remaining mercs, their speed stunning as they converged from three sides. Drake slammed the butt of his rifle into one man's face, always wanting the death toll to be as low as possible, and fighting against elements of old training that urged him to never leave a live enemy behind.

The world was different now, and it was hard not to change with it.

Dahl rendered another merc comatose to the side, then Smyth disarmed a third. Hayden shot a fourth an instant before he fired on her, his loosed shot slamming into a nearby pylon. Kinimaka was down, struggling with another but using his considerable weight, twisting the man's arm until he let go of his weapon.

Dahl surveyed the facility. It seemed an RPG had been brought to bear on the main door, blasting it right off its hinges. Hayden's phone chirped, much to her annoyance.

"Fuck's sake! Even in the middle of a battle they can't leave me well alone!"

Drake hauled up one of the survivors and pulled off his ski-mask "So tell me, matey. What's going on?"

The mercenary struggled. He was a battered-looking individual—face crisscrossed with old scars and an odd "broken" look to his jaw, as if had dislocated once and never properly reset. His eyes fired bullets as violently as any old Uzi.

"Go fu—"

Drake shook him, then realized how futile the gesture was. "Not even a cryptic clue?" he asked. "A tidbit?"

"Like I said, asshole—"

Smyth stepped in just as Hayden cursed. The entire team turned toward her as she stared in dumb disbelief at the facility all around them.

"It's a ruse," she whispered. "This entire attack. These men . . ." She gestured at the dead and wounded. "The poor bastards who work here . . . it's all a fucking trick."

"*What?*" Drake couldn't stop his eyes practically bulging.

Dahl clucked, disbelieving. "Not a chance. This is a *full scale assault,* Hayden."

"I know. And the mercs who blasted their way inside? They ran straight through, leaving by the rear even now, according to those stuck inside. *While an even larger force is currently attacking the main San Jose substation.*"

"I don't . . . get it," Lauren said through the comms.

"Neither do I. Clearly . . . our informant . . . either lied or was fed false information. This attack is all subterfuge whilst the Pythians hit their main target."

"But we're in San Jose," Yorgi said. "How many substations are there?"

"Many thousands," Hayden said. "Karin. Where's the principal San Jose substation?"

"Not three miles from you," Karin said. "And get this. That same substation was hit by a sniper attack, disabling it a few years ago, and then suffered another security breach a few years later. The Pythians appear to have targeted a facility that has a long history of breaches."

"Three miles?" Dahl heard only what was currently relevant

to him. "Then let's get over there."

Drake nodded and raised his weapon as sirens sounded close by. "What are we waiting for?"

Hayden was already stalking away. "Get the fucking transport ready. This time we'll be going in hot."

CHAPTER EIGHT

Hayden had ensured all combatants were in the first of their two SUVs, whilst communications would be handled by the second. That way they could drive as far inside the power plant as they were able.

Reports indicated that the second assault force was even larger. Drake began now to realize the size of the new problem they were up against.

"Beauregard told us that they'd swamped the ranks with mercenaries," he said. "I guess we didn't fully understand how many until now."

The SUV jounced along the badly asphalted road. Hayden grunted. "He might have been right about that point," she said. "But why send us to the wrong substation?"

"We can't answer that now," Dahl said. "Let's leave the questions for later and work on getting a step ahead of our enemy this time."

"Better still," Kinimaka muttered. "Our focus should be on finding this asshole, Webb. Put an end to the threat at its source in one big swoop."

Drake agreed. "He's right. Cut off the head and the body dies. We're not talking a terrorist organization here, folks, we're talking a bunch of rich autocrats."

"As much as I agree with both of you," Hayden said, pointing ahead. "We already have our main focus right now. Webb has been firing attack after attack at us since the Pythians began. He will implode soon. He has to. Right now we have this facility and the ghost ships to focus on. Our job, for now at least, is pretty clear."

The San Jose substation bore every resemblance imaginable to its smaller sister. PG&E, it seemed—the people who owned the facility—weren't big on change.

Smyth, driving their SUV, aimed for the demolished outer wall. No mercs guarded this entry point and the vehicle bounced through, riding the rough terrain presented by the scattered heaps of bricks. Drake clung on to the grab handle whilst scanning the area ahead.

"There."

Smyth saw it too, aiming the SUV around the gravel track toward the jagged hole in the building's wall. A man was staggering out of there now, a man, wearing a blood-soaked shirt and tie.

"Hurry!" Hayden cried.

Smyth juiced the throttle. The vehicle eventually slewed to a halt before the wavering man. Drake leapt out of the door.

"Where are you hurt?"

The man fell to his knees, holding his chest. Hayden dropped beside them.

". . . came through about ten . . . ten minutes ago . . ." the man gasped. ". . . crowd of them with guns, all screaming . . . I didn't drop fast enough . . ."

Drake saw the bullet wound and quickly put pressure on it. "Ten minutes?" he glanced worriedly at the others.

"Not good," Dahl said.

Hayden attended the man. "Go," she said. "I'll look after him. You guys need to hurry."

Drake hurdled the rubble and landed inside the building. Alarms blared and emergency lights shone. He raced down a narrow corridor and then through an already blasted-apart door into a spacious high-ceilinged room. At its far end stood a complex of offices and it was from this direction that a barrage of bullets erupted. Drake dived to the floor, rolling as the air was crisscrossed with death. As he did so, mercs fell from above and jumped in from the sides.

An ambush.

A forest of feet obscured his vision. Pain erupted where boots kicked at him. Then two enormous pairs smashed among them—Dahl and Kinimaka laying waste to their enemies. Drake rolled and jumped up. A foot smashed him in the ribs but he ignored the pain. He caught the arm of his attacker and broke it, then twisted and engaged another. A merc landed a blow on the back of his neck, making the joints creak. Drake saw stars for a moment, turning amidst half a dozen enemies all intent on stamping him to mush. Bullets still hammered above their heads, probably fired from gung-ho assholes. Drake somehow managed to stay on his feet, using the crush of the mercs themselves to remain vertical. This was close combat like he'd never dreamed of. A blow to the ribs at this distance was a mere slap, a "love tap" as Drake used to call them. He pushed and fought to gain some room, wary of knives but unable to see much of anything.

Shouting came from the far side. More alarms began to bay. Through a brief gap between the bobbing heads, Drake saw the alarm room light up like the Fourth of July, and men bent over flickering screens. Something significant was going on in there. Then, Dahl and Kinimaka were back, physically grabbing hold of mercs and pulling them out of the crush of bodies, launching them through the air. Smyth knelt and shot the flying bodies as they landed.

"Like shooting tin-cans in a field," he murmured, shifting his sights to take out a soaring merc as he might a clay pigeon. "Next!"

Dahl obliged, hefting a struggling ski-mask covered man out of the throng and then flinging him into space. The next merc caught the Swede by surprise, hammering a closed fist at his solar-plexus and then immediately grinning.

He'd fully expected Dahl to go down after that enormous hit.

The mad Swede bellowed in anger, picked the man up and used him as a battering ram to take out three more. At last, Drake began to see some light. Ducking and rolling he escaped the crush, swinging his weapon around as he went.

"Fire!"

Drake, Dahl, Kinimaka and Smyth were all on the outside of the merc pack now and, upon seeing guns swiveling toward them and no sign of enemy surrender, immediately opened fire. Bodies fell and twisted. Blood sprayed and then curdled on the floor. Shots went off as mercs folded, now just lead fired up at the roof. Drake turned to check the state of what he believed was the main operations room.

Mercs were piling out and forming a perimeter. Other men moved within that perimeter, guarded, making swiftly for a far door. *The bastards have already taken what they came here for!*

"Attack!"

Drake knew there was no alternative, and that single word would convey all he wanted to say. *No option, no surrender. Take these fuckers to hell!*

Fanning out and moving slowly forward, the four men opened fire without relenting. Their Sig MPX's barked and spat with fury, emitting the fire of devils desperate to be unleashed. Bodies collapsed all along the mercenary line and at least one of their dependents keeled over, his blood spraying against the office wall. Return fire was hesitant, the entire line now in two minds and intimidated under fire. The four-man SPEAR team increased their speed, unconsciously working as one, fully aware of the men at their sides and what they might do next. Some bullets flew between them but they did not flinch. The force of their fire decimated the mercenary line. Behind that line several men ran and hit a far door, booting it open, one with a package strapped to his back. Drake forced the advance even more, feeling the risk was worth it, and riding their wave of luck.

Until it all crashed down.

Smyth took a bullet to the chest. One minute he strode with them, a solid and proven link in the chain. They were invincible, unstoppable. Then a well-aimed slug kicked him off his feet, depositing him onto his back with a heavy grunt of pain.

The sight of their comrade falling hit the rest of them hard. Memories of Komodo were fresh in their brains. When Smyth was hit, Drake instantly dropped to his knees beside the man only to find both Dahl and Kinimaka doing the same.

Their eyes met above the groaning body.

"Thank God for Kevlar," Drake breathed, voicing the thought that came to them all at the same time.

"Isn't it time for something new?" Dahl wondered.

Smyth grimaced as he tried to sit up. "Fuck me, guys. What the fuck are you doing down here? The assholes are getting away!"

Drake breathed out long and carefully, tempted to let his fist give the explanation but quickly rising above such crassness. Instead he leaned on Smyth's impact zone as he stood up.

"Shall we?"

With Smyth carping after them Drake, Dahl and Kinimaka ran headlong for the far door. Drake picked off a covering henchman. Dahl turned as another leapt from the shadows, knife in hand. The blade passed by the Swede's neck, drawing a single speck of blood but not an ounce of reaction beyond swift retribution. Dahl left him motionless, head canted at an unhealthy angle.

Drake slowed quickly as he reached the door, wary of booby traps, but there were none. The comms system crackled and Lauren reported the arrival of a huge contingent of cops and agents and ambulances. Kinimaka shouted that they should be redirected to the building's rear.

"They will be too late," Dahl intoned.

Drake thought about the sprawling office they had just passed. Not surprisingly it had been crammed full of multi-colored screens, computers and other monitors. Was this station an electrical hub? If something was stolen—either physically or electronically—how would they know?

He saw the tripwire at the last minute, pulled up before the single glistening thread, and held an arm out. Kinimaka, almost inevitably, noticed way too late and had to launch his huge bulk through the air and over the wire. The Hawaiian crashed down, sliding, coming to a halt a hair's-breadth from a second shimmering cable.

"Crap," he breathed, nose almost touching the cord. With great care he shuffled back and tried to pull his feet underneath him.

"Wait!" Dahl suddenly shouted. "There's another wire at shoulder height and it's right above you!"

Kinimaka froze, left in an ungainly position. Drake examined one wire whilst Dahl leapt over to the second. Within a moment they had disarmed both. As Kinimaka finally gained his feet, the Swede made short work of the third.

"Thanks guys," Mano said.

"None needed," Drake said. "It's what we do."

The delay had cost them. By the time they traversed the rest of the corridor, moving slowly in case of further traps, their quarry was gone. One more merc lay bleeding out to the right of the farthest door, but Dahl categorically stopped anybody from approaching him, fearful that a grenade might have been wedged beneath his body.

"I guess that's part of reaping what you sow." Drake thought about the previous snares, still feeling a twinge of guilt at not being able to help the merc.

"Let's move." Smyth was with them again. "And quit being such pansy-ass pussies."

The door opened into cool night air. Drake went first, gun up, checking every direction, squinting again in the harsh glare of artificial light. It took a moment for his vision to adjust.

"There," he said.

They headed toward something that gleamed in the dark, the only thing Drake could see that didn't quite fit. As they approached, a heavy motor coughed into life and rotors began to whir. A chopper rose, its cockpit blacked out, another shadow in the dark. Now Drake saw other choppers, maybe as many as five, most of which were redundant now so many mercs hadn't made it. As they approached the rising bird cops and other forces streamed around the side of the building, yelling for all and sundry to "eat the fucking dirt and lace their hands together over their heads!" Drake knew there was no point arguing. He lowered his weapon.

The chopper banked as it rose, audaciously passing over the running cops. Then Drake saw why.

"Get down!" he cried. "Down! Now!"

Leaning out of one of the doors was a man holding a chain gun. Heavy caliber rounds thunked into the ground and the building, causing mini explosions wherever they hit. Mercifully the rounds all passed between the cops but the message was abundantly clear.

Stay the fuck down.

The chopper ascended and then took off to the north. Drake watched it go with a sense of unfinished business ricocheting around his mind.

"Your time will come," he said under his breath. "And soon."

CHAPTER NINE

In the aftermath they sat and stood around the SUV, taking stock of what potentially had been stolen.

Hayden stood washing her hands free of blood, using water she poured out of a small Evian bottle. "We have no idea what they took. Engineers are going over everything right now. Hopefully it will be glaringly obvious."

Drake harbored doubts and said so. "Any news from the guys deciphering our own Z-box yet?"

"Not a squeak."

Dahl nodded toward the overwhelmed facility. "I feel like we both won and lost here today. The amount of mercs we took down put a dent in their resources, but they still managed to escape with what they came for."

"We lost," Smyth said pessimistically.

"And remember, Beauregard told us *three* substations will be hit," Dahl said. "Any clues as to which is next?"

Again Hayden shook her head, upending the rest of the bottle over her face. "The investigation is underway."

She indicated Karin inside the rear SUV, already tapping away at a laptop with Lauren seated beside her. "It's time to move ahead."

Drake chewed his lower lip. "Do you think? Splitting our forces in the light of what we just saw? Is that wise?"

Hayden shrugged. "Like we said before: Grabbing a Pythian might end this entire fiasco. It'll get us several steps closer, for sure. And right now we know where at least one of them is. We also have to cover this ghost ship angle in case it turns out to be even worse than the friggin' Z-boxes. We can't allow them to just take anything they find."

Drake saw her logic. "Okay, agreed. So I guess we're headed to Arizona." He glanced at Dahl. "You be okay without a hand to hold?"

The Swede grimaced. "Would you like a hug before you go?"

Drake raised both eyebrows, his expression deadly serious. "Considering the specter of where we're going, the spookiness of what we're chasing, and all those ghost stories and apparitions I think a hug might be good about now."

He moved in. Dahl almost tripped over his feet in an effort to escape. Subdued smiles flickered across all their faces.

None of them wanted to split the family up right now.

CHAPTER TEN

Yuma was a city in the southwestern corner of Arizona, first settled by Native Americans whose reservations still exist in parts of the state. Expeditions later saw the trade and living opportunities offered by the narrowing of the Colorado River at this point, and during the California Gold Rush the Yuma Crossing became known as the gateway to California.

Drake found himself pacing the hotel lobby wondering where the hell the rest of the crew had gotten to before realizing this was it. This was all—the extent of his current team—Lauren, Smyth and Karin.

The decision had been made to arrive low key. There was no telling who the Pythians had enlisted or paid off, no guessing how many spies they had dug in around the area. Thus, the four-strong group were vacationers, stowing what military gear they may need in oversized backpacks. Once their rooms had been allocated they trooped into the elevators, all heading for Karin's room.

Drake voiced everyone's thought. "So give us a clue. Where do we start?"

Lauren spoke up. "Where did Nicholas Bell start? With stories, I guess. So short of flying over all of Arizona and California with a spotting scope we'd best put our resident genius to work." She patted Karin's shoulder.

Karin grunted, still far away. Drake wondered for the thousandth time if she should even be here. But then, where else? Grieving alone? Therapy? There were far worse places to be than following lost treasure.

Just ask Alicia.

Drake again found himself thinking about the Englishwoman and her endless march forward. It was at times like this that a separation of weeks felt more like years.

Karin silently plonked a laptop onto the room's only table and logged onto the free Wi-Fi. The width of the room prevented the rest of the team from standing too close so Lauren offered to make a coffee run and Smyth elected to go with her. Drake found himself suddenly alone with Ben Blake's sister, Komodo's girlfriend.

"Anything," he said. "Anything I can do to help just name it. Even if it means putting a gag on my stupid mouth."

Surprisingly, Karin turned around to stare at him. "I'm starting to believe there may be something you can do," she said. "But I'll let you know."

Drake nodded, a little taken aback. She was working through stuff and needed to ponder. He watched her pound the keys for a while and then stepped away. Lauren and Smyth returned, comfortable at each other's side, and offered strong black coffee all round. Drake liked the new Smyth; the man seemed more at ease, though the old irascibility still hovered just underneath the surface. As the group perched awkwardly on the side of the bed, Karin began to speak.

"Ghost ships of Arizona," she said. "It's no more than a bunch of legends passed down from old Red Indian days. Scary campfire stories or lost treasure mythologies—your choice. The main story," she breathed, "centers on an old Spanish galleon."

Smyth leaned forward. "Was it haunted?"

Karin continued without an acknowledgement. "Stories started springing up after the great Colorado flood, sightings put it forty miles north of Yuma. Of course, that was back in the 1860s..."

Drake wasn't sure whether to smile or knit his brows. Was she suggesting it might—somehow—have *moved*?

"These places back then had various names—Indian Springs, Soda Springs, Bitter Springs. The Salton Sea is another popular place for myths since this grew out of an even larger inland sea over the centuries. There were and are many myths that said this galleon was none other than Sir Thomas Cavendish's *Content*, filled with pirate booty. Now we're talking—a pirate ghost ship."

"Who relates all these old stories?" Lauren wanted to know. "And who remembers them?"

"Old timers." Karin shrugged. "People who grew up listening to them. Ear-benders. Entrepreneurs."

"What's so special about the *Content*?" Smyth tipped his coffee back and drank.

Karin also drank, her mind engaged in the task. "Well, Cavendish was an English explorer and privateer. He purposely tried to emulate Sir Francis Drake by raiding Spanish towns and ships and then returning triumphantly to England by circumnavigating the globe. Successfully. He became a rich man, capturing rich prizes in silk and treasure from Spanish ships he attacked. He captured a six-hundred-ton ship called the *Santa Anna*, and this was all on his *first* raiding run. Queen Elizabeth I knighted him upon his return."

"And the *Content*?"

"During Cavendish's second run and circumnavigation he encountered a little more than he bargained for. The man died at the age of thirty-one from an unknown illness whilst his navigator sailed on to discover the Falkland Islands. But the story of the *Content* actually arises from the first voyage. Cavendish had two ships near the Gulf of California—the *Content* and the *Desire*—and both were put to good use chasing down the *Santa Anna*, which was a so-called Manila galleon. Now, firstly these Manila galleons only sailed once or twice a year and carried *all the goods* accumulated through an entire year's trading. Goods from the coin mints in Peru and

Mexico to the Chinese for silk, spices, gold and other luxurious materials."

"All on one ship?" Drake said.

"Yup. In any case Cavendish got wind of this Manila galleon and hunted it for days, at last spotting and then capturing it. The *Santa Anna* struck her colors and then the English swarmed aboard, taking enough treasure to fill *both* their ships. Cavendish did allow the Spaniards food, water and weapons and put them ashore, then he set fire to the *Santa Anna*, before sailing away to continue their voyage across the Pacific. The *Content* was never heard from again. The *Desire* spent the remainder of her voyage hiding from every skirmish."

"Never heard from again?" Drake repeated. "How could that be with a ship carrying so much loot?"

"Is anybody else here wondering how a Spanish *galleon* ended up wandering the friggin' desert?" Smyth grouched. "And especially how this *English entrepreneur and privateer* sounds like nothing more than a marauding pirate?"

"Ships being marooned in the desert is not unheard of," Drake said. "Storms. Great tidal bores. Even hurricanes and typhoons can deposit ships miles away from where they were. And that includes onto solid ground."

"A tidal bore is most likely in this area," Karin stated.

Now Smyth shook his head. "I'm lost again. What's a tidal bore?"

"A wall of water moving fast up the stream bed." Karin finished her coffee and deposited the cup in the bin. "The Gulf of California's topography, incoming tides and river outflow produced the potential for unparalleled tidal bores. The basin was more than two hundred and seventy feet below sea level, perfect for flood waters. The flood could have skipped the land barrier, cresting over the natural dam and down into the Salton or Cahuilla Sea. In addition, it seems that the Salton

Sea and Gulf of California were once connected."

Drake whistled. "I bet those poor sailors had a bit of a shock."

"Early surfers," Lauren agreed. "But without the boards."

"I never heard of such a great tidal flood," Smyth said with suspicion. "Surely it can't only have happened that one time."

"These days a tidal bore can no longer occur," Karin read. "Due to the depletion of water from agriculture and municipal use before it reaches the gulf."

"Gah. Always a freakin' answer."

Karin glanced around at him. "You can always try this yourself." She picked up the laptop.

Smyth quickly held his hands out, muttering an apology. Lauren frowned in his direction.

Karin sighed. "Sorry. I'm not myself at the moment. Bores occur in relatively few locations worldwide and are generally nothing to write home about. You only hear about them when a tragedy occurs or a rag newspaper needs some sensationalism to help sell a few extra copies."

"Okay," Drake said. "So in the right conditions the ship in a desert phenomenon could occur. What we have to do now is to find it. I know you said 'old timers', but where in particular have all the ghost stories come from?"

"The Red Indians," she said. "Or Native Americans, as they're now called. They started it. Legends were expanded when the local prospectors and explorers of the time decided to make their own investigations. One man named Charley Clusker. Another named Colonel Albert S Evans. Another called Fierro Blanco. These men knew natives from every tribe of Baja California of that time and attest that the local tribes never once lied to them. The kicker here is that—just like the peculiar worldwide dragon myth—everybody tells the same story and offers the same descriptions. The myth has persisted. It's always similar, and survives both in Native

American and frontier lore. It's spookily uncanny."

"Why has it never been found?" Lauren wondered. "Surely a well-organized flyover would do it."

"The desert's an astoundingly large place. Wind-blown sands from the desiccated delta of the Colorado River generate vast sand dune systems that are constantly shifting. Storms spring up in seconds. Then there's mud near the inland waters and other dangers. It's entirely possible that the things one storm uncovers, the next completely eradicates. And, supposedly, it *was* found. Several times. Only to disappear again."

"But not recently?"

"The last sighting occurred in the 1970s," Karin related. "Though it wasn't corroborated. Ground penetrating radar would reveal a ship's remains but nobody has managed to accomplish such an undertaking yet."

Drake made a noise. "Except possibly our new potential friend, Nicholas Bell."

"That seems likely."

"And if we sought to replicate his activity?"

"It would undoubtedly reveal us to him."

"Then what's the answer?"

Karin closed her laptop, staring with more than a little regret at the slim black case. To Drake it seemed as if it might be for the last time.

"Are you okay?"

"We go old school," Karin said. "Seek out the old timers. Head into the desert. We find the ghost ships the old way."

Drake thought of all the times they had used modern technology to solve their problems, their ancient quandaries. "That should be different."

"It's the only way."

"An expedition?" Smyth was clearly trying hard to keep his voice neutral. "Campfires and tents? Trail guides? Sleeping under the stars? Not sure I like the sound of that."

"Are you scared?" Drake asked. "Scared of the desert's ghosts?"

"Fuck, yeah. Aren't you?"

"I'm more scared of getting swallowed and buried in a sandstorm."

"And yeah, there's that too!" Smyth jumped onboard Drake's theory as if it were a million-dollar yacht. "Mostly that."

"Don't worry." Lauren patted the back of his hand. "I'll keep you safe. Us New Yorkers don't take no shit from anyone, especially ghosts."

"Questions need to be asked locally," Karin said. "And quietly."

Drake took a quick look out the window. The sun was descending in the west but hadn't set yet. "No time like the present."

"I'll come with you," Smyth said. "Get me out of this pokey old room."

Drake winked carefully at him. "I'd prefer to take Karin," he said neutrally. "A man and woman would look more natural than two burly old blokes."

"Old?" Smyth protested but got the point. "No worries."

Karin stroked the lid of her laptop once more. "I'll come with you, Matt."

Drake wondered just what the hell was going on in her head.

Yuma basked beneath a clear sky full of sunshine, even as sundown approached. Karin told Drake that this town was officially the sunniest place on earth, with clear skies for 90 percent of daylight hours. Drake stared at the wide, scorched streets.

"Think there's an old timer's bar around here, love?"

"Probably a hundred. But why bother buying 'em drinks when they advertise their services on the web?"

Drake barely stopped his mouth from falling open. "They do? Where?"

Karin tapped her head. "All in here. Eidetic memory, remember?" She smiled at the small joke.

Drake grinned more than he should. "Amazing. Lead on."

Karin surveyed the area. "I'm not too sure about this bloody 'old school' thing," she said. "What we need now is some kinda satnav."

Drake pointed out the white-walled building flanked by trees off to the right. "Old school satnav right there," he said. "I think they call it a post office."

Karin nodded. "Use to be the corner shop that gave you directions," she smiled, "where I grew up."

"Me too." Drake set off. "Along with a pound's worth of Black Jacks, Midget Gems and kaylie."

"Kaylie?"

"I guess you're too young. Kaylie was like sherbet, only better. Rainbow kaylie was the best; all you did was dip your finger in the bag, get it covered, and then pop it in your mouth. At the end of the bag your finger always ended up bright yellow."

"Sounds great," Karin said in a non-committal tone. The pair entered the post office, requested directions, and were on their way to a meeting point in just a few minutes.

"How did you know which old guy to choose?" Drake asked.

"I didn't, of course. I just went for the oldest of them all."

"Oh. Well remember, we don't want him to expire out in the desert."

"Then he shouldn't be advertising his services."

Drake stayed quiet, making sure they made their rendezvous in good time. Far from a dingy bar, it turned out to be the lobby of one of the town's classiest hotels and it was clear from the start that the man they met only wanted to fleece them, asking for money upfront within the first five minutes. Karin asked a few pointed questions and then they parted company, heading for rendezvous number two. The second man turned out to be almost as shameless, but when he found out they seriously meant business, he went quiet for several moments. Subsequently, the face he turned upon them was thoughtful.

"All right. I can tell you're not the usual fare we get through here. There's a man," he said. "There are two or three if I'm being totally truthful. No shit, I can point you the right way and I can see you're havin' no part of me. That's fine. But you won't find ole timers like him on the Web, Miss. That's for amateurs. These ole guys are strictly word-o-mouth."

"And I imagine you want paying for pointing us in the right direction?" Drake asked.

"Tell you what . . . *I'll* trust *you*. Don't matter to me either way. If you get what you need come find me—pay me what you think the information was worth."

Drake shrugged. "All right. But don't even think about trying to lead us out into the desert and laying an ambush, old man."

"Never crossed my mind, friend. Trouble is though . . . Kelly . . . he's the kinda guy finds you."

"Meaning?"

The old man chuckled. "Meaning you head out into the desert, friend, and he'll find you. I can arrange it tonight."

"Seriously? Do we look like we were born yesterday?"

"Nope. Well, she does. You—not so much."

Drake wasn't entirely sure he shouldn't be offended. "Hey!"

"I know. Long paper round. Old before your time. So, ya gonna meet my man or what? You won't be getting a better offer today."

Drake stared into the watery eyes for a time, then turned to

Karin. "I can't believe I'm agreeing to this."

"He seems cool. And it's the best chance we've got."

Drake bit his tongue. That may be true, but it was no way to move forward. His mind flicked over alternative choices and found them startlingly sparse. Without a local, first-rate guide they would be lost in the desert—quite plainly. On the other hand, Yuma, and these old men, hardly seemed likely to imperil his team. The risk was negligible. "Why should we hit the desert?"

"The ghost ships are out there," the old man said, nodding dreamily. "An' I'm making no bones about it. Not blowing yer skirt up neither, excuse me, Miss."

"Don't worry." Karin almost smiled. "I've heard—and seen—worse."

"Then I'm mighty sorry about that. An' as I said—those ships're out there. Galleons. Longboats. A schooner. Set eyes on more'n one of 'em meself."

"Have you?" Drake wondered how much more embellishment the tale could get. If the reports of Nicholas Bell's actions out here in Arizona weren't so reliable he'd have moved on to more important things by now.

Then again, he'd once set eyes on his own set of fanciful longboats.

Karin's voice broke his musings. "How do these boats move around?"

The old man's eyes were speculative. "They don't, of course, young lady. The geography moves around them. Dunes become valleys and hills turn into basins. No two storms leave the landscape untouched. And you never wanna get in the middle of a dust or sand storm out here, not a bad one. They whip up like wraiths, bad genies that wrap around you and take you down, deep into the desert. You get turned around, lost, buried. They would never find you."

"And that's why the ships are so scary." Karin nodded in understanding.

The old man looked at her through slitted eyes. "No, young lady. They're scary because at night, when it's full dark, they creep, they loom, they threaten and sneak. They haunt the desert, Miss, and if you don't respect them they will spirit you away forever to your doom."

CHAPTER ELEVEN

Hayden snatched a moment with Mano, taking him out onto the balcony as Dahl spoke to his wife inside their suite. Her purpose was manifold, but first she wanted to reassure him.

"We'll get past all this," she said. "The Pythians. Webb. The stalkings. Even Kono, I hope. We're strong, Mano. Stronger even than that new body armor we're trialing."

"Speaking of trialing—how did you find the new Sig?"

Hayden made a happy face. "Kick ass."

"Sure. Me too. And we've sure had our canoes sunk more times than I can count lately," Kinimaka said figuratively and looked down at her. "Do you think the Pythians have much more in the tank?"

"Not if we cane their asses this time," Hayden said. "They can recruit more leaders by the dozen, by the hundred, it doesn't matter. Webb is gonna explode big time."

"Which I for one want to see."

"We will."

"Together."

"Together."

Hayden held the big Hawaiian tight, pressing herself into his body. In an odd way, standing as they were exposed on the balcony, she felt less scrutinized than in her own street and home. And safer than in her own state and government buildings.

Webb's puppet string ran twisted and extensively.

Kinimaka winked more than a little suggestively, his hand hovering lower than was appropriate at that moment. "Maybe we could . . ."

Hayden wriggled a little. "Ooh, Mano."

"Not being under surveillance and all that maybe we could be a bit more . . . experimental?"

Hayden closed her eyes in anticipation. "Mano!"

Dahl, standing right beside them, then spoke up. "I'd save your energy, pal. I'm sure you'll need it soon. What have you learned of the Z-boxes, Hayden?"

She had spent the last few hours liaising with their team back in DC who were carefully decoding their only device. Of course, it was a clever piece of Chinese engineering and nobody wanted to be responsible for breaking it.

"It's at least as bad as we feared. They are intricate code-cracking machines, able to extrapolate complex cipher strings and encryptions in minutes, but even they have their limitations, we think. Much of the time—unless they're decoding basic stuff like public passwords, email accounts or hacking computers—they'll need a base hardwire from which to hook in."

"Do we think that's why they hit San Jose?"

"Probably." Hayden shrugged. "It's the best guess so far."

"But what could they possibly have stolen to help with that?" Kinimaka said.

"Maybe nothing," Hayden said. "Maybe they left something behind. On a server. We have a team inbound."

"And Beau told us three substations would be attacked. So maybe they need more data first, or whatever."

"Beau also told us the wrong friggin' substation," Hayden said irritably. "But I do agree. We're putting together a list of places they're most likely to hit next."

"And by next . . ." Dahl's big hands clenched with a sense of impotence.

"Yeah, I mean now. Today. Tomorrow."

"The geeks in DC," Hayden said quietly. "They're worried this is an Aurora Vulnerability situation."

"Sounds bad."

"Worse than bad. Back in '07 Idaho University discovered that within the United States' electrical grid system there exists a vulnerability to cyber-attack, a vulnerability that could result in the destruction of essential components. It found that any attacker who can gain access—the hardest part—could communicate with the device, control it, or use the Aurora Vulnerability to damage or destroy it. Now, the electrical people say a failure of just one single generator could result in extensive outages and a *possible cascading failure of the entire electrical grid*. Just like the northeast blackout of '03."

Dahl visibly held in a curse. "Do these people never learn?"

"Oh, they learn well enough," Hayden said. "They know. And then they claim their dividends and bonuses and go buy a personal jet."

"So it's a very real situation?"

Hayden nodded. "Add to that the second vulnerability—it could take a year to fix."

"How does it work? This Aurora attack?"

"I was told it's an out-of-sync opportunity. Imagine you rev a car's engine in neutral and then, as it reaches maximum, you shift into drive. That one moment when the engine goes out of sync—going from neutral to incredible power—is when it's most vulnerable. That's when the attack is initiated."

They turned and walked inside, Hayden giving Kinimaka a "down boy" look. She stopped after a minute to stare around the hundredth, or possibly thousandth, hotel room she'd stayed in during the last few years. Eventually, they all looked the same.

She waved toward Dahl. "Johanna okay?"

He nodded, knowing instantly what she meant. "No strange happenings at the Dahl household. I think we stalker-proofed it just in time."

Kinimaka headed for the kitchen counter and his own phone. "I'll try Kono."

Hayden flung herself headlong on the room's only sofa. "What we have managed to determine is that the substations have to be relatively close together to communicate properly on the same system."

"Relatively? That means . . ."

"California."

"Ah, is that all?"

"It's been narrowed down to substations in Silicon Valley, Sierra Nevada, Santa Clara and Palo Alto. Something to do with them being on the same data streams and hard lines."

"Bloody hell." Dahl began to blink rapidly. "So what are we waiting for? They could be in danger even now."

"Webb lost a lot of men in that last assault."

"Yes, and he flooded his ranks, remember? A pleasingly pliable army."

Hayden had opened her mouth to speak when Kinimaka came rushing across, his free hand waving for attention. He pointed dramatically at his cellphone.

"Are you okay? What the hell happened?"

Kono's wavering Hawaiian tones filtered through the speakerphone. "First, I heard noises in the house. Creaks. Little knocks, you know. Like timbers settling. It's common in wood-frame houses in Hawaii and didn't bother me. Then I realized I wasn't renting the wood-framed house that I'm used to. It's a brand new brick, mortar and concrete build."

"Could still be rafters." Kinimaka couldn't help but correct his sister.

"I realized then that the little knocks and settlings sounded more like stealthy footsteps. I listened. I lay in the dark with my eyes wide open and listened like . . . never before, just staring up at my ceiling with the tiny lamp switched on. Have you ever tried that? Both ears straining so hard you could hear the sound of a feather floating through the air? Time passed. The sounds stopped. I realized I was lying on top of the sheets in just my underwear, cold, tears in my eyes, and that's when I saw it."

Kinimaka stared Dahl straight in the eyes. "Saw what?"

"On the ceiling where the main light fitting hangs, holes had been drilled to secure a previous fitting, I think, and one of them blinked."

"*What?*"

"Somebody was up in my loft, Mano, watching me through the ceiling and they had been there for a long time. Nobody gained access to the house in the last week, at least since you increased the security detail."

Kinimaka swallowed. "What happened?"

"The owner of the eye knew I'd seen him. Suddenly, the noises were loud, the sound of somebody standing and moving and then part of the ceiling came down where he miss-stepped. His foot came through. I was screaming, running for the door. The foot was above my head and then I realized he was stamping down, trying to knock me out. The heel of his boot slammed my head, unbalancing me and I ran right into the door frame, falling to my knees. At that point the boot drew away and I just knew he was headed for the hatch. But my head was woozy, my vision blurred. I climbed to my feet, screaming now, hearing the door rattle as the detail entered. But the man was already before me, leaning over, breathing heavily. He was huge and bare chested, sweating and dirty. A monster." Kono paused, her own breath coming in sharp gasps.

"That's enough," Kinimaka said. "It's enough that you're—"

"No. I have to get this out. The detail reached him first but he batted them aside. Then he walked towards me, feet stomping so loud my already pounding head almost burst. I slithered down the door frame, not only woozy but scared to death. I'm not strong, Mano, not like you or the women you work with."

You used to be, Hayden saw the words forming on Kinimaka's lips and vehemently shook her head.

Not now. Save the interrogation for later.

"The brute grabbed my hair and threw me to the floor, then knelt at my side. His lips were dry and they brushed my ear. He said, 'We'll always be watching you.' Not *I. We!* Then he grabbed my neck and the detail shot him."

Hayden blinked. Kinimaka sighed in relief. "So you're okay?"

"For now." Kono sounded like she had finally run out of steam. "Where are you? Have you guys found the asshole who's doing all this yet?"

Kinimaka grunted. "We're on it."

Hayden nodded, speaking up. "We have a lead, Kono, and we're headed out right now."

Kinimaka mouthed, "We do?"

Hayden held up her phone to show the incoming text:

Mercs seen massing near Silicon Valley. Too many to count. They came in convoys. We need help!

Hayden blanched as she digested the message. *They came in convoys?* What kind of fucked up assault were they mounting now?

CHAPTER TWELVE

Steeped in overstated luxury, the blacked-out Maybach cruised the busy streets at a leisurely pace. Tyler Webb enjoyed getting out into the world, and into Washington DC in particular. This way, hidden from prying eyes and curious cameras, he could sit forward and feel the adrenalin start to rush through his body; a living, breathing, squirming snake of dark passion, as potential new victims caught the attention of his warped radar. Here, a businessman too involved to notice the enormous pitch black Maybach and waving irritably at the driver who had braked hard to avoid crushing the man's legs. There, a family of four where the woman struggled with two kids as her husband chatted and gesticulated on his cellphone. Webb immediately snapped the man's picture—he would make a good candidate for incense and provocation. Elsewhere, a man in an open-top sports car racing between lights whose registration was taken down, and a group of youths laughing at a homeless man.

Webb saw them all as serious applicants. Not because he was by any means a bleeding heart but because these people tried hard to exude confidence. Taking every last shred from them would literally make the hairs on his arms stand up. His mouth would dry out. His toes would most likely curl.

Being chauffeured around for hours didn't put him in the best of moods. This entire Pythian thing wasn't going as well as he'd hoped. Here they were, only months into their campaign, and already key personnel were dead or lost and they had been forced to hire a goon army. Not that he didn't enjoy the expendability of his subjects—sending men to die helped dramatically boost his ego. Sometimes, he did it just for fun.

Earlier that day he had met all three new Pythian candidates—Zoe Sheers was a round-faced, wide-eyed stunner who instantly put him on his guard. The brunette appeared savvy, forward to the point of annoyance and hungry for action. Julian Marsh visibly struggled to contain his exuberance, the clothes he wore didn't quite match, and his parting was in the wrong place. His watch was on the wrong wrist, his shoes the wrong color. His smile twisted the wrong way. Webb was a little unnerved by Julian Marsh, though he buried such idiocy beneath untold layers of sinful shadow, ignoring it and tasking the man with the very next Pythian event to keep him busy. Marsh's resultant grin was entirely wrong.

Finally, Lucas Monroe, whom Webb at least knew a little of, was the blandest, quietest and least inspiring of them all. *Seriously,* Webb thought, *if the man stood in a corner for too long people would stick a lampshade on his head.*

Not a bad bunch though, and certainly no worse than the last lot. The problem was that now Webb was having serious doubts about how long the Pythians could continue. His greatest goal, the ability to seek out the great treasures of Saint Germain, was at hand.

A few more weeks . . .

And the Pythians might be no more. Maybe even now the group was actually redundant. No mind. Nicholas Bell was off seeking ghost ships and Bay-Dale was with him. Good. It gave Webb time to concentrate on the Saint Germain plan—but first he needed a vital component.

As luck would have it word had recently reached Webb's ears that the final and greatest arms bazaar hosted by the royal prince of terrorism—Ramses himself—was being planned, and soon. Webb planned to attend with his uber-bodyguard and secure the component. The top-secret guest list was already a terrible who's-who of international intrigue and terrorism, but once that was done . . .

The world will change.

The car continued to pick its way through the congested streets, courteously, carefully, with precision. Webb turned his mind back to people-watching for sixty seconds and noted one more person—a bouncer pushing a woman to the ground and grinning as he puffed up to his colleagues—before starting to ponder the Z-boxes and their current role. They were essential to the plan, a fortunate addition to Bell's escapade. Showing America the might of the Pythians would distract its leaders from the true agenda at hand. It might even cow them for a while, although Webb would have liked a weaker president than Coburn. Still, you worked with what you had. The man's underlings were more than malleable in every way.

Another thing and another godsend . . . he knew Matt Drake and Co. were wandering around the desert, seeking the ghost ships and trying to determine which electrical facility would be hit next. That gave Webb some wonderful freedoms, though it did limit his stalking capabilities—Hayden Jaye and Mano Kinimaka were off the list, at least for a while. But back to the freedoms—new prey, for example, new hunts.

Pleasure coursed through him.

Take Topless Sports Car Man, for example. If he returned to his car one day to find a sidemirror smashed, what would he do? Put it down to vandals. Then, a present left in the back seat. *One of his own discarded belongings.* Then the cogs would start to turn. A small snake in the footwell. A mound of ants perhaps. Later, attention would turn to the bank account, mortgage and other financial considerations. A slow leak, a few letters. Life would start heading downhill for Mr. Topless Sports Car. His girlfriend might desert him. Then, embarrassments at work and at the mall. Objects moved around back at the house. A stint in the man's loft, spying and planning. The game would then grow serious . . .

Webb realized he was breathing too hard, growing too passionate, and let it go. For now, the hunt was enough. It would have to be.

The car's inbuilt cellphone controls lay just below his right hand. He waited one more moment as his mind flicked over Mai Kitano—the Japanese woman had disappeared. Something about heading to Japan and trying to help her new protégé—Grace—whilst seeking out the young woman she had wronged when she killed her father. That young woman was named Emiko and even Webb had been unable to find her.

Mai Kitano though, he knew where she was right now. Which was a whole lot more than Matt Drake could say.

Webb allowed a self-satisfied, smug grin stretch out his face. Then he tapped a pre-programmed number.

"It's me."

"Yes, sir?"

"As soon as you can, kill Drake and send the US back to the dark ages."

"Yes, sir. That's the plan."

"It's the plan *now,* idiot. Now that I have given it to you. And not until then, do you understand?"

"Of course, sir."

"Let's beg to differ on that, shall we? Just get it done, man. And report. The sands of time are running out."

"There's a shitload of sand out here, sir. Not sure it's ever gonna run out."

Webb sighed, fighting off a moment's despair. At least his uber-bodyguard, Beauregard Alain, could hold down a conversation. Not like this prehistoric freak.

"Kill Drake," he repeated as though addressing a deaf old man. "And use the Z-boxes. Do you understand?"

"Yeah, I do."

Webb signed off, ignoring the final effrontery since his radar had just honed in on a new victim—the best yet. A tall, thin woman in a black pencil skirt who actually had her assistant following her, clutching cellphones, handbags, sheaves of paper and a small, yappy dog.

Oh, that's just perfect. This day ain't so bad after all.

Webb snapped her picture, trusting his powerful facial recognition software would lead him in the right direction later. The woman's assistant, looking harassed and sweaty almost tumbled, eliciting a grunt of disgust from the tall woman. Webb felt an entire flood of pleasure as the thought of stalking her swept through his body.

To hell with the Pythians, he thought. *All I need is Saint Germain . . . and this.*

And Matt Drake dead, of course.

CHAPTER THIRTEEN

Mai Kitano loved Tokyo, it was the one true home that filled her soul, but lately each homecoming had been worse than bittersweet. This one, she knew, might be her last, but the dire knowledge was offset by just one thing.

Chika.

The two sisters stood hugging in the street, Mai experiencing a moment of disbelief that she was able to stand so openly without fear of assault. That was taken care of now—though the final reckoning was coming. Dai Hibiki stood just behind her, an open smile on his face, and Grace stood off to the right, staring into the distance. Some brand new, bright red headphones covered her ears, the wire trailing down and attached to her equally new Android phone. Grace's head was nodding to an unheard beat, mostly missing the happy reunion.

Mai stepped back and allowed Hibiki a quick hug before grabbing hold of Chika once again. "We never seem to meet under happy circumstances. It is so good to see you!"

Chika spoke into her shoulder. "And you. But what is happening now? Have you heard?"

Mai took her sister by the hand and led her toward the house. "This looks nice. Have you two bought it?"

"We're renting. But, Mai?"

"You should buy it. I mean, come on, you two should have your whole lives together."

Chika pulled away as they reached the middle of the garden. The sun flashed past her right shoulder—a hot, glaring light of interrogation.

"The Yakuza are sending their best warrior to settle the score. It is probably not worth ignoring that, Mai."

The Japanese woman sighed. The road of her past stretched out behind her. The road of her future didn't stretch anywhere—it lay broken at the edges, shrouded in drifting fogs. Since hooking up with Drake and the SPEAR team during the Blood King exploit her life had developed more meaning, rounding out all the rough edges and finally making sense. She had remained deadly, hard, yet surrounded by caring friends and colleagues, now whole. But life never let you live the way you wanted to. It threw hurdles and complications your way like a gleeful jester performing for its uncaring master. Through their adventures from Hawaii to Germany, from Iraq to North Korea, from ancient Babylon and Sunnyvale UK to Washington DC and Hong Kong and now Japan she had grown more and more accustomed to the new life. It had molded her, and she had happily invited it in.

Then—her parents, Grace and murder. Everything had changed. The knife-edge of life was more dangerous than any opponent she had ever faced. At least Grace seemed to be quickly growing for the better.

Mai regarded Chika now with Grace in the background. Instead of answering her sister she focused on Grace. The young woman had blossomed during this trip and indeed during the danger that came before it. More than the actual danger, Mai knew it was the purity of living life that helped Grace shrug off her old fears and nightmares. It was experience, involvement, interaction. Get dirty, get complicated; immerse yourself in life's entangled web.

One life, she thought. *Live it.*

Bloody hell, I'm starting to sound like Alicia!

Maybe Grace's flourishing good moods were starting to have a positive effect on her. Maybe she could get past all this.

Maybe . . .

Chika thrust her hands onto her hips, the no-nonsense look reminding Mai of a much younger girl and a much more innocent time.

"I love you," she told her sister suddenly, openly.

Chika's face crumbled, the sisterly affection shining through. Despite their years apart they were bonded forever. Nothing could ever change that. Grace finally noticed and bounced into their embrace, clueless to what she was interrupting and all the more lovable for it.

"Group hug!" she cried, beckoning Hibiki.

When they broke, Mai turned away and addressed Chika. "I have accepted the Yakuza's terms and am awaiting notice. It won't be long now."

"Shouldn't you be . . . training . . . practicing or something?"

Mai smiled. "I doubt I will improve my abilities in a day or two."

"They say he's their best. He will be no pushover, Mai."

She refrained from telling her sister that she did not expect to win. "He's human. I have had nightmares far worse than anything any human could ever do to me."

Hibiki inclined his head. "Haven't we all?"

"I guess." Chika looked between them as if searching out an answer. "But Dai told me he was a Ninja master, unbeaten. A devil."

"Everyone's a Ninja." Mai faked a laugh. "Or so it seems lately. You would think the brotherhood never really died out."

"Maybe it didn't. That is actually the whole *point* of Ninjas. That you don't even know they're there."

Mai turned away quickly, again surveying the house. "I really think you two should consider buying this place. It's lovely. And safe—for when the kids come."

Chika almost choked. "Kids? Whoa, give us chance. I haven't lived *my* life yet."

"There are many who believe life truly begins when your first child is born."

"And I get that. But, hey, let's cook supper first."

Chika and Hibiki led her toward the large dwelling. Grace looped her arm and skipped along, grinning at everything, including a bed of roses. Mai wondered briefly if she had eaten too much chocolate for lunch and then found herself back in the whole "kids" state of affairs. Was she visualizing Grace as her surrogate daughter?

Later that night, she managed to draw Hibiki aside. "Did you hear anything about Emiko?"

The Japanese policeman instantly darkened. "That window has long since closed," he said. "Where we might save or rescue her. It is many weeks since she vanished from our custody, as you know. I'm sorry, Mai, but I wouldn't expect to hear anything relating to Emiko again."

"She could turn up."

"Do any of them ever turn up? Do you ever hear of children or adults who vanish on the streets—who are sold into slavery or work gangs or forcibly turned dependent on drugs—ever returning weeks or months later? I don't, Mai, and I'm a cop."

Mai swallowed down a rising, expanding bubble of guilt. "I wronged her family."

"Maybe, maybe not. You can't do anything about that now, so get on with it."

Mai imagined Drake might say the same. That thought made her think of the two people who had the most impact on her life.

Ah Matt, she thought. *And Alicia. Where are you now and who are you royally pissing off?*

CHAPTER FOURTEEN

Truth be told, Matt Drake felt more than a little foolish. People told him the Bones of Odin quest sounded a little far-fetched, but searching for a five-hundred-year-old sunken ship in a barren desert really unhinged something inside him. He understood the logic, even the reality of a ship being deposited out here, but then someone had to go and label them *ghost galleons* or some such and spoil the entire bloody thing.

Bollocks.

He'd have an easier time seeking out an investment banker's market stall in the middle of Pontefract, Yorkshire.

As darkness fell across the desert he found himself seated with Karin, Lauren, Smyth and Yorgi around a hastily laid campfire. Blankets were spread beneath them, backpacks sitting alongside. The heat that had palled the day was thankfully beginning to dissipate as though someone had left the oven door open. Drake took a long swig of water and surveyed the landscape.

Sand dunes of varying heights undulated all around them, forming a natural valley for their rest. Nobody was under any illusions that the same dunes might last until morning, but the good news was that no storms were incoming. None that could be forecast anyway.

Yer take yer chances, their guide had told them. *I ain't stayin' out here.* And he had slunk off with that slightly terrified blank stare across his features.

So now they sat awaiting their mysterious new guide— Kelly, the old man who would find them in the desert. *The Ghost Ship Whisperer,* Drake thought with a silent chuckle.

The landscape wasn't all sand. It was composed of dried roots and barren, gravelly paths. Brown straggly trees. Flat, austere land. A featureless plain lay beyond the dunes, home to few but master of all. The falling night came down like a hammer to an anvil, fast and hard, and soon the lands were blanketed in darkness. A heavy silence descended with it that soon became broken by odd, anomalous sounds.

Drake broke a tense silence. "So, who's up for Scrabble?"

Karin didn't look up. Only Yorgi glanced over at him. "Is it you being serious? You did not bring Scrabble, no?"

"No mate, I didn't. But I did bring this." He whipped out a silver hip-flask. "A bit of west-coast grit."

Smyth held out a hand. "I'll take some of that."

Drake threw him the flask. "Since we're here for the night how about a game of 'I Spy'?"

Now Lauren threw him a withering look. "Really, man? What you gonna say? Something beginning with the letter 'S'? 'Cause that's all I see round here."

Drake rose up on his haunches. "All right, all right, so I'm bored. Look, I'm off to take first watch. Shout me if, you know, one of those bloody galleons rises or jumps out at ya."

He climbed the constantly shifting hill and studied the backdrop. It was uniform to the degree of pointlessness. Of course, this kind of backdrop made it harder to stand watch. Everything looked the same, ergo nothing moved. And now the darkness was lightly caressing every horizon, blotting out the light and forcing him to rely solely on hearing. He crouched down, getting accustomed to the surroundings and the "normal" sounds that infested the night. A faint wind scuffled through the sand, sending tiny rivulets streaming downhill like a miniature dry river. His friends chatted quietly. A small animal ferreted nearby. Like any other place on earth, the desert had its patterns and its laws. Drake respected and learned them. Below, the campfire crackled and sent a thin, twisting spire of gray smoke into the air. The land was quiet and non-threatening, if a little stealthy. It took ten more minutes for the old man to find them and when he did Drake knew exactly where he would appear. Carefully, he escorted Kelly into the camp.

Smyth eyed the Yorkshireman. "Kudos, dude. I thought he would slip by you."

"Never happen," Drake said. "Though it's so quiet out there it could put a zombie to sleep."

Kelly stepped to the center of the camp, close by the fire. His hair was white and hung down past his shoulders, straggly to a strand. His clothes were dark, dirty and creased whilst not being torn. Drake, the closest, smelled no odor emanating from him so maybe the rumpled front was just that. When he spoke his voice was rich, intelligent and resonant, as if he'd once been used to lecturing on a circuit.

"I am Kelly, your guide. I can't promise that you will see the ghost ships, but I can promise that I will try my best to show you. Monies may be paid at the end of our trip. You," he stared at Drake, "and you," he nodded at Smyth, "are not like the usual type."

"Usual type?" Smyth snapped straight back.

"Non-combatants." Kelly chose an odd description. "You have seen action."

Drake coughed. "We all have."

Karin lifted her face from a contemplation of the flames. "And you? Have you 'seen action', old man?"

"More'n my fuckin' fair share," Kelly rasped with gusto.

Drake clapped him on the back. "And now you're a ghost ship hunter. Congrats."

"Ah, so you're a cynic and a non-believer, yet here you stand. Your mission has to be larger than you."

"Quick deduction. It is."

"The ghost ships then," Kelly took a moment to seat himself

and request the hip-flask from Smyth's tighter-than-usual grip. "Five hundred years ago an abandoned ferry was seen moored in the desert. A huge ship, it broke banks during a violent storm on the Colorado and drifted here. Stories tell of the screams of its crew being battered around the deck, broken and fragmented by the intensity."

Drake rubbed tired eyes. "Fragmented?"

"Imagine being tossed so violently you don't know which way is up or down, left or right."

Drake stared. "Wow, dude, you are *so* lucky Alicia isn't here."

"The ferryboat now resurfaces to the sounds of thunder and the screams of its crew can be heard still."

Drake listened to the old man's voice, pitched perfectly to a level just above the crackle of the flames. Timbers spat deep in the fire and, as the desert temperature plummeted, the little group huddled closer as darkness pressed all around.

"The Pearl Ship was seen again only a few years ago. Said to have vanished in the 1600s when a young explorer was carried away by a tidal bore, the craft was beached, full of black pearls and ransacked by the American Indians of the time. They skinned and scalped the man alive, leaving him chained forever to the Pearl Ship as an offering to their gods. When it rises from the dunes he can still be seen, bound to the rigging."

Drake felt a little shiver despite himself. Kelly was good at creating atmosphere, lowering his voice so even Smyth had to lean forward. Darkness and the snapping, popping fire added to the scenario the old man was creating. Drake himself took a moment to scan the dunes and then listened even more closely, intrigued.

"Of course, the stories of lost galleons are as plentiful as waves in the sea. Add to that a bay that was once attached to an inland sea and an undeniable confirmation of a vanished Spanish treasure ship in the area and you have the stuff of which legends are born. At least, for the fanciful. My own opinion was much the same as yours—" he indicated Drake "—until I saw one for myself."

"You've seen a ship?" Lauren asked. "Out here?"

Kelly nodded vigorously. "I have, young lady. The Spanish galleon of old, I saw, with me bare peepers. And ethereal it rose out of the gloom, as intact as the day it were lost, a wraithlike wooden structure that almost seemed to ride the sand dunes like waves. I stood and I could not move. It was as if I were stuck in quicksand. My heart—it fair beat out of my body. My face, it must have been as white as the specters that inhabited the deck."

Now Drake broke the mood with a cough. "Specters?"

Kelly shrugged. "P'raps it were me imagination. P'raps not. But something moved on that deck. All around me was a mist, slowly rising, and I couldn't get no bearings. More than once I felt icy fingers at the nape of my neck. I struggled forward and the ship stayed still. Only now do I realize it was real, not an illusion. This was a tangible vessel, its creaking timbers not the stuff of supernatural nightmare. I approached its huge side and imagined I could see vaporous, impossibly long arms reaching down toward me—either to help me up or drag me into their cold embrace and an eerie doom."

The old man sat back, swigging from the hip flask, and not even Smyth uttered a sound. Drake frowned as he evaluated the story. Take away all the embellishment and yes, such a thing was possible. But still . . .

"Still another story recounts of a Viking ship," Kelly went on, to Drake's surprise. "Described by the local American Indians as an open boat with round metal shields along its side, settled somewhere in the Badlands. Several people were given directions to its location but an earthquake prevented them from reaching the site, swallowing two of the party whole. If we do find the lost ship during our travels, guys, please be careful. Disaster always lurks close by any sighting."

"How would you even know where to start?" Karin asked quietly, indicating the all-enveloping dark that lurked just outside the influence of the flames and seemed to creep closer with every passing second.

Kelly nodded at her, as if acknowledging an intelligent question. "This is my home, Miss. For many years I have lived here. It can change its appearance in the passing of a storm, as may you and I, but underneath everything is still the same."

Drake wondered if that was really an answer, but Kelly at least appeared genuine. He noticed the man carried no belongings, no backpack. "You say you *live* out here?"

"I have an abode not too far away. I'll be fine for a couple of nights."

"Wouldn't it have been easier to meet us at your house?"

"Me space is me own," Kelly said. "And not to be blatantly publicized."

"Fair enough." Drake nodded. "So what's next? We set out at first light?"

Kelly tipped the flask until no more liquid fell out. "Ya got any more of this?"

"No, mate. But I could warm you a plate of beans."

Kelly wrinkled his face up. "I'll pass. Unless—"

Suddenly Drake was up and on his feet, listening hard, as desert noises became scrambled and made no sense. The balance had been broken.

By someone.

Or some*thing*.

CHAPTER FIFTEEN

They came over the dunes, descending on the small camp like desert apparitions; silent, black and lethal. Drake saw their intent, the weapons they carried—knives in hands that knew how to use them. He kicked at the fire, spreading glowing embers far and wide and spiraling up into the night. Smyth didn't waste a second meeting the enemy dead on, engaging the first as he hit level ground and grappling for his weapon. Behind him Lauren took out a pistol. Drake met his first attacker, wincing at the thought of a shot ringing out in the desert silence—now *that* might wake the dead.

But Lauren wasn't the first to fire. Gunfire shattered the dark. Bullets kicked up sand around his toes.

"Get among them!" he shouted.

There were snipers atop the dunes.

As they separated, more shots rang out. Drake ducked and made to drag Kelly along with him, but several bullets kicked up around the fire . . . and one slammed into the old man, knocking him onto his back. Blood flowed from a stomach wound. As he lay there, a split-second later another projectile hammered into him.

"No!" Drake struggled across to him.

Life had already left his eyes. His chest was still. Drake closed his own eyes for a second, but then his sense of imminent danger sang out—a soldier's sixth and seventh sense.

Drake caught a knife thrust, averted it, and smashed its initiator on the bridge of the nose. Only a grunt came forth and the man wrenched his arm free, thrusting again. Drake sidestepped, caught him under the chin and tipped him backwards. His body hit the ground with a thud, slipping a little in the streaming sand. Drake was aware of another attacker at his side, registering a misstep even as he fought the first. Quickly, he diverted to the second, striking while the dark-clad man faltered, breaking his windpipe before he even knew he was a target. Drake then heard Yorgi's warning shout, and glanced beyond the first attacker to see another man had launched himself into the air, using the slope to gain momentum. Drake hit the sand in less than a second. The man flew over, landed at Yorgi's feet and one more gunshot rang out.

A frantic battle ensued. Drake kept his pistol tucked away and drew his own knife, dispatching two enemy combatants almost immediately. To his left Smyth followed suit. At Karin's urging, still only minutes into the battle, they angled to the left where a smaller, unmanned sand dune offered a way out. Lauren used her pistol to pepper the top of the dunes, giving the snipers up there plenty to think about. Drake witnessed her lightning-quick magazine change and knew Smyth had spent many hours coaching her.

Not the most obvious way to impress a girl. But then Smyth is hardly typical.

He sidestepped at a rapid rate, taking care to allow for the unstable surface. A bulky figure came straight at him. Drake dipped and hurled the man past his right shoulder, straight into the remains of the fire. A bullet cleaved the air in front of his face, right where he would have been if he hadn't taken time to deal with the larger figure. Karin was already near the top of the slope, taking risks, urging Smyth and Lauren after her. Yorgi fired into their pursuers. Drake made sure they gained several feet of clear ground.

"Run!" he cried.

With a last look at the old man's motionless body, Drake pounded up the short slope, seeing Karin and Smyth flying over the top. Yorgi fired his pistol as he ran, but Drake urged him to concentrate on getting his head down and putting some distance between them and their attackers. The darkness around them became absolute as they escaped the vicinity of the still smoldering fire. Drake knew from earlier reconnaissance that running dead east from this position would lead them to a dried-up river bed within minutes. Hopefully Smyth remembered the same. Their pursuers thumped after them, some tangling with fallen bodies, others clearly unsure of their orders now that their quarry had escaped the net.

Drake saw now that there was a little illumination offered by a new sliver of moonlight, its eerie glow adding to the desert's sinister appeal as it slipped between passing clouds, a hide-and-seek specialist. Smyth hit level ground and stopped to allow the group a chance to reform. Drake risked a look back, and saw dark bodies not far behind.

"We'll lose them ahead," Drake said, voice low, showing the way.

He pushed Karin, Lauren and Yorgi ahead, making sure at least two of them were armed, then brought up the rear with Smyth.

"How'd the Pythian assholes find us?" Smyth breathed.

"You think it's the Pythians?"

"Who the fuck else could it be? They know we're searching for the ship."

Drake considered this as he ran. Nicholas Bell was leading this operation and had probably scouted the entire area for miles around, leaving spotters behind. Finding and gaining access to a lost desert ship wasn't a small-scale operation—it was relatively huge and he'd want first-hand knowledge of any interlopers who might be heading his way.

It was a theory anyway.

The train of thought brought him back around to poor

Kelly. Drake had wanted the old man to fulfill his dream of finding the lost galleon, and wondered briefly where his 'abode' might be. Somewhere close by. The Badlands out here were so unpredictable it might be an old dwelling or even a cave. He checked behind as they ran, and saw a bunch of darker night following them.

"Yorgi. A couple more bullets please."

The Russian obliged, aiming into the pursuing throng. Drake saw the land dip ahead just in time as shots were returned. The group raced down toward the dry stream bed, their boots slipping in shale at the bottom. Smyth muttered for them to follow, choosing a direction and heading out. Drake heard scrabbling at his back and knew one of their pursuers had broken from the group. Quickly, he turned, bringing his knife up. The man ran straight into it, but, wearing a knife vest, merely grunted. A haymaker smashed into Drake's jaw, staggering him. Without going down, he kicked out, hitting the exposed pistol and sending it flying through the air. Even this close the man's features were nothing more than shifting forms of shadow. Precious seconds were slipping by. Drake kicked out the man's knee and then punished the other place he had no obvious protection—his skull. A sharp cry demonstrated a direct hit. Drake instantly whirled and set off at a sprint, catching up to the others.

"They're too close," he said. "We either stand and fight or find a place to hide before we start getting shot in the bloody back."

"Yeah, maybe this arrow-straight stream bed wasn't such a good idea," Karin said.

"How many did we put down?" Lauren panted at her side. "Surely they'll drop back when they start losing men."

"Not these guys," Drake said. "Not if it's the Pythians. It's all about overwhelming force now."

"It feels—" Karin said. "It almost feels like they've hit the self-destruct button. Man, I hope so."

Drake grunted. "Something new will always come along."

"Man, I hope so."

Drake eyed Karin, learning nothing in the dark contours of her face. *What did that mean exactly?* Ahead, Smyth spotted a break in the river bank and aimed for it. Within seconds they were scrabbling and scrambling up a short slope and then headed back into the desert wilderness, the high empty vault of the cool night above.

Drake and Smyth carefully cast around for another mercenary force, one that might be trailing them from above, but it seemed their leader hadn't thought of such an obvious idea. Drake eyed Smyth with quiet surprise.

"And again we overestimate our enemy."

"Ain't the worst thing in the world, bud."

Drake urged the others past, setting out into the desert. Scraggly brush littered their path, threatening to upturn them and break an ankle at every step. Still, they could not slow down. The sounds of their pursuers were almost as close as ever. It occurred now to Drake that if the team had been at full strength they would already have ended the chase. Here, right now, was a strong argument for never splitting up the group. Not that he could actually do anything about the likes of Alicia or Mai. Both were off fighting their own battles.

Something rose up out of the shadow-strewn darkness ahead. At first, Drake almost stumbled, heart pounding, convinced the sudden appearance was an insubstantial ship, a ghost of the desert. But then a haphazard structure revealed itself: a tumbledown cluster of walls and empty doorways.

Smyth jumped behind the lowest wall and drew his weapon, taking a bead on their pursuers. Drake ran hard, opening the gap even more. A gnarled root caught his foot, sending him staggering headlong and shoulder first into an upstanding wall. The impact knocked the breath out of him.

"Crap."

Smyth started firing fast and accurately, if the screams were anything to go by. Drake ducked behind another wall, seeing the others pressed behind vertical pillars of bricks. Even then a bullet smashed off stone, sending slivers and dust right past Yorgi's nose. Drake added to Smyth's firepower, sending shadows dipping to the ground, but the sheer numbers of their attackers soon proved too much.

Yorgi ducked out of hiding, as did Lauren, both emptying their clips. At last they saw an end to the chasing group, but those who still lived were suddenly within the stone dwelling. Drake smashed a man to the ground and elbowed another. Still another leapt at him, bowling him over. His head hit a fallen pile of rubble, sharp edges splitting skin. For a moment there were more stars in the sky than before. He rolled away, groaning. A man landed where he had been, cursing. Drake shot up randomly into the night sky. In another moment Yorgi was at his side, new clip loaded and in full use. Drake sat up too fast, taking a few seconds to allow his head to stop spinning. The man who had initially struck him knelt at his side, staring, seemingly also dazed. For a second neither he nor Drake made a move and then they both exploded into action.

Drake punched an ear, then the neck twice with lightning strikes. His opponent tried to twist away. Drake grabbed his arm and spun him back. The man rolled but now with a small handgun tucked within the meat of his enormous left paw. Instant reflexes born of years of battle saved Drake's life. The quick shot zinged past his head and on toward the moon. Acting as best he could in the dire situation he jumped atop the gun hand, preparing to take bullets to the vest. As Dahl would say—*they're only bullets. It's not as if it's a fucking cruise missile.*

The man's hand was trapped though, the gun pointed at the

desert floor. Drake took advantage and smashed down until the eyes glazed and then, on Yorgi's warning, rolled clear. Another man landed hard an instant later, this one already shot dead. Drake twisted around to take in the scene.

Stragglers were now coming toward the crumbling structure, but these more warily and spread out. Drake counted maybe five shadows and knew there might be more. Smyth picked one off as he watched. To a man all the others fell to the floor. Were there more out there in the crawling darkness?

"Sit rep?" he called.

"All good," Smyth came back. "And well rested."

Drake allowed himself a grim smile. The dilemma was whether to break cover now they'd stumbled across the ruin's moderate security. If the Pythians had more men in the area they could easily ambush the ruin from all sides. Probably best to keep moving.

"Fall out," he whispered. "Quietly."

Smyth withdrew, ever the soldier. Lauren followed as carefully as she could. Karin waited for Drake who fired off three more bullets before loading his final mag.

"We should kill these bastards," Karin whispered. "All of them."

"I'm not entirely sure we could," Drake said evenly. "Live to fight another day, love. They caught us by surprise tonight. It won't happen again."

"I hate to leave even one alive."

"That's not the way we do things and never will be." Drake, staring up, noticed a faint lightening of the skies. "So come on. Dawn's coming. They used the dark to ambush us; now we'll use the last of it to escape from them."

He pulled Karin along, worried now that all the recent suffering might have changed her disposition forever. The team used several minutes of enemy misunderstanding to open a substantial gap, picking up pace the further they left the ruin behind.

Drake felt for a compass. "Time to head back to town and stock up before we even think about heading out again. Put this all down to a bad loss. We should catch up with Hayden too, see how they're getting on. This desert trekking's a bit more perilous than we thought. Lauren, you spoke about Nicholas Bell as a man who might be turned. Do you still think so?"

"Well, yes, I do. Despite everything, he seemed nice and still does. I liked him. I'm convinced it's merely circumstance that keeps him with the Pythians."

"Circumstance?" Smyth said sarcastically. "Doesn't turn you into an expedition leader. He might have even ordered those mercs to move on our position."

"He's worth a try," Lauren said with conviction. "That's all I'm saying."

Smyth sent a look of disgust her way.

"I wonder if poor Kelly left anyone behind," Lauren said, changing the subject.

Smyth took her arm. "We'll ask when we're safe. Now keep moving."

CHAPTER SIXTEEN

Hayden, Dahl and Kinimaka headed for Silicon Valley at a rapid rate of knots. Weapons were prepped on the way, teams armed. If the last assault was anything to go by, the one on Silicon Valley would be huge.

Even then, they couldn't have guessed how huge.

Hayden leapt down from the still hovering chopper, taking care to step away from Kinimaka's landing spot. They had put down at the side of the road—a two-way carriageway now crammed full of cop cars and black vans. Sunshine beat down hard at the asphalt, but even that had a hard time outshining the array of flashing lights. Hayden quickly sought out the man in charge.

"Hayden Jaye." She shook hands with a tall, spare man wearing a flak jacket, her words almost torn away in the tumult.

"Jack. Jack Crews."

"What do we have, Crews?"

After taking an extended look at her badge and then Kinimaka's bulk and Dahl's obvious European features he made the clear decision to cooperate. "Large group of mercenaries have stormed the Silicon Valley electrical facility. We've taken the area where they discarded their vehicles, without much incident to be honest. It's almost as if they broke in without expecting to get out."

Hayden scanned the skies. "Unless they have options on the way. Do you have an estimate as to their numbers?"

"At least forty. Possibly as many as seventy."

Hayden turned to Dahl. "Thoughts?"

"These guys will have to wait." The Swede motioned at the milling throng of authorities. "Doesn't mean we have to."

Hayden nodded.

Crews frowned. "Wait. What?"

"Worry not, my man." Dahl grinned. "The less you know the better."

"What the hell does that mean? And there's no way I'm letting a Brit take the lead on this. What the hell is SPEAR anyway?"

Hayden made a show of blinking at all the questions as both Kinimaka and Dahl made a last check. Finally, Dahl addressed the agent.

"I'm not British, or English. Or even Australian. The best thing you could do is accept what's about to happen. Oh, and look the other way."

Hayden tapped his shoulder and they were away. Clumps of trees sat adjacent to the high metal fence that circuited the facility, offering a welcome area of cover. As they ducked under the overhanging boughs, Kinimaka took out a small pair of heavy duty clippers and set about the fence. A notorious fact was that security was mostly for display at electrical facilities around the US and the world, despite the numerous sniper and other armed attacks of recent years. *Power companies,* Hayden thought, *clearly don't make enough of a profit to afford better security for their staff and customers.* Of course they didn't.

Kinimaka clipped a hole and the three crouched down together to survey the interior. Similar to the San Jose plant, a large open-plan area was home to many electrical stations, transformers and pylons, with an office building sitting at the far side. Unlike the other plant this one was extensive and its machinery immense.

"This is a major facility," Hayden said. "And if the mercs are following the same orders as San Jose they'll have headed right for the control room."

"So what do we do?" Kinimaka rumbled.

"Fifty mercs between us and them." Dahl took an estimate. "What are we waiting for?"

He set off first, pushing through the gap with Hayden a step behind. Kinimaka grunted. "It'd be easier with a full team."

Hayden agreed but said nothing. Not only was the separation of their family group personally incapacitating it made every operation that much more dangerous. Crucial decisions were made differently; outcomes changed. Dahl ran ahead of her, staying low and stopping behind a bank of machinery. Two more swift runs and they were within distance of the entrance doors. Hayden glanced back at the perimeter and the gaggle of cop cars parked there. Quickly, she radioed Crews.

"Any contact with the inside?"

"Yeah, one guy has a cellphone. He says most of the mercs are armed to the teeth, not afraid to use force and massing close to the central office. I'd say look out for guards though. All the civilians have been herded and barred inside their locker room."

Hayden turned the radio off, relaying the news to her companions.

"No exfil?" Dahl asked.

"Not yet."

"This feels like a last gasp scenario," Dahl said about the last few days, sitting back on his haunches for a moment. "An entity throwing everything they have at something just to see how it turns out, maybe get a result."

"Or that they just don't care anymore."

Dahl sighed. "There is that, too."

Hayden reached the entrance without incident and glanced inside, surprised at the lack of guards. Her brain screamed at her to be careful, that this wasn't right, but one quick flick of her eyes around the inside explained why.

"It's laid out differently," she said. "Pretty much one vast room full of machinery and it looks like they have guards perched on the gantries above, watching over. There's no easy way in, guys."

Dahl cursed. "Then we take the hard way. The civilians are safe inside the locker room. Let's take this facility back."

With that, the Swede flung open the door and charted the interior with nothing more than a quick glance. Raising his weapon he slipped inside, then flung grenades in two directions at once. Shots rang out. Dahl returned fire, racing fast around the inside perimeter of the open shell. Hayden tried to keep up, with Kinimaka at her back.

Explosions shook the structure. Twin gouts of flame rocketed toward the ceiling. One of the gantries shook as its foundation wobbled. Two snipers, clinging to its side, fell as the entire scaffold collapsed. Another metal stanchion rocked from the impact of the second explosion. A gunman fired at them even as his footing slipped, the shot striking a spot twenty feet above their heads. Dahl raced down the center of the vast room and tucked in underneath the central support beam. Mercenaries stationed above tried to lock him into their sights. Hayden and Kinimaka fell to one knee.

Firing, they picked two more guards off. Dahl hurled another grenade, this one exploding immediately as it struck another support beam. More gantries leaned and tipped. Cries of alarm went up. Hayden saw a knot of mercs squeezing through a far door that led to the building's main office block.

She fired off three sharp shots, hoping to keep them pinned down. Kinimaka ran to shelter, then covered her as she ran to his side. Dahl held a grenade in each hand with his gun slung over his shoulder. To their left another gantry tumbled, the metalwork shearing down and crashing to the floor in a deadly splatter. A merc who survived the fall turned his weapon upon them.

Dahl dived away as Hayden picked the man off. As he rolled

he threw one of the grenades toward the advancing force, then rolled back. The subsequent explosions shook foundations and rafters, and made the mercs dive for cover. Kinimaka stared upward, seeing the entire inner metal framework wobble.

"Umm . . . shit."

Dahl wasn't done, not by a long shot. Terror? He'd give these fuckers terror all right. Some were bought and paid and gave a fuck about the money, others did it for the depraved thrill. Then there were those who did it to make a difference . . . but none did it better than Torsten Dahl. Diving headlong beneath the array of gantries with bullets peppering the ground just inches from his every extremity, he rolled and hurled one last grenade. The bouncing bomb came up against another support member and instantly exploded.

The entire structure came down.

Dahl scrambled away. Kinimaka took hold of Hayden and flung her to a corner. A mercenary plummeted first, smashing hard into the ground beside Kinimaka's feet, splattering his trousers with blood. The Hawaiian turned away, eyes fixed on Dahl and the far office.

The Swede was already up, dodging collapsing rafters and falling gantries. One metal walkway tumbled, end first, its spear-like edge impaling a merc who was lying injured. A metal box hit the floor and exploded, shards and sparks bursting like the Fourth of July. Dahl ducked and darted among it all, brushing sparks off a shoulder here, extracting a metal splinter there, and concentrated on the office with its emerging military force. The grenade he'd thrown earlier had sent them into disarray and they were even now still trying to reassemble.

Around the side of the building came Hayden and Kinimaka. A piece of framework swung against the wall behind them, shattering the plaster and block work. Kinimaka dealt with an errant merc, assessing that the injured man was mostly faking it and finishing the job Dahl had started.

The three soldiers came at the force of mercenaries hard, and from different directions. Dahl's new MPX was on full-auto, his patience well and truly worn. Still firing he waded among the enemy, forcing Hayden and Kinimaka to switch to their Glocks for more accurate shots. Dahl fired with one hand and punched with the other. A man rebounded off his solid arm, nose bloody. Another fell underfoot and received a face full of Swedish boot. Reacting far faster than any of his opponents, the Swede cut a swathe through them.

On the other side he paused, sending a fast glance into the office itself. Men wearing backpacks and sidearms were bending over computer consoles, tapping away, and even as Dahl watched they straightened and signaled that they were done.

"I really don't think so."

At that moment a blow staggered him, making his ears ring. Dahl turned to see a fleshy mountain at his side, slobbering and sweating profusely with the effort of wearing weapons and body armor. The stench of body odor was almost as deadly as a lead projectile.

Dahl smashed the barrel of his gun across the man's nose, drawing blood, breaking cartilage, but gaining only a slack grin for his effort. His opponent's arms opened wide, hoping for a hug. Dahl jammed the business end of his rifle into the enormous belly and fired, seeing no other way out. Even then the beast barely flinched, lumbering on. It was only when Dahl squeezed off the fourth shot that he started to falter.

Dahl skipped aside. Jelly-man descended to the floor with a flop and a crash that put the gantry collapse to shame.

But the distraction had allowed the office mercs to exit and start moving toward the back of the vast room. For once, the rest of their team acted in unison and shielded their retreat. Hayden and Kinimaka ducked behind fallen machinery, suddenly under heavier fire, and Dahl barely made it to the open office door before bullets started rattling around his heels. Hayden saw him duck inside even as the glass all around him shattered.

"Only friggin' thing these guys're good at is laying down covering fire," Kinimaka growled.

"But *how* are they planning to escape?" Hayden said.

"They're not," Dahl's voice came over the comms. "At least not all of them. It's much easier for one or two men to escape whilst the main force remains."

"But why would they even consider that? I mean, jail?"

"Far as we know they haven't killed anyone. Ten years or less and they'll be out and millions of dollars richer, I bet."

"You're saying the payoff is worth the stretch?"

"Most career criminals consider those odds first."

Hayden flinched as a burst of gunfire rattled all around her. Dahl was keeping an eye on the mercs from inside the office.

"Some are leaving by the fire exit at the back. Radio it in."

Hayden thumbed the mic, changing channel and informed Crews.

Kinimaka thrust his gun out blindly and let loose a salvo. Grunts attested to the foolishness of the mercenaries yet again, having grown complacent in the last few minutes. Hayden saw the facility's locker room door crack open and waved furiously at the emerging man to get back inside.

"They've taken big losses," Dahl said. "But they still won. That's the second grid facility they have infiltrated. Hayden, America is under attack. We're at war."

Hayden stayed low, nodding to herself as she came to a similar conclusion. "I have to call Robert Price." She fished out another cellphone.

Kinimaka stared. "Is it even worth it? The new Secretary of Defense hasn't exactly been a constant ally so far."

"I have to, Mano. It's protocol. And he hasn't hindered us either."

The Secretary answered on the third ring. "Hello?"

Hayden explained the situation as succinctly as she could, ignoring the occasional volley of gunfire designed to keep her pinned down. "It's a major attack, sir. The grid is under increasing danger. Z-boxes are in play. We need military help."

As Price asked questions she couldn't help but flick her mind back to when the traitor General Stone had practically accused Price of being in bed with the enemy. A while back now, and nothing further had happened, but Hayden would never forget it. Price ended up stating he would "come back to her".

Jonathan Gates would have taken her at her word.

"I'll be here, sir," she said, signing off a little sarcastically because she knew he couldn't possibly understand the irony. Kinimaka fired blindly again and Dahl discharged several rounds from the office.

The mercs were all clustered around the fire exit door. As Hayden chanced a look she realized most of them had now vanished.

"They're aiding somebody's escape," she said, moving fast and firing hard. "Come on!"

But Dahl's frustrated voice put it all into perspective. "They've already gone."

CHAPTER SEVENTEEN

Drake sat in the dirt and with his back to a wall at the rear of a safe house in the center of Yuma, and stared through the holes in the rear chain-link fence at the drifting, broiled, barren folds of desert land that stretched endlessly beyond.

There was only one thing he could think of to do.

Her name was Alicia Myles.

And, despite their dire situation, coming to that conclusion gave him a sudden jolt of happiness. If only she would answer her bloody phone.

"Yeah?"

"Yeah?" he repeated. "Whaddya mean 'yeah'? You bloody know it's me."

"And what? I'm supposed to squeal? My loud noises are reserved only for exceptional bedroom antics as you may remember."

"Balls, I haven't interrupted have I?"

"Nah. Haven't seen the appendage in a while."

Drake shook his head. "Does Beauregard know you call him that?"

"Who cares? Really though, dude, there isn't much more to him. Honestly, he's about 90 percent appendage."

Drake definitely didn't want to go there. "Where are you?"

"Sat outside a nice little café in Knightsbridge. Watching the world go by." Alicia sounded almost wistful for a moment. "But judging by the sudden warning twitch in my loins I'm guessing you need me. Got yourselves in trouble again?"

"It's an odd mission," Drake admitted. "Entirely different to what we're used to."

"Well, so long as there's no sand involved. You know how I feel about sand and those spidery things."

Drake winced but kept it professional. "Hardly any sand at all. Honest."

"Wanker."

"Bitch."

"All right, ya had me at 'balls'. Less of the fuckin' sweet talk. I'm getting tired of sitting around all day anyway."

Drake knew her latest mission had only just ended. Still, Alicia would not, could not, stop moving forward. The singular explosion he had been expecting still hadn't happened and the Englishwoman was becoming more pent up, more angry and disturbed by the week. The demons of her past, riding their chariot of war, were close to catching up.

If only he had known then *how* close, he might never have made the call.

Drake explained a little of their mission. "The stories of these ships," he said, "are uncannily accurate across the board. Embellished, yes, but most likely true. I'd doubt that Bell and his freaky friends expect to discover much more than treasure chests inside but even that, when you calculate how much it's probably worth, is a scary addition to their wealth."

"You haven't mentioned Webb."

"He's not around. Probably back in DC sniffing panties."

"Now there's an image. So how many ships have you seen?"

"Well, none."

"Ah, and you lost your guide, your ammo, and your Swede. I can see why you need me."

"We're hiring Jeeps," Drake told her. "Tracking them down the old fashioned way. Ain't no other choice. A chopper would probably be shot down, same for a small plane. And the Internet can't tell us what's happening out in the middle of nowhere. So it's gonna be us, a few Jeeps and an ancient treasure. Up for it?"

"No need to lay it on so thick. I'm already walking," Alicia said. "Can't you tell I'm walking? Just crossing Sloane Street on my way to the underground. I'll be there as soon as I can, Drakey."

"Good. Track me using the GPS signal. Failing that, track Hayden. We should join up again soon. With the team so depleted it's becoming a hell of a struggle."

"I get it. Without me you're weak, horny and depressed. It's understandable. Say no more, Drakey, I'll liven y'all up a bit."

Drake ignored the fake accent and concentrated on what truly concerned him. "And that kinda worries me."

Even from several thousand miles away he could tell she stopped walking. "What?"

"Stop standing and gawping at the phone." Drake found himself reverting to his native accent. "It's nowt, just an old tosspot speaking out of turn. Forget it."

Alicia was quiet for a moment, then: "It's okay. I do know what you meant and, well . . ."

"What is it?"

"I think it's about time I got all this off my chest."

Now Drake gawped at the phone, imaging an atomic explosion. *Oh fuck . . .*

"The desert's not a bad place for that," he tried.

Alicia laughed, thank God. "Don't be a knob end. Coming to terms with my life is not exactly something I can plan out."

"I understand. Just one thing . . ."

"Yes?"

"I'd like to be there when it happens."

Alicia now definitely had a smile in her voice. "You do? Wow."

"Despite it probably being the most dangerous thing I've ever done—yes. We've been together since the beginning, Alicia. You and I. From the early days of the Ninth Division. Africa. The shit we did in the late nineties. And now—"

"And we *were* together. I still know what makes you squeal like a girl."

Drake laughed quietly. "And I—you."

"Don't *ever* call me that again," Alicia said in mock exasperation.

"Or else?"

"Else you might not regret it," Alicia whispered.

Drake found himself staring at the rugged desert, the glare that frazzled the middle-distance, the silent swoop of a kestrel. The world was practically motionless out there—in stark contrast to the refurbished pinball machine that had just turned on inside his own head. A volcano could lie dormant for many, many years but sooner or later . . .

"I'll see you soon," he said without emotion.

"Yeah, soon."

The call ended.

Drake considered the desert with unseeing eyes.

Later, when the Jeeps were ready and the team had refueled, reloaded and repacked, Drake considered their situation. This was truly the oddest mission of his life. Motivated, intelligent people were out there, wading through sand dunes seeking something huge and preposterous. Forget the Grail, El Dorado and Atlantis this was off the nutball scale.

Or is it?

Documented evidence existed that ships had somehow made their way inland. Why couldn't one of them lie somewhere within this vast, barren expanse? Explorers and sensationalists and publicity-seekers—not to mention the local councils—played up the ghost ship part as much as Scotland played up its 'monster', so maybe the real truth lay somewhere in between.

And perhaps the treasure was genuine.

Nicholas Bell and his Pythian pals believed so. They were

looking to fund some kind of mega end-game. *Saint Germain?* Drake wondered. *Or something else?*

And what more did Webb need to put it into motion? The niggling, bothersome part of his mind pointed out that Webb was strangely absent from this party, and when the chief party planner didn't turn up . . . something bigger just had to be underway.

The finale was close and the Pythians would either rule or be completely destroyed.

Drake walked away from the safe house and contemplated his companions. Smyth sat in the passenger seat of the second Jeep, tooled up, hard-faced and capable. Lauren had the seat behind him, her hands resting on his seatback as she leaned forward in conversation. His own Jeep was being driven by Yorgi with Karin in the rear. He climbed up next to the Russian.

"You ready?"

Yorgi nodded, eyes practically taped to the windows.

"Stop staring at the new girl," Drake said. "She'll get nervous and leave us."

"Did you *talk* to her?" Yorgi whispered reverently. "I doubt even Dahl could make her nervous."

Drake frowned hard. "What the hell do you mean 'even Dahl'? I'm pretty sure I made her a little nervous."

Yorgi started to smile and then clearly thought better of it. "Of course," he said in a thick accent. "Of course you did, my friend."

"Whatever." Drake stared across at the other Jeep where Smyth sat next to the new girl, the driver. Her name was Jenny Rathe and she was a short-haired redhead with a smooth pale face and blue eyes that glinted like menacing icebergs. Outwardly, this woman appeared safe and approachable and even cautious. Underneath this outward demeanor, Drake gauged she had the potential to be entirely treacherous, hard and jaded. The jury was out, but people he trusted vouched for her as the best, hardest and most reliable guide in the business. The fact that she'd been in California wasn't entirely down to good fortune—the US government were more involved in searching out old legends than they would ever take credit for.

Jenny was no trained fighter, not a soldier, but possessed a sharp tongue and could hold her own in a mean fist-fight, or so she said. She was also extremely healthy and in great shape; at twenty-eight possibly the best shape of her life. A gym enthusiast, a sport fanatic, and an American car lover, Drake instantly knew she'd be the best guide for them. Maybe she could dodge bullets too. Indeed, her only debatable quality was that Price had sent her.

So far Karin had barely noticed her, Yorgi was drooling and Smyth was doing his best to remain professional. Lauren was watching Smyth, predictably. Drake wondered if those two were sleeping together yet. He kind of hoped so—they were both good people.

Yorgi slipped the Jeep into gear and gazed through the windshield. Drake rested a hand on his arm.

"I think you should let our guide go first."

"Ah, yes. It is good that one of us is on the ball, yes?"

"A nice football reference, mate. We'll turn you into a passable Englishman yet."

"Oh please, no."

Jenny eased forward, aiming her vehicle toward through the gates and toward the road. Yorgi followed slowly. Drake's mind became focused on the utter silence that emanated from the back seat. Karin Blake was more than a physical passenger back there, she was a blunt force, commuting through life vacantly, indifferently, showing no indication that she might know the way back from the sharp turns her consciousness had taken.

Drake wished that he could help. As of now, he didn't want to make it worse but as with Alicia, a crunch of some kind was inevitable.

The desert opened out on both sides, as deadly and barren and lonely as the worst kind of grief.

Drake waited for the onrushing storms.

CHAPTER EIGHTEEN

Mai Kitano prepared for the greatest battle of her life.

A Yakuza communication turned up before sunrise that morning. It conveyed that their warrior had arrived near Tokyo and suggested a time and a place for their engagement. Mai liked the simplicity of the words—it inferred nor assumed anything. It was plain. And there could be no misunderstanding.

It gave her time to reflect, to prepare her mind and body for what was to come. There were no outcomes in her mental arrangements, only designs. She allowed Dai Hibiki to be her second, the one who would accompany and observe, the one who would be forced to deal with the aftermath.

Before departure, she spent a few final moments with Grace.

"I will be back soon."

The young girl stared at the floor, her new, now natural bounciness depleted. "Will you?"

"If I do not do this a war will begin. It is a credit to my enemies that they even make such an offering."

"A credit?" Grace looked over, her brow creased in confusion. "You're crediting your enemies? I don't get it."

"There is nothing to 'get'." Mai didn't explain how she was doing this to keep Grace and the entire SPEAR team safe. How much the safety of her sister and Hibiki mattered. How much she loved the new emerging woman that Grace was becoming and wanted to protect her at any cost. It wasn't something she felt she could explain succinctly.

"Please. Be careful." Grace's eyes watered.

"I know of no other way to be."

"I don't know what I would do now if you . . . you . . ."

Mai struggled to hold onto her composure. Grace's words raised in sharp detail Mai's foremost concern. The young girl was doing so well, growing and developing in mind and body every day. The healing process was as well advanced as anybody could expect. If she suddenly hit a hairpin curve the terrible regression might be even worse than before.

There was no way out. This Yakuza sword was well and truly double-edged. *But it also gives me the greatest reason in the world to fight hard. To win.*

The actual departure was even worse, Grace clinging as long as she could and Mai struggling to keep the tears from her eyes. *I have made you my ward, my conscience, my life, and now I am leaving you.*

The congested road through Tokyo was almost as hard. Hibiki drove, taking the journey slowly. He knew by heart the place they sought. It was an old mountain monastery situated at the end of a steep winding road. Above the monastery was a flat plateau rarely visited, sealed off from tourists and where the resident monks occasionally worshipped.

Tonight, at sunset, it would be the unhallowed ground for Mai's conclusive rite of passage. Mai watched Hibiki from the corner of her eye but saw no emotion there. It put her in mind of how Drake and the others would almost certainly deal with the same difficult problem—it was a soldier's reaction minus the camaraderie and leg-pulling that came naturally to most Europeans.

Time slipped by and the roads grew less busy. The sun passed its zenith and began to wane, turning a burnished gold for what were possibly her final few hours on earth. She was thankful for it, and spent the time contemplating the events that had led her to this appointed moment.

Finally, she cleared her mind as all roads led to the

monastery, with its plateau at the very top. Beyond a certain point they had to park up and walk, the twisting path passing under overhanging trees and growing narrower by the second. A cool breeze caressed Mai's countenance as, finally, Dai Hibiki turned his overwrought face toward her.

"It's just beyond that bend in the path. Mai, there *is* no point of no return. It does not have to be this way."

Mai touched the Japanese man's fair face with the back of her hand, looking infinitely sad. "Tell Chika I will always love her," she paused, "and that I am sorry."

"For not saying goodbye?"

"We did that last night. It did not need to happen again. I am just sorry it all ended up this way. Violence and death have been my mentors from a very young age."

"The Yakuza can be beaten in other ways."

"But not without further bloodshed. Let mine be the last drop spilt in the name of all this madness."

Mai eased past Hibiki and negotiated the final bend in the path. Beyond, a flat paved area bordered with wooden benches extended into a wide, circular grassy expanse. Its borders were cobblestones, its boundary a sheer two-hundred-foot drop. A small contingent of Japanese men stood silently at the center of the clearing, but only one man mattered to Mai.

The Yakuza warrior, the very best of the very best, the unbeaten devil, stood with both arms crossed. More than a showdown, this truly was a battle to the death and the warrior looked more than ready. A scarred face topped an almost naked, absurdly muscled body. He did not speak but regarded her as though she were already dead.

Mai stepped out, leaving her coat on a bench as she passed. Without even a backwards glance at Hibiki, she approached the clearing. "I am here."

"Then it is time to settle this matter." One of the Yakuza leaders moved aside, gesturing at her. "In combat we seek justness. In death, an impartial outcome. Let it begin."

Mai waited until the Yakuza men departed before approaching the great warrior. His name, they told her, was Aoki and he bore no arrogance, no pretentiousness and no rage. She stood in silence before him and waited for the signal. If everything she was came down to this then it was an ignominious, inglorious end and one quite befitting.

No further thoughts entered her mind in that final moment of contemplation. In absolute silence and total emptiness there was a kind of cleansing.

"Fight."

Mai sidestepped twice as the powerful figure loosened himself up. The head rocked from side to side, slackening neck muscles. The fingers flexed in anticipation. Aoki locked gazes with her.

And struck. The act had been mere misdirection. Mai deflected his clenched fist with an upraised arm, his rising knee with one of her own. They came together briefly, breath intermingled, before stepping apart once more. Mai tested the ground. The grass and soil beneath was firm, not slippery. The air was thin. The extremities of their battleground were always going to be precarious. The pack of men to her right constituted a point of reference, Hibiki another.

Aoki's knee rose, but it was his fist that drove at her, glancing off her temple as she ducked aside. Instantly, the Yakuza warrior spun and planted a turning heel into her abdomen. Mai felt the impact and tensed her muscles but still she staggered. Pain exploded around the partially healed bullet wound. The blow was no accident. Incensed at such trickery, Mai ignored the pain and pounced before Aoki had a chance to right himself. Delving her right hand into his ribs she also chopped her left down on the back of his neck. Aoki's muscles were large enough to absorb both blows but he certainly felt them.

Silver flashed, and two gleaming swords landed on the green grass.

Aoki leapt for the closest. Mai ignored the weapons and again hit the warrior hard. Two blows made him groan—a chest blow and another neck punch. Aoki would already be bruised there. Mai then dived headlong as Aoki swung his entire body, sword extended. The blade barely whistled over her ducking head and even from here she heard Hibiki's sharp intake of breath. Mai allowed her momentum to become a roll and then revolved to her feet. Aoki came fast, swinging the sword fast like a blade in a Rotavator, scything the air with each deadly stroke.

Mai saw her death approaching. The avenue of evasion was just too narrow. Last ditch efforts came to mind and Mai took up the fastest. Against all of her—and Aoki's—instincts, she fell to the floor, kicked out and rolled. Her heels slammed into his knees, her momentum took her under the sudden downswing of the blade. Still rolling she knew she just wasn't fast enough to gain her feet.

The blade was already slashing toward her—the killing stroke. Mai twisted in mid-roll, brought her arm up and caught the blow of Aoki's sword on the blade of her own. She'd barely had time to snatch it up and the angle wasn't right—so his blade slid down hers, its progress only halted by the wide hilt. The slip made him lose his balance, his face coming down until it was an inch away. Eyes of hard unfeeling granite met her own. Impossible strength pushed the blade of his sword closer and closer to her face. Her sword was trapped between them. Mai kicked her legs and jack-knifed her body but to no avail. The man was immovable, a boulder, ensnaring both her hands between their bodies and pushing down with every straining sinew.

A collective gasp of victory went up from the assembled Yakuza. But she wasn't done yet. Mai twisted her shoulders, flung her head back. Aoki rotated with it, and every second brought the edge of his sword closer to her face.

Mai felt the cold touch a moment later. Her body was held immobile, preparing for the inevitable. The razor-edge was cold as it pressed against her, first a mere presence and then a major concern. The first trickle of blood slipped down her face, spilling down her chin and across her throat to soak into the cold grass. From here, Aoki could only get stronger. His muscles bulged. The blade sank a millimeter further. Mai gasped in pain. Blood poured, the gash now over two inches long, the skin parting. If she stopped pushing back he would slice her face clean off. This knowledge as much as anything made her fight harder, channel more strength than she knew she possessed into her arms. If only . . . if only she could twist or curl one more time.

But Aoki was a hardened warrior and knew all her tricks. The only emotion he showed was when he thrust his face even closer, intimidating even her final moments. The blade sank further into her face, more than a gash now, an open, flowing wound, a grievous injury. Blood turned the grass into a deep, crimson mud. Not a sound could be heard. Mai saw the sunset waning to nothing in the skies above and a darkness starting to appear.

The day was over. All the light in the world had diminished, faded forever.

CHAPTER NINETEEN

Mai suddenly flashed on the best part of her life. It wasn't now, it wasn't recently, but it *was* a great portion of the last few years. It was the dumb Yorkshireman and all his eccentricities, his intelligible language and odd foibles. His successes.

His quirks.

And so the only idea wedged inside her head at that moment suddenly offered a slight chance of a way out. He often referred to it as a Yorkshire Kiss. Something about—*it's been donkey's years since I last saw a good Yorkshire Kiss.*

Mai gathered herself, expecting the pain for her action would force the blade even deeper. But it would be fast and it would be hard. It would be the best Yorkshire Kiss of her entire life. Pushing her skull as far back as the soft soil would allow she met Aoki's eyes, saw him come another inch forward and then let it all loose. Striking incredibly hard she smashed her forehead into Aoki's face, aiming directly for the bridge of the nose. The impact was huge. Blood spurted from Mai's already deep wound but Aoki, experienced warrior or not, reacted as anyone would—his hands flew to his face, blood erupted from the broken nose, and he screamed.

Mai slithered free, but she didn't escape his clutches, had no intentions of doing so. With blood streaming and flying from her deep laceration she jabbed again and again at Aoki's eyes and neck and cheekbones. Another bone broke. An eye almost dislodged. More screams came from the warrior.

This was pure down-in-the-dirt survival combat now, no fancy moves, and Mai was as comfortable with it as she was with breathing. Both hands struck directly and hard, fingers and palms. As Aoki rolled Mai went with him, now targeting an eardrum and popping it, now mashing lips and dislocating the jaw. Aoki began to forget his training such was the mounting pain. Mai bled and never gave up. Her blood coated his face, his hair. Two knuckles broke against his cheekbone as they shattered it. Aoki's elbow flew backward, connecting with her left eye, instantly blackening it and causing an unexpected lance of pain that caused her to scream. She staggered onto hands and knees, momentarily blinded by the agony. She collapsed onto her elbows. Her breath came in shallow bursts as she fought for more. Aoki's face swam into focus, distorted and broken and bloodied, no doubt a mirror of her own. One huge arm scrabbled for a sword.

Mai went flat as the sword came down, swung almost blindly. The blade passed over her horizontal back, digging into the grass. Mai rolled quickly on top of the flailing warrior.

"No quarter," she heard from the Yakuza head. "This is our judgment."

Mai knelt with her knee across Aoki's throat, pressing down. The sword rose behind her. Its length made impaling impossible but its cutting edge could be brought to bear. Mai bore down with every ounce of strength she had left, watching the fight die from Aoki's eyes. The sword came closer and then the blade was again at her skin, cutting through her clothes to her shoulder blade. Aoki sawed as if he was carving a turkey joint, strength waning. Mai ignored it all, using every ounce of her old training and focus techniques to compartmentalize both the peril and the pain. Everything would pass and when the end came she would be where she was supposed to be.

Then came the hammer blow. Aoki had been distracting her with the sword, gathering his strength for one final effort. His right fist struck the side of her head like a hammer striking an anvil. Stars exploded and they would for an eternity. *Where did he find such staying power, such incredible will and admirable potency?* The unbeaten devil had tricked her at the final moment.

Mai toppled off Aoki, barely conscious. Her body toppled to the ground, arms flopping. Her eyes closed. Did she breathe? *I no longer care.*

Blood pooled all around her. Muscles had seized and an incredible blackness floated into her brain, overwhelming all. Without conscious thought or even the benefit of vision she sent her fingers searching through the grass.

Aoki struggled to his knees at her side. Through experience she knew he was evaluating her. The decision would be quick. Blindly, painfully, optimistically, she clasped the hilt of the discarded sword and brought it around in the instant that she believed Aoki would strike.

Instinct. Nature, inbred at birth. Reflex. A true sixth sense.

Aoki's lunging body impaled itself on the thick blade. Mai forced it all the way through before collapsing into unconsciousness.

Dai Hibiki's guttural cheer told her the real truth.

CHAPTER TWENTY

Drake settled back as Yorgi operated the Jeep, watching the horizons as best he could and hoping Jenny Rathe kept them to the less dusty dirt roads. The Jeep bounced along. His heart was buoyed, expecting Alicia to arrive within the next day or two. Maybe they could even join up with the rest of the SPEAR team. Of course, even as a group they were far from invincible—the young woman seated behind could attest to that—but there was something about having your soldier family with you, something . . . unassailable.

Brown, barren landscape spread out in every direction. Jenny was leading them on a roundabout route to the vicinity of where they had been attacked. Her methods should give them protection, concealment and forewarning. Jenny was old school clever, taught hard by her wilderness-living father even before the government acquired her. The Jeeps would take them so far and then she would be able to track any quarry she liked. Drake was of no mind to completely trust her at this point but so far she seemed to be the real deal, if a little on the quiet side. She appeared to be either quick-tongued or largely discreet. Maybe it was the red hair, or that some people just took a bit more bedding in than others

On a different note, the noise, or complete lack of it, from the back seat was worrying. Drake wished he could stop his surveillance to have a deep and clear conversation with Karin. He wished he'd already done so. What was she leading up to?

The Jeep was equipped with a two-way radio which crackled into life. "I'm calling a halt," Jenny said. "Time to camp."

Drake evaluated the terrain. "Are you sure? We have a couple of hours of daylight yet."

"You wanna drive around half-cocked or with a least a semblance of safety? If it's the latter pull the fuck up and let me scout."

Drake blinked.

Yorgi mouthed: "Half-cocked?"

Drake sighed. "It means 'with your head up your ass', and she's right. Stop over there, Yorgi."

They pulled up behind the lead Jeep, basking for a final few moments in the air conditioned interior. Drake tried to put some comforting words in his mouth, something heartening, but his brain wouldn't play ball. Whatever words could be said to Karin had already been repeated a hundred times. If Drake was being honest he would have to admit that she was in the wrong place.

Yorgi cracked the door, wincing as the hot desert air rushed inside. Drake followed and watched as Jenny strode toward him.

"Make camp here. Use the vehicles at the perimeter but not too close. Prepare a campfire and some food. I'll be starving my ass off by the time I get back."

"Where the hell are you going?" Smyth hefted a rifle. "Tijuana?"

The redhead threw him an irritated look. "You think you can do better, soldier boy? Be my guest. Just don't fall into the quicksand or get eaten by sandworms."

Smyth was setting himself to square up to the guide when Lauren laid an arm across his shoulders.

"Just let her do her job. Yes?"

"Whatever."

Drake nodded at Jenny and set tasks. The sun's orb was already dipping low, accelerating it seemed as night approached. The black vehicles ticked, the only noise in the vast stillness. Drake was already tired of the desert landscape, the dust and the heat, the sand in his boots.

"It's such a vast wilderness," Karin surprised him by saying. "How can we hope to find anybody out here?"

"That's why Jenny's here. She's the best of her kind."

"A fiery redhead?"

"If that works for her I'm good with it. People tend to go with what works for them, especially if it helps them get through the slog of the day."

Karin walked uphill to the camp's perimeter and dropped down onto a patch of infertile ground, a faint path. Before her an expanse of desert stretched, endlessly bleak, seemingly lifeless, and Drake found himself likening it to Karin's heart and soul, if not the entire team's. How fitting that they ended up here in the wake of Komodo's death.

It suited his mood. "As bleak as it gets," he said, sitting beside her.

"You think?"

Probably not. He kicked at the tiny rocks. "How do you feel about getting drunk?"

Karin turned, eyes open and focused upon him for the first time. "There's a time and a place. It sure didn't work for you."

Drake winced. She had him there. In the wake of Kennedy's death he had degenerated into a whisky-swilling piss-head. True sobriety was undoubtedly the way to go in the long run. But Karin hadn't grieved openly even for just one night. Didn't she need to let it all go?

"One drink," he said.

"You really want to help me? I might have an idea."

It was everything he'd been hoping for. Disturbing memories of Ben Blake, Karin's parents and Komodo assailed him from a dark corner of his mind. After Kennedy's death he had sworn not to promise anyone *anything* anymore, and it had worked.

But this . . . this was entirely different.

"Tell me."

Karin lifted her head up. "I want to be trained up. Like you. As a fighter. I want you to train me up to be a soldier."

Drake drew a breath. It was the last thing he had expected. "Say again."

"I have the experience. Some even in the field and under fire. I can fight already, but yes I understand that my civilian training is of little use. I'm an office baboon, but I want to be a field expert. I want to honor Komodo and Ben and my mum and dad. I want to do it my way."

Drake watched her as she spoke and, at that moment, couldn't speak if he wanted to. What he saw in her was an awful lot of Ben Blake's youthful enthusiasm. The young lad's drive and cheeriness shone through in his sister, almost as if Ben spoke to him from beyond. Drake felt a string of words choke in his throat.

"Will you help me?" Karin leaned forward in earnest.

He thought about all the promises he had made to Ben Blake. "Yes," he said finally. "Trust me. I will get you to where you want to be. I promise."

Another vow broken.

Karin put an arm around his shoulders. The sun turned to a deep crimson before them as Jenny finally returned. It was going to be a long night.

CHAPTER TWENTY ONE

Hayden woke with a start, quickly reaching out for Kinimaka's reassuring bulk at her side. The Hawaiian grunted and rolled, slipping an arm around her. Hayden didn't like to struggle away but something was definitely bugging her. Some kind of intuition. Sunlight flooded through the closed hotel room curtains but that didn't mean it was late. A quick glance at the Pulsar on her wrist told her it was a little after 7 a.m. Knowing Mano was difficult to wake at the easiest of times she slid backwards in the bed until she sat upright and surveyed the room.

Shit, perhaps it was Tyler Webb's stalking back in DC or getting their butts kicked twice already, or even the reports of the ghost ships that Drake was tracking through the desert, but an unsettled sensation stole over her. Kinimaka snored, face to the pillow. Hayden slipped out of bed, suddenly feeling exposed in her underwear, and shrugged on a bath robe. Water dripped in the shower. Traffic roared outside the slightly cracked window. Someone walked noisily past along the hallway. All normal and natural noises for a middle-of-the-road hotel room, nothing sinister. But having reviewed all forms of stalking she knew that the worst and most dangerous forms were those where the victim wasn't entirely sure if it was happening. The ones that haunted people, made them edgy for no obvious reason.

Why were the hairs on the back of her neck standing up?

Were her clothes piled differently than she remembered? Her pants folded along a new crease? Her shirt arranged so that the arms were flung up in a classic "hands high" pose? Or did she leave everything that way? Was that bathroom door left wide open last night? Because she knew damn well that she'd closed it to reduce the noise from the dripping tap. Maybe Mano had—

Wait. That wasn't right.

Hayden padded over to the bureau. Sure enough her Glock sat in the center of the desk. The problem was, she always slept with it under her pillow, ever since her father explained it was the only place in the room she could reach it easily and a perp might not be able to steal it away as she slept. Old fashioned, yes, but as true as the coming of night and day. There was nothing subtle about this situation now.

"No!" How could this keep happening? And in such a random hotel room. Shivers crept up and down her spine. She knew very well that Webb possessed endless and multi-layered connections. It wouldn't be too tricky for a man of means and he clearly got off on the danger.

Kinimaka was struggling toward consciousness. "Wha—"

"It doesn't matter," Hayden said. "Get dressed, Mano. We have a job to do."

With the CIA's and NSA's mega-boffins investigating the inner workings of the Z-box and studying what the Pythians were trying to achieve by so rapidly targeting energy facilities, the proactive competence of Hayden's team was severely limited. It was with exultation then that they received the best guess of the NSA—that the third and final facility to be assaulted would be the electrical grid and major substation of Sierra Nevada.

Hayden immediately jabbed the ongoing call onto speakerphone and motioned at Kinimaka and Dahl. "We have a lead," she said, as she walked along the sidewalk to their vehicle, shop fronts to her right. "They're saying Sierra Nevada will be next." She paused, then stared at the phone. "How can you possibly know that?"

A small voice hissed from the microphone. "Deduction and possibility. We weighed the options. Nothing endgame has materialized as yet so that means these people do not have everything they need. Perhaps they need as many as three entry points, then—"

"Entry points?"

"Ways into the main system. Yes, they have been gaining access to substations and taking nothing away. That means they're leaving something behind. But why?"

Dahl coughed. "We were hoping you might tell us."

"Yeah, the question was a rhetorical one. We believe they're creating a back door—a way into the system but we don't yet know how. Quite probably something to do with these Z-boxes. Anyhow, both San Jose and Silicon Valley were primary junctions for the electrical grid. The only other one in your area is Sierra Nevada."

Dahl flung open the door. "We're on our way. Let's hope this time we can beat them to it."

Hayden ran around the other side, giving Kinimaka the back seat. "A plan would be useful."

"I have a plan. Take down any motherfucker toting a gun near an electrical substation."

Kinimaka checked his weapon. "I can get behind that."

Hayden thanked the NSA techie and hung up. She stared through the windshield as Dahl pulled into traffic, wondering if even now they were being observed. Dahl questioned the whereabouts of the Sierra Nevada plant and Hayden looked it up. With a few jabs she programmed it into the satnav. Then her cell rang once more.

"Jaye."

"This is Robert Price."

"Mr. Secretary. What can I do for you?" She was relatively pleased he had come back to her without needing to be chased.

"You have your reinforcements. I'm sending a large force

your way, formed from various military divisions. I left the dispersal in their hands, but I'm guessing—contact in four to six hours."

Hayden was grateful and said so. "The Pythians seem to be throwing everything they have at this so it's good to have the backup."

"Use it well, Miss Jaye. We'll speak the next time you're in DC."

Seeing that as a dismissal, Hayden severed the connection and looked around. "I wonder what that's supposed to mean."

"He's not Jonathan," Kinimaka said. "But then nobody could be."

"His way of ending a conversation and moving on to the next." Dahl shrugged. "Impersonal, but effective."

"We might never be in DC again."

"There you go."

Hayden checked the nav for the arrival calculation. "Forty two minutes. Step on it, Dahl. We have to beat the asshole brigade this time."

"The foot is down."

CHAPTER TWENTY TWO

Tyler Webb considered the evidence that lay before him, sheaves and sheaves of paper and thick manila files. The man he had chosen to use was the man he was most wary of, but even that development piqued his excitement. Out of all the ideas offered by the new Pythians, Julian Marsh's proposal was the most devastating. It also coincided beautifully with Webb's final launch of the Saint Germain operation.

Marsh entered and sat down. Again, Webb was struck by the oddity of the man. One trouser leg was immaculately pressed whilst the other was hopelessly creased. Were the socks different colors? Crazily he thought the hands might be different shades—one more tanned than the other—but thought it best not to stare.

"I like your plan, Marsh," he said agreeably.

"Thanks, man. I've been liking yours so far."

"Well, they're not all mine."

"Oh."

"I'm going to give you the green light," Webb said quickly, deciding he wanted shut of Marsh in a hurry. "Bring it up to speed and implement it within the next few weeks. This will be the last before Saint Germain kicks off."

"Sounds like you're going to be playing the truant, Mr. Webb."

Perceptive bastard. "I have two vital components to pick up from Ramses' arms bazaar. As carefully guarded as that will be nothing involving terrorists is ever straightforward or without risk. I'll be taking Beauregard, of course, but still . . ."

"Understood."

"Hopefully Bell and Bay-Dale will return soon armed with all the spare money we need for the final push. The greater times are upon us, Julian."

"I hope to further enrich those words, sir."

"I'm sure you will." Webb rose and extended a hand, pleased that he prevented a wince as the decidedly darker left shot out for a shake.

"Thank you, sir."

"Just don't fuck it up."

Marsh nodded and walked out. Oh hell, the man was limping slightly now. Webb would bet his life that he hadn't limped *into* the room or at any time before. Webb also imagined that the man used a different cellphone for every day of the week, each programmed to call forward to the next.

Weirdo.

Webb shrugged it off and took a quick look out of the window of his hotel room. Hayden Jaye's vehicle was gone now. He wondered where she was and wished he'd had the chance to plant a tracker on her. Or that muscle-bound walrus she slept with. Last night's escapade had been stimulating to say the least but soon the real fun would begin.

Soon . . . like now. Today.

Webb pressed a button on his cellphone and told the man who answered to come straight in. Eight seconds later the door opened and a lithe figure slipped around, approaching softly.

"Beauregard Alain," Webb said. "As you know we must soon leave for—" He left the destination unsaid, mindful that even the loyalist of accomplices might one day turn against him. "The bazaar. Prepare for at least three days there, in constant danger, and possibly more if we get invited back to Ramses' . . . castle. I need to be at ease, able to make my decisions and locate the best components, and that's why I have chosen you as my bodyguard. I take it you understand the honor?"

Beauregard nodded in that complacent way of his. Webb

never understood if the man was being subservient or arrogant but his prowess spoke for itself. There were none better in the known world.

"But first . . ." Webb allowed the biggest of smiles to break out across his face. "First I have a new job for you. And what a grand exploit it will be. The best yet."

Beauregard angled his head to the side. "Sir?"

"The stalking of Hayden Jaye is about to pass its zenith. I will need you for the fallout."

"When?"

"Tonight. For as long as it takes. Now, sit down. I need to talk to you. We should plan this together."

Webb underwent a swift makeover in his soul. Gone was the Pythian leader. Gone was the multi-millionaire company boss. Everything that was left was all that he was, all that he wanted to be, and it was the stimulated, aroused youth who had become a menacing stalker, the portentous haunter of the shadows.

Thrilled, practically overwrought, he explained the plan to Beauregard.

CHAPTER TWENTY THREE

Drake ruminated as they crawled northeast across the desert, occasionally passing within a few miles of small towns or asphalted roads but ignoring them and keeping to Jenny's take-it-or-leave-it style instructions. Drake took it, but with every bouncing, juddering mile he regretted it that little bit more.

Even more so with Smyth's growling tracery of complaints trickling through the two-way. "Even my ass-crack has sand in it. This air-con's too friggin' cold. Whoa, was that a roadrunner?"

Eventually even Lauren had reached her limit. "Shut the hell up. *My* ass-crack has sand in it but you don't hear me complaining like a six-year-old on a road trip!"

"It does?" Smyth said into the radio. "Want me to get that for you?"

"Gross!"

"Ha, says you. The New York—"

"The New York *what?*" Lauren's voice dipped dangerously.

"Umm, shit, hey these radios are open. Fuck." Smyth turned back to his irascible ways.

Drake watched as Yorgi drove. Truth be told the sighting of a distant town or twisting back road was the only brief variation to their constant monotony. So far though, there had been no sign of gun-toting mercenaries—a sign Drake took as entirely positive.

Whilst partly feigning a toilet break he wandered off into the desert during a short halt and made a phone call. His contact was an old friend, stretching all the way back to the days of Wells and Crouch, Sam and Jo. The world had seemed quieter, more innocent then. But all that was mostly down to youth and inexperience and the lack of a properly functioning Internet.

"Fort Bragg."

"Could I speak to Colonel Rudd please?"

"On what business?"

"Tell him it's Matt Drake and it's personal."

"Hold."

The minutes ticked by. Drake shaded his eyes from the heat.

"Drake?" An American twang focused his meandering thoughts. "Is that really you? Shit, man, I heard all about your exploits. Thought you'd forgot about lil' old me."

"Course you did, *Colonel*. It must truly suck to be you."

"You have no idea. But I'm sure you understand it's not all pancakes and maple syrup at the top."

"Oh, I do."

"And Matt," the Colonel's voice lowered, "I was sorry to hear about Sam and Jo. And even Wells."

Drake nodded to the desert. "Thank you."

"But Crouch is still out there. One of the good old boys, that one. A stalwart. Called in a favor only a few weeks ago. I'm pretty sure he owes *me* now but I would never tell him so."

Drake was silent, contemplating all that had gone before. It was odd how the quiet and stillness of a desert panorama brought forth his inner thinker. He was still musing when Rudd spoke up.

"Drake? You still there?"

"Aye, I mean yes. I was just lost in all that has already slipped by."

"Don't even think about that scary shit. Now, what can I do for you?"

Drake responded to the change in tone as Rudd knew he

would, the brusque tenor catching his attention. "Well, I have a strange request."

And he launched into Karin's story, telling as much as was relevant and ending with her request and his own promise to help. Rudd listened carefully without interruption and when Drake was done probed him with some hard questions as to her mental and physical health and prowess. Drake heard a shout—Jenny's raucous summons—and realized time was short.

"Can you help her?"

"Matt, this is a fully functioning, hard-learning military base. If she does come here there can be no special favors."

"That's exactly the point."

"And she has some idea what to expect?"

"Karin has been around soldiers for years now. Acted positively in some of our worst situations. I will vouch for her."

"Well, what can I say to that? I don't like it but I'm not gonna refuse you. Try again, but if you can't change her mind send her here immediately, but once she's in—she's in. Get me?"

"Affirmative. I'll explain it to her."

"Be clear. This ain't the fuckin' World Championships and she ain't that Ennis chick, Drake."

"I understand, I think."

Rudd sighed long and hard. "As if I ain't got enough shit to contend with. If this fucks up, Drake, if she fucks up in any way, I'll come looking for you."

Drake knew it was no idle threat. "I appreciate this, mate, more than you will ever know."

"All right, no need to bring out the English-isms. That friggin' language of yours is hard enough to get your head around with referring to me as your 'mate'. Shit, I'm military. Talk to your friend, Drake, and if she still wants in—send her."

Drake signed off. The small convoy sat beyond hearing

distance, now clearly waiting for him. What he would have liked right now were many moments of contemplation. An hour of examining morals and needs and plain old gut instinct. What he actually had was no time at all—not even a minute. Brushing himself off he rose and jogged back to the cars, climbed in and made ready. The two-way crackled into life and Jenny's raucous tones lit up the air.

"We all good now?"

"We're good. Let's kick this mother into action."

"Say what?"

"Let's go."

The cars rolled out. Drake immediately turned to Karin and relayed the conversation he'd just had with Rudd. The expression of relief that took residence in her face said it all—she needed this more than anything in her whole life. From far too young an age Karin had been losing the people most dear to her. The simple fact was that by taking control and earning confidence and training to win she saw the way to becoming the manager of her own destiny.

"First chance," he promised. "You're out of here."

Yorgi piloted the car, saying nothing. Jenny broke in over the radio at random intervals, explaining their route, crossing an actual road to continue into the wilderness and avoiding human contact at all turns. The satnav told Drake they were heading in an unwieldy direction for the large body of water known as the Salton Sea, what used to be a much larger inland sea at the time of the American Indians. What even might once have been connected to the Gulf of California. The area around there was as connected with lost desert ships as much as anywhere in the world.

Karin spoke up. "An interesting thing about Thomas Cavendish, the man who attacked the Manila galleon and divided her treasure between the *Content* and *Desire*, is that he limped back into London a year later, obviously minus the

Content which was never heard from again, sporting new blue sails of pure damask—he was a huge success financially and by all other means, and at twenty eight faster than Sir Francis Drake, and then knighted by the Queen—"

Drake wondered for a moment where she was getting all this information. No laptop sat open on Karin's knee. Then he remembered. "It's so odd knowing someone with an eidetic memory."

Karin ignored him. "And then being dead three years later."

"Three years?"

"Yes, buoyed by his overwhelming success Cavendish set off on a second voyage of circumnavigation and died. Unknown causes. Unknown place. His name lost through time, remembered only by a brand of pipe tobacco."

"That is thing about time," Yorgi said. "It erases everything."

Drake nodded wistfully. "Eventually, even heroes turn to dust." He spoke before his brain caught up, then kicked himself. "Bollocks."

Karin laid a hand on his shoulder. "It's all right."

Drake, embarrassed, fished out his cellphone and distracted himself with a call to Hayden. The unofficial boss of SPEAR told him that in addition to their attempting to stave off a third mercenary assault she was in touch with a local facility that was studying ground penetrating radar images of the entire Arizona/California area in question, seriously searching for anything out of the ordinary, but had so far come up blank.

"You don't realize the size of the area you have to cover," Hayden said.

Drake grimaced at the windshield of the car. "Y'know, I think I do."

"The old fashioned way not so good?"

"There's a reason it's called 'old fashioned'."

"Fighting for the US government has turned you

marshmallow soft," Dahl chimed in.

Drake laughed. "I couldn't have put it better myself."

"Not that you Brits ever get far past soft, given the limits of your training."

"Don't even go there, pal."

Dahl's laugh drifting away told them he'd won that particular head-to-head, easily getting a rise out of Drake. Hayden returned and Drake explained what was going to happen to Karin. Hayden's questioning eventually came back around to the subject of the ghost ships.

"So nothing's jumped out at you yet?"

"Nothing that's been buried in sand for five hundred years anyway."

"Maybe it's all a hoax designed to split us up." Hayden sounded disappointed.

"And on that subject I think we should rejoin. We're stretched. Alicia's on the way, but still . . ."

"As soon as we're done at Sierra Nevada we will rendezvous."

"Good. Then *you* can take the ghost watch after midnight."

"Sounds spooky."

Drake was about to say, "It can be," then heard Dahl mimicking a moaning ghost in the background. "Maybe you leave the Swedish chef behind? Do us all a favor."

Jenny called a halt over the two-way as a glistening body of water came into view off to the left. The perimeter alone stretched further than the eye could see and there were stories that most of these reportedly lost ships were now *underneath* this actual sea, buried in its darkest depths. Drake suddenly felt a little overwhelmed.

"There has to be an easier way than this."

Jenny clucked at him. "What? Ya don't trust me now?"

"There's one last thing," Hayden said quietly. "We do have reinforcements on the way, but the sheer weight of enemy numbers tells us the Pythians have no concerns over that and no thought about the welfare of their men. We feel exactly the opposite. I have the ISN—the Institute of Soldier Nanotechnologies—on board. They're based at MIT but have been tasked to supply us with their latest awesome invention—nanofoam body armor."

Drake had heard the rumors. "It exists?"

"Of course it exists. We only hear about these things when they're old news and the military experts have moved on. Yes, they're still being tested but we might be able to get our hands on some."

"I'm not sure I'd want to."

"Trust me, you do. But hey, I'll let you know."

Drake ended the call, wondering just how many mercenaries were out there waiting, how big his reinforcement company might be and just what would happen when the showdown began.

CHAPTER TWENTY FOUR

Hayden joined Kinimaka and Dahl in the lobby of their hotel. The trio had just arrived back from Sierra Nevada, having spent the entire day prepping for an attack that hadn't happened. With nothing more to be done they had decided to get some rest. Hayden was too tired for a sit-down meal and opted for taking a sandwich to bed. Kinimaka looked gutted.

"You stay." Hayden pointed to the well-lit archway that led to the hotel's restaurant. "Order a horse. With chips."

The Hawaiian looked suspicious. "Are you saying that I've put on weight?"

Hayden laughed. "Of course not. But I do know you like your food."

Kinimaka admitted defeat and headed inside. Hayden said goodnight to Dahl and took the elevator to their floor. Withdrawing her gun she entered her hotel room, eyes flicking left and right. A cursory check told her the room was empty and nothing appeared to be out of place. That led to a detailed check which also revealed nothing. Even so, Hayden didn't undress when she went to bed. Instead, she kept the lights on and slipped under the top cover, logging onto the Wi-Fi and flicking randomly through her cellphone. Gradually, the automated exercise began to dull her mind and send her to sleep. There was a reason these phones were called Android, she mused, considering the robotic nature they implanted into their user.

Kinimaka came in not long later and never saw Hayden's hand under the pillow, gripped around her Glock.

"Lock the door, Mano. Double lock it."

"Always do." Kinimaka gauged her weariness and then began undressing. "You tired?"

"I'm never too tired for that," Hayden laughed at his obtuse question. "But, in truth, you did just choose a meal over me."

"Eating's important." Kinimaka climbed into bed. "Gives you energy."

Hayden knew the reply should be "you're gonna need it" or something naughtier that might green-light their private carousing but the thought hit her then: *private?*

Inhibition pierced her like a long needle. Tyler Webb had the uncanny knack of being fully able to invade and spy upon her most private life and God only knew what he had already seen. Right now, she was drawing the line. There would be nothing more before they brought the bastard to cold, hard justice.

"Actually, Mano, I am a little tired. I think I'll go to sleep."

"Okay. Maybe in the morning then."

Kinimaka slid in beside her, not noticing that she lay fully clothed beneath the sheet. He switched the light off without checking her wide-open eyes. Within seconds he was asleep, leaving her to make sure her phone was switched to "loud" in case the facility was threatened, to set her alarm and, with a deep breath of fear, to turn out the light.

Hayden woke early the next morning, feeling oddly refreshed. She stared at the ceiling, at the light flooding through the imperfect windows. The sunshine invigorated her; maybe she could slip onto the balcony and bask in it. A rumbling mountain lay at her side, most likely the reason she had awakened.

Did I really sleep so long?

Considering her final thoughts of the night it surprised her. Pleased though, she sat up.

And met the eyes of the stalker standing at the foot of her bed—the man with the smug grin, the man whose eyes spoke of an infinite horror, the man who haunted her dreams and tore strips from her soul, the Pythian leader—

Tyler Webb.

CHAPTER TWENTY FIVE

Hayden screamed and then went for the gun, but found her hand grasping only air and pillow. *How the hell had this bastard gotten so close without waking me up?*

Never mind. Webb had outplayed himself this time. Trying to ignore the chagrin she felt at screaming—a sense of embarrassment and failure that months of this kind of torture naturally fostered—she threw off the single sheet and jumped to her feet. Webb grinned soullessly at her.

Something wasn't right.

Kinimaka was suddenly in motion, shifting the bed with the sheer force of his instant momentum. Webb grinned even wider. Hayden would get to him first, but every forward move she made was stunted by a wave of caution. *What are we missing?*

She grabbed his shirt, hauled him toward her, ready to vent months of frustration and feeling a moment of elation when the other great fact occurred to her—

This was the Pythian leader! Captured . . .

"The end is coming," Webb hissed in her face. "But not today."

His tongue flicked out, touching her cheek, and then the great bulk of Kinimaka was there. Except there were *two* bulks, and one was considerably more sinuous and deadly than Mano's.

Even without seeing the face Hayden knew.

Beauregard Alain.

It was the reason Webb remained so calm, so infuriatingly smug. Beauregard had already removed their guns and they were no match for him in hand-to-hand. Still, that didn't stop them trying. Hayden shoved Webb into the far wall and spun with a straight elbow to the face. Beauregard dipped and glided away, straight into Kinimaka's bulk. The Hawaiian grabbed eagerly, then grunted as striking blows hammered against pressure points. Webb stayed up against the wall, watching. Hayden kicked at the back of Beauregard's legs, digging into his calf. The Frenchman jumped as if hit by a cattle prod, lashing out in mid-air and catching her a painful blow on the arm. He came down on the bed, jabbed Kinimaka with a right and Hayden with a left just below the ear.

Both swayed, the pain momentary blinding them. Hayden struggled to shake it off.

It was at that moment that Torsten Dahl entered the fray.

The door to the room clicked open—the trio having asked for extra keys in case of a crisis—and the Swede filled the space. Hayden experienced a silent moment of rejoicing.

"Mr. Dahl," Beauregard said. "This party is already full."

"Oh, no," the Swede growled. "I don't think so. I've been looking forward to this for a bloody long time."

Webb stepped forward then, looking to intervene. "Then you will have to wait a while longer. This exercise is over."

Hayden paused in her fast and silent deliberations over the loyalties of Beauregard Alain. "Exercise?"

"To prove that at any time, and anywhere I can get to you."

"Fuck you."

"Look for me soon."

As if by prearranged signal Beauregard burst into sudden, violent action. A charge at Hayden brought Dahl into the room and Kinimaka leaping hard, whereupon Beauregard merely tangled her feet, tripping her to the floor. Webb eased toward the door as Beauregard maneuvered Kinimaka straight into Dahl.

"Tricky little bastard!" Dahl grunted, a muffled shout as the Hawaiian took him to the floor.

Beauregard took hold of Webb's arm and finessed him around the struggling pile. Webb looked like he wanted to say more but the Frenchman dragged him even harder. The deadly assassin's worst fears were realized when Dahl, never one to lose hope, threw Kinimaka to the side and reared to his feet.

Webb found himself flung into the corridor. Beauregard faced Dahl, all concentration. "One on one," the Swede said. "No tricky bollocks. Fight me."

"It's coming," Beauregard said. "Soon."

Dahl lunged, a fist already in full flight. Beauregard stepped back and closed the door. The entire piece of wood and its frame juddered as Dahl punched it closed. "Ow!"

Outside, swift feet spirited Webb away. Hayden rushed to the door and flung it open, saw Beauregard headed down the stairs. Should she give chase? Yes, but all that had just transpired had served only to drain her. Shockingly, the will wasn't there. *Is this how a victim feels?*

With the fight inside her leeched away she retreated back into the room. Two pairs of eyes stared at her.

"We have real work to do," she said firmly. "Get dressed and let's get back to the Sierra Nevada plant."

"We just let the Pythian boss get away," Dahl moaned.

"No we didn't. We allowed Beau to stay undercover for when he's desperately needed. I assumed that's why you let him slip away?"

Dahl gulped slightly. "Umm, yes, sure. That works."

"Good. So get the hell outta my bedroom so I can shower and change. And make yourself useful—try and think of a way to own that Webb asshole once and for all."

"Yes, ma'am."

"Fuck ma'am. You trying to shit me, Dahl?"

The Swede thought better of any more banter and quickly retreated. Kinimaka gave her a slightly hurt look.

"You want me to go too?"

"Unless you wanna do it in the shower with Dahl in the adjoining room?"

Kinimaka nodded. "Gotcha."

Hayden waited until the door was closed before she sat on the bed, gripped her head between her hands and sobbed.

CHAPTER TWENTY SIX

Tyler Webb was truly ecstatic. What a way to leave things with Hayden Jaye! *Utterly superb.* The hotel room visit had been the culmination of the current phase of stalking and now, with her wits in tatters, he intended—actually circumstances were forcing him—to take a relatively short break.

No mind. The bitch will be thinking of me every hour of the day and especially through the night. Wondering . . . feeling my eyes upon her . . . imagining what isn't even there. Every sound, every admiring or odd look. Every turn of phrase from a stranger.

The game was set then for a grand finale. But first he had important matters to attend to. Ramses had been in touch and the great bazaar now had a date if not yet a venue. Still, Webb knew the approximate location and that he had to get his real life into gear if he was to attend. Beauregard was prepped. The components would, hopefully, be acquired without incident.

And Julian Marsh's crazy plan was, quite literally, soon to go nuclear.

Interesting.

Webb seated himself behind his makeshift desk, still trembling with excitement. He even let out a little giggle to ease the tension. But there were jobs to do. First he organized a flight for himself and Beauregard, the jet even now being prepared on a private runway ten miles from his current location. It would fly them anywhere in the world at a moment's notice. Then he arranged the fundamentals for the next and probably final stage of his plan—he would be moving to New York as soon as he returned from the bazaar. DC was entirely too hot right now and this backward hovel just wouldn't do. The New York office was perfect, even loftier than his office back in DC where he enjoyed his daily scrutiny of the ants scurrying below. It would be a fitting palace from where to end the Pythians.

And it would end, he had decided. The Pythian ideal, the anti-shadow organization, did have its place—but it was just too much hard work. Webb meant to cut everything loose. But only when he could go out with a huge bang.

Of course, the culmination of the Saint Germain exercise would have the entire world chasing him. Not an enviable situation by any means. But the world would soon forget . . . and he would live on. The biggest thing that had ever happened in the world would make him—

A knock at the adjoining door interrupted his meanderings.

"Yes?"

A long-haired brunette entered from the room next door. "I have Nicholas Bell on the phone for you, sir."

Webb waved. "Fine. Put him through." He needed an update on the ghost ships anyway. Their discovery would add the funding he required to advance his plans exponentially. As he waited for the connection his mind flicked to Zoe Sheers. The newest Pythian had yet to offer up any proposal. Well, he could always send Beauregard round to accelerate her thinking.

"Hello?"

"Bell? What do you have? The ships? C'mon, man, time is short and so will be your lifespan if this doesn't pan out."

"Again, we believe we are in the right area, sir. Drake is on the case, actually here somewhere in this godforsaken scorch pit. And I'm told that the Sierra Nevada facility is about to be taken apart."

Webb held on to his excitement. "Oh? Excellent. That will be three."

"And then it's 'Goodnight, America'."

"Let us hope so. The Z-boxes are of Chinese manufacture and unproven. It would not surprise me if they hadn't programmed in a back door of their own and are copying everything we do. It certainly wouldn't surprise me if they could track the devices somehow."

"Do you think they might alert the Americans?"

"That depends on many things—the mood of that day's official. What meat he had for lunch. Who overtook him on the way to work. One day they cooperate the next they hack each other to death. I would not like to forecast tomorrow."

"Then we'll keep digging."

"Dig harder."

Webb hung up. Everything was coming together nicely. He called up Beauregard and told him to make ready to leave. Ramses was next.

CHAPTER TWENTY SEVEN

Mai Kitano struggled to remain conscious. The battle with the devil, Aoki, had robbed her of more than just strength. It had taken her last shred of mental energy along with her blood, her flesh, her will and her clothes. Only Dai Hibiki was present to help her. The Japanese cop rushed to her side, covering her as best he could and tearing off his own shirt to help staunch the flow of blood that came from the gash across her face. When he saw the Yakuza step toward them he reached into the back of his waistband for a gun.

The older man held up a hand. "It is finished," he said. "Mai Kitano defeated our best in fair combat. She is absolved of her sins against the Yakuza. Let this be an end to it."

Hibiki nodded; Mai barely registered any of it. All she knew was that Dai and she were soon alone and he was struggling to lift her, to maintain her dignity, and curtail her blood loss all at the same time.

"Not far," he whispered, most likely reassurance for himself. "Come on."

He carried her back to their car, laid her in the back seat and then bent over her for a while. Mai faded in and out, unsure what he was doing. The shirt pressed hard against her face. The next thing she knew they were driving for a time and then screeching to a halt. Hibiki ran around the car, hefted her and carried her up a path. Mai felt nothing but a sense of numbness, not entirely unpleasant.

It was Chika's voice that pierced her cloudiness and then the resounding slap that stopped Hibiki in his tracks.

"You both left it this long to tell me! Neither of you is going to get away with that."

Hibiki grunted. Mai attempted to speak but couldn't seem to make the connection between mouth and brain.

"Shit, and she's almost naked. What the hell have you been doing to my sister?"

Hibiki pushed past Chika, then knelt and deposited Mai very gently on the couch. "She fought as hard as anyone I've ever seen," he said. "And she won. The threat is lifted. Now, I need to grab my kit. Wait here with her."

Mai tried to focus, but the room swam so much it made her feel nauseous. Chika's voice kept her grounded, kept her tied down to this place. When Hibiki returned she felt the shirt being gently removed from her face and knew there was more pain soon to come.

Why?

You are dying.

She knew the best way to stitch a facial wound as well as Hibiki, and now that she knew what was happening she was better able to focus. The longer the wound stayed open the greater the chance of infection. Hibiki could have taken her to a hospital but how many questions would that have raised? It was better this way. Hibiki would use skin adhesive or liquid stitches on her. He lowered his face to hers now, washed the wound and then pinched both sides of it together. Mai struggled, the pain almost impossible to bear. As Hibiki pinched even harder she sent her mind away, back into her consciousness and searched for a subject to consider. *How about Hayami?* The deadly, tragic issue that had started all this. In an odd way the forgiveness of the Yakuza had eased her inner burden, and the pain in her face made a great escape channel for the pain in her soul. She guided it out. Hibiki applied the liquid stitches, keeping the surrounding area clean and directing Chika to hold Mai as still as she possibly could. Mai didn't feel the pain anymore. Part of this demon had already been laid to rest.

Where was Grace?

Mai flicked her eyes to and fro. As if by sisterly telepathy Chika appeared to understand exactly what she was thinking. With a dip of her head she whispered into Mai's ear.

"Upstairs. Asleep. She knows nothing of your return."

Additional good fortune. Grace had already suffered more than enough. No need to extend that suffering now that she was well and truly on the mend. Hibiki then entered Mai's field of vision, his face staring critically at hers.

"It's gonna scar."

No shit, it was a fucking sword not a tenderizer.

But the scar . . . it was fitting. She would wear it as a tribute to the man she killed and the family he lost, the daughter who was still missing. She deserved lasting damage of some sort. Chika then held a bottle of water to her lips and Mai regained presence of mind enough to drink.

Already, a semblance of energy was starting to return. Hibiki and Chika were fussing over her other wounds, the sister firmly telling the boyfriend to attend to matters above the waist, not below. Mai felt the slightest of smiles curl her lips.

Life goes on. And people go on. And their mannerisms, quirks and personalities are the true heart that keeps the world beating.

She could live now.

A croak escaped her throat, low at first but then gaining in volume. "Ce . . . celebrate."

Chika looked up at her. "What?"

"We should celebrate."

"Give us chance to put you back together," Hibiki said. "And we'll do a Godzilla on Tokyo, believe me."

"And we'll take Grace." Chika smiled, again reading Mai's thoughts before she even uttered them.

Mai smiled. The world had turned and it was good. Who

could have guessed she might come out on the other side with a chance at a real future?

Matt Drake, probably. And before the guilt of leaving him began to eat at her she buried it hard, covered it with a sense of achievement. Tomorrow was always uncertain and anything beyond that could wait.

Anything.

As Mai relaxed, allowing the painkillers and her friends to do all the work, she saw movement in the hallway. It was a fleeting shadow, possibly less—the mere suggestion of an outline, but it was most certainly there. Her eyes refocused and her wits returned instantly. Mai had been trained hard to be the best and not pain, nor stitches, nor a mix of alcohol and Tylenol was ever going to dull her responses. She knew where the closest weapon was, where the best cover was, how to save Chika from harm. She knew the fastest escape route, the lay of the land outside both ways, the time she could expect to pass before her opponent acted.

She braced herself.

But then the shadow moved and Mai saw by its very outline that it was Grace. *My Grace.* A moment later and she caught the girl's breathing, the nasally rasp she had developed from a slight head cold. She relaxed.

Grace popped her head around the corner. "Guys?"

Still wary, still unsure of herself, Grace was well on the way to a wonderful emotional comeback. The horrors of her childhood were receding; the worst of the returning memories mostly dealt with and compartmentalized. They would never pass away, but they could at least be managed. Grace's way of managing them involved copious amounts of fun, food, laughter and shopping, much of it at the same time. If Mai had thought it wasn't helping Grace she would have gently eased her in another direction, but the young girl seemed to be flourishing. The next step would be a more stable environment and Mai began to think for the first time about heading back to the US, maybe sending her to a DC school . . .

"Come here," she said, and Grace did. Mai explained everything, sensing that she needed full disclosure. At first Chika and Hibiki winced a little—their synchronized shying away actually a little comical—but as they read Grace's understanding they soon warmed up.

"It is over," Hibiki said. "We can all return to our lives again. Or start new ones."

Grace snuggled into Mai. "Thank you," she said. "Thank you so much."

Mai tried not to gasp as movement tended to elevate her pain levels. "Together, we will make it work."

"Oh, sorry!" Now Grace pulled away, realizing that her friend was still in pain. "Hey, that's a mega scar!"

Hibiki grimaced. "Maybe it's best not to—"

"No, no! It's a warrior's scar. A sign of victory in battle. And well earned."

Mai grunted. "Whatever happens *don't ever* tell me you want one."

"Jeez, you kidding? Imagine what the boys would say."

"Thanks," Mai said drily, then: "*What* boys?"

"Umm, nothing."

"Believe me, boys are bad for you. They stink, they scratch, they drive too fast. They forget, they develop hormones and they don't shower properly. They're pack animals, always—"

"Excuse me," Hibiki said a little huffily.

Mai laughed. "Oh, you're okay. I don't class you as a boy."

Now Chika laughed. "Really? What is he then?"

"More a big sister." Mai leaned into Chika and they smiled at each other. Grace bounded in between them, right across their knees. Hibiki finished cleaning Mai's cheek, now eyeing the liquid stitches.

"I'm no doctor, of course, but I think *that* will be a warrior's scar of major import, a talking point."

It was good that they could make light of it, Mai thought. Being dejected would not change anything.

"Wait until Drake sees you," Grace said. "He won't be able to keep his hands off you. Not that he ever could anyway."

Mai felt her face soften. "Ah, well, I don't really know how things stand there." She knew she should at least have kept in touch with the SPEAR team. "Maybe he has a new girlfriend," she added lightly.

"As long as it's not that Alicia!" Grace burst out. "Blond bimbo said she'd give me a lesson in the birds and the bees when I'm ready. I don't even know what she means!"

Mai gulped slightly. "Yeah, avoid that one at all costs." But she wasn't entirely sure Matt Drake would. They had been the original couple, the original team, and Alicia had come a long way back to normal over the last few years.

Chika drew their attention to the clock. "It's beyond late, my friends. Maybe we should call this morning and breakfast time. I'm certainly famished."

Grace nodded eagerly. "Me too!"

Mai couldn't keep the smile off her face, despite the pain that it caused. Grace was perpetually hungry and could eat at any time of the day or night, even minutes after declaring herself "full to the brim". Hibiki caught her eye and shared the joy of it and then grinned as there came a quick knock at the door.

"Postman's right on time," he said. "We ordered Grace something."

Postman's early, Mai almost said but didn't want to disturb the playful atmosphere. There was a time when a ninja soldier should remain dormant, if only to promote peace and happiness, and this was it. Hibiki walked over to the front door. Chika paused and waited and Grace stared between them with wide eyes.

"What is it?"

"Wait and see."

Grace pouted on hearing the time-honored parental phrase.

Hibiki swung the door wide open, smiling. "What do you have for us?"

It was all so easy in the end. She had planned and planned. She had waited and waited. She had run away and stayed quiet. She had known this day would come from the moment she received news about her poor father. She had eaten garbage from the street and evaded tramps and sex-slavers. She had gotten lucky more than once, but then she deserved that kind of good fortune didn't she? Her name was not known to those people. Her name was no longer important to anyone, for she had no family. Her name was mere fresh air, a lifelong gift of pure nothingness.

And the moment, quite suddenly, was here. Right on this doorstep. Her name *did* matter for this passing of a few seconds. It *did*. They did not see the danger. They were all so blind and uncaring. But she cared, and she would prove it right now. The cop, Hibiki, was even smiling as he stared at her. The sister, Chika, seemed so happy and secure. Mai herself, the great ninja warrior, would never be a threat.

Not to her.

Emiko was totally sure of that.

The gun, an enormous Magnum, raised and the deadly barrel pointed unwaveringly at Mai Kitano, the woman who had murdered her father on his yacht and then sent the Yakuza after the rest of her family. Mai Kitano would not evade the bullet, Emiko knew, she would welcome the absolution of it.

Hibiki was still smiling—in that split second—for he recognized the girl and probably believed she had found her way back to the light. But his features began to falter as his instincts registered the gun. Chika's eyes were widening, her mouth turning into a huge 'O'. There was only one who reacted.

Mai screamed as she recognized Emiko and the huge gun she held in her right hand. There was no evading it and, even now after everything she had won back, she believed this was her fate. It had been all along.

But nobody factored in the streak that suddenly intervened. Nobody banked on Grace reading the situation perfectly—even before the door opened she had realized the hour was too early—and throwing herself at Mai to try and make her move.

The gun boomed, deafening and deadly. Hibiki screamed. Chika screamed. The bullet flew straight, unerring and fatally.

Mai flew back with the impact, staggering to her knees. Hibiki drew the gun he always carried and shot Emiko dead on the doorstep before she could squeeze off any more shots, even as Emiko staggered back from the initial recoil. Chika turned toward Mai, shrieking.

"No!"

Mai cradled Grace's dead body, the blood already blooming from the bullet hole in her back, soaking through her clothes and staining Mai's shaking hands. Staring down into Grace's lifeless, unmoving beautiful eyes she felt her body clutch so tightly she could not breathe. Shock destroyed her. In less than a minute a bright new world had turned to ashes.

"What . . . what has she done? Oh no, oh, no." Chika scrambled over on her knees, distraught. She clutched Grace's shoulders and laid her head down and began to sob.

Finally Mai found her voice. "My beautiful . . . my . . . beautiful . . ."

The word *daughter* was spoken in her mind only.

CHAPTER TWENTY EIGHT

Mai crumpled. Grace was gone and two worlds had died with her. Two futures. Throughout her life she had known despair, but this . . . *this* . . . it simply destroyed her.

She collapsed onto the floor, oblivious to all else. Grace stayed with her and she would never let go. She heard Hibiki's movements and Chika's crying but none of it was starkly real. Only one stark truth existed.

There would be no more life for Mai Kitano.

Deep character traits bloomed up, forcing her to look at the truth, to accept the facts, showing her that moving forward was possible. But how much could one person take? How much *should* one person take?

"Mai." Chika's voice at her side. Her sister's arms wrapping themselves around her.

She said nothing, barely able to breathe. All she knew was the lifeless presence in her arms. All she felt was despair.

And Emiko? The girl had survived all this time just to kill Mai Kitano. Now she was dead too. And Hibiki? How would he handle this?

"Mai!"

His shout penetrated her fugue only marginally. Chika was so close now her breath was hot in Mai's ears, her tears streaming down Mai's own face. Blood coated Mai's hands and forearms, lifeblood.

"Mai!"

Digging deep, calling on every ounce of strength she ever possessed, the Japanese woman raised her head. Everything was blurred until she blinked her eyes and then the water cleared.

Hibiki knelt before her, holding Emiko. Blood covered his face too.

Chika knelt beside them both, horror etched so deeply in her face it formed furrows.

Mai saw her family, but still felt overwhelmed. As powerful as she was she could not protect the people she loved. None of them could. *Nobody* could. Disaster and tragedy lurked around every corner, every curb, every main road and every schoolyard. Not so long ago it had been safe to let a child visit the park alone. Now, even the presence of parents couldn't keep them totally safe.

Mai looked up at the ceiling, feeling certain she would never move again.

Hibiki's voice brought her back down. "Mai!"

She glanced at him instinctively, recognizing the tone of utter urgency. "Just leave me with her," she said finally. "This was not supposed to happen."

Anger raged inside. *What chance did Grace ever have? And she had been such a fighter . . . so spirited . . . taking all the bad and trying to turn it to good.*

"Mai! I saw her move. I saw her fucking *move!*"

The words jolted her like machine-gun bullets. Mai flicked from Hibiki to Grace and took it all in. The blood. The body. The eyes that had closed long ago.

"Wha—"

There! Mai saw the movement too. Grace was moving her fingers ever so slightly. The fingers of her right hand. It wasn't a cruel vision nor a sudden spasm.

Grace was alive!

CHAPTER TWENTY NINE

Hayden entered the Sierra Nevada electrical substation in a sub-zero mood. It didn't matter what anyone said, Hayden found a way to pick a hole in it. Her colleagues looked as though they'd both been hit by icy daggers. The facility's security had been beefed up, along with two other lesser ones that were close by—but Hayden was taking zero chances. Approaching the entrance and shading her eyes from the sun and heat, the first cop who met her gave a little attitude—especially on seeing the unfamiliar SPEAR badge—and almost ended up in a heap on the floor.

Dahl intervened. "We're a covert agency," he said in a rush as Hayden's fists clenched. "So covert we're practically unknown."

"That work out well for you?" the cop drawled, oblivious of his near-death experience.

"Almost never."

Hayden pushed past and Kinimaka followed. Dahl forestalled any wisecracks from the cop by verifying the extra security.

"How many, bud?"

"Thirty," the cop said. "Includes a Special Ops team."

Dahl had been about to squawk *"thirty*?", knowing that wasn't nearly enough and dreading how Hayden would react in her current mood, when the final part of the cop's answer registered with him. "Special ops? Now you're talking."

He moved off, keen to meet the elite team. Hayden stopped him inside the facility. "How many?"

"Well . . . they're still counting but we do have a Special Forces team."

"We do? Well, thank fuck for that. About time Robert Price started getting his act together."

Dahl sauntered past, having averted the explosion quite nicely, he thought. Kinimaka's shrewd glance didn't go unnoticed. The inside of this particular facility was relatively cramped—a wide open space crammed full with offices, electrical boxes, small pylons, and gantries. It was a maze, but thankfully one in which you could always see all four walls.

Cops stood around in huddles, disorganized. Dahl followed Hayden to the main control room where a diminutive bank of CCTV screens minded the facility. Immediately, he saw the men he was looking for.

"Torsten Dahl." He nodded at the group.

"How ya doin'?" To a man they eyed him suspiciously. "You in charge here?"

"Nope. She is." Dahl nodded at Hayden. "We're part of the *other* Special Forces team here."

"What?" a man said. "All three of ya?"

Dahl conceded that point. "It's been a rough one."

Hayden quickly scanned the screens. "We need some of the cops outside. Those two police cars ain't gonna be enough. Don't these people listen to the news?"

"The important part is to prevent them from gaining access to this room," Dahl said. "We think they're planning to enter the system by leaving behind a back door. The harder we make it the better the chance they'll give up. So let's make it very hard."

A rugged soldier stepped forward, addressing Hayden. "Where do you want us, ma'am?"

"First—the next person who calls me ma'am is gonna be walking funny for about three days. It's Jaye or boss. I mean, do I *look* like a friggin' ma'am? Second—we need to get those cops organized. I don't want any dead officers today."

"I'll do it." Kinimaka turned on his heel.

Dahl nodded at the screens. "Thirty minutes and we should have this place pretty well sewn up."

Hayden sighed. "Yeah, ahead of the game at last."

"Don't count on it," the Special Forces leader said. "You told them how many mercs assaulted the last station, yeah?"

Hayden nodded, already ahead of him. "I did. And our boss sent a few cops and you guys. No offense, but that ain't enough."

"And there's a bigger problem," the leader said.

"Which is?"

"The mercs are already here."

Dahl reacted faster than anyone, lunging for a weapon rather than reaching for his own. This way he got among them and caused a little havoc. A weapon came free, its owner stumbling as Dahl wrenched hard. These men were not Special Forces then, and as he tackled them he immediately knew it. They were slow, and poorly trained. They were unsystematic. Dahl swung the weapon hard, connecting with the side of a skull. The first merc toppled at his feet, the second went flying. That left four, all drawing guns.

Hayden swept the desk clear of junk, aiming it straight toward the mercs with a powerful sweep as she drew her own gun. The facility workers froze in place, eyes wide. Hopefully Kinimaka, behind them, would bring the cops running.

She fired instantly, her shot going wide. A merc lunged at her face, grabbing for the gun. Dahl swept another weapon aside, grabbed its owner, and slammed him against the wall. The man battered both his ears with fists the size of soccer balls. A sixth sense warned him of a blade zinging in toward his spine but he knew the stab-vest would deflect it, waited, and used the ricochet to gauge where his cowardly attacker would end up. Dahl's arm was ready, wrapping around the neck and squeezing. With the other hand he jabbed his first opponent, keeping him against the wall.

Hayden struggled as her merc caught her in a bear hug, their faces pressed together. The gun was trapped between them. His strength crushed the breath from her body. They were too close to enable her to maneuver, but she drew her head back and used her skull. The merc was clever, having dipped his head so she couldn't reach his nose. The blow still smashed against his temple though, a wallop that he felt all the way down to his knees.

Hayden pivoted and smashed him into the bank of TV screens, then bore down on his spine. With a little room now she brought a hand up, stiffened the fingers, and dug them into his windpipe—harder and harder, each second applying more force until the choking drowned out all else. He was a stubborn son-of-a-bitch, but nobody could resist such pressure forever. At last he pushed her away, staggering. Hayden vented much more than frustration with a sharp kick to the head.

She whirled. Dahl was dealing with two mercs, and that left just one unattended. Yes, they had been outplayed but the odds were certainly changing. The merc waved a gun in her face.

"Step back, *ma'am*. Sit your pretty little ass down on that chair and put your hands behind your back so I can tie 'em together."

Hayden backed away meekly, holding her hands slightly apart. "All right. Just calm down. No one needs to get shot here today."

"Well that depends how good you are at keeping us happy, ma'am. Now sit the fuck down."

Hayden bowed her head, still meek and subservient. The man stepped forward menacingly and it all fell into place. Or rather his testicles fell into place. Now at the perfect range she made good on her earlier promise and drop-kicked them from his groin to his throat. The man collapsed with a high-pitched squeak, scrambling about the floor. Hayden collected his gun.

She turned again. Dahl had already choked one merc into unconsciousness. The other batted futilely at him, already knowing he was going to lose. Quickly, Hayden spun toward Kinimaka and the cops.

The day is ours! Even now we've thwarted the Pythians...

Kinimaka didn't look happy, being prodded in the back by four handguns and surrounded by thirty grinning mercenaries dressed as cops. More than twenty weapons were leveled at her and Dahl.

"Now," grated a swarthy man with a face and arms as dark and wrinkled and hard as a tree-trunk. "Get your ass down on that floor. And you too, big guy. One wrong move an' you'll get to see yer fucking brains across them TV screens."

CHAPTER THIRTY

Matt Drake would never admit to it, but as he ventured closer and closer to the eerie ghost town the hairs on the back of his neck bristled more and more. It wasn't any Scooby-Doo mentality, nor even a boyhood fear, it was the unnerving fact that everything looked like it had been deserted just yesterday. As they approached the main street he saw a children's swing set moving gently in a garden, creaking and swaying as if a child had run inside just moments earlier. A timber-built store sat dead ahead at the street corner, its colors as bright as any new store shouting "Motherlode Mercantile" and "Tomahawk Tours". Tree stumps, dusty and gray, sat all around, old signs tacked to them. An overgrown yard lay behind. The main street was nothing but a gravelly dirt track, but smooth and tidy as if had been raked over just this week.

Jenny appeared between the buildings. Having been gone for over an hour she finally returned with a frown. "Nobody living here as I thought. But there *has* been activity over the last few weeks. Footprints, shuffle-marks and used condoms aplenty out back there. Handprints—female—against the door. Somebody had themselves alotta perpendicular fun."

"Kids?" Drake wondered.

The redhead grimaced. "Doubtful. Kids woulda left McDonald's wrappers and more. This was someone trying to be reasonably careful. Probably slipping away from a large camp."

"Mercs," Lauren said. "Maybe Alicia got here early."

Drake grinned. "Nice. But I gotta say—it doesn't mean it's our lot."

"If that means it might not be the people we're searching for then I agree. But it is someone, and I can follow their trail." Jenny nodded at the jagged wall of mountains set dark against the blue sky. "That way."

Drake pursed his lips. "Well, it's as good a direction as any, I guess. And within the grid we're searching. Let's do it."

"I was going to."

Jenny hitched her jeans tighter and strode off toward her Jeep. Smyth stared for a moment before Lauren put an arm around his shoulders. "Ready?"

"Oh yeah. Umm, I mean, sure."

Drake blinked rapidly. "Well, I guess we're going to have to follow her."

Yorgi smiled. "Not a problem. I now see what is meant by your phrase—second skin."

"Quit it." Drake tried to remain objective about the new arrival, unsure what her motives were beyond getting paid for a good job. The redhead was short-tempered, tetchy and easily able to incite annoyance among other team members to be sure, but she was also proving to be highly capable and surprisingly knowledgeable. The world out here was a land of expiry and sand, a drifting monument to mortality. Jenny knew it well, and guided them without acknowledging their shortcomings. Her ability to track was beyond any that Drake had ever known, to his own great surprise. He wondered how she might handle herself in a crisis.

He took another look around the silent town, still unable to shake a sense of creepiness, of being watched through unwashed windows. If he stood there long enough he might see a curtain twitch, might even see it slide open . . . and a skeletal head peering out at him with a grinning death-mask smile.

Drake shivered. Karin, at his side, shuffled her feet. "Do you truly believe in ghosts, Matt? That our loved ones are, even now, at our side?"

"I can't answer that. It's a bloody loaded question. No more promises, Karin. You were the last. All I know is these ghost towns are very well named."

"A village of the damned," she said.

Drake studied a huge, three-pronged cactus that rose up like a unique signpost at a four-way junction ahead. Lush and green, it contradicted all that stood around it. The ramshackle, haphazard clutter of buildings should be occupied, and not only by the undead. A lady should twirl here, a gentleman tip his hat there. An old timer should be lying back in a chair, watching the world go by, not creeping through the netherworld, reaching for all that he had lost with cracking, emaciated fingers of dead bone.

Drake shook himself out of it. Jenny started up the lead Jeep and rolled out, keeping the revs low. Yorgi waited for Drake and Karin, and then followed. Silence hung like an oppressive curtain. Drake wondered how many more of these ghost towns sat out there, soundless grieving tombstones gazing out at the world through hollow eye-sockets, as unnatural as black rain and more peculiar than moonstone. Someone had painted an old brown sign at the edge of town.

Up here ends the sidewalk
And the Old West begins

Drake focused on the job at hand, keeping his eyes peeled especially now that Jenny had found real signs of a human presence. *Human?* He thought. *Fuck, I hope so.*

They came at length to the enormous inland Salton Sea, a shallow rift lake located directly on the San Andreas fault line. Created by accident, its salinity was higher than that of the Pacific Ocean and was once much larger and called Lake Cahuilla. As the vehicles found the marina, Drake saw an abandoned boat stuck in the ground.

"I hope we haven't gone through all this for that speedboat, guys."

Jenny didn't even chuckle. "We'll be beyond here in just a few minutes, heading west again."

Drake stared at the pure white earth, bright under the blazing sun. Buildings dotted the marina sparsely and it felt like another ghost town. He was happy to spot a young man leaning out of a window, watching them.

"Another weird area," he said.

"Dude, this is America. Get used to it."

"Well, passing an abandoned-looking auto shop painted with the words 24 hour repair doesn't give me much hope."

Beyond the Salton Sea, the barren landscape encompassed their horizons once again, dotted and dappled here and there by twisted tangles of green. The marina and its odd lake were left far behind as the day wore on. Jenny forged her own path, staying stealthy and hugging the dunes. How she found her way in such a featureless landscape, Drake never knew but he was glad she was along for the ride. Her progress was sometimes slow, sometimes even stealthy, but always considered and careful. Of course, even his soldier's patience was beginning to wear thin. They had been out in this wilderness for far too long. Before they crested any hill of significance she always halted the convoy and inspected ahead. It was about thirty minutes later when her standard reaction suddenly changed.

Drake saw her hit the dirt and stay there. At first he was horrified, thinking she had been shot, but then she rolled over, giving them a small signal.

Get out of sight.

Immediately he took charge, guiding Yorgi to drive their Jeep to the nearest cover and then beckoning Smyth over. The small stand of trees huddled up against a dune would work with a lazy, careless observer—aka the Pythians' new bunch of mercs—but not with anyone of even the slightest prowess.

Nevertheless, Drake and the rest of the team crawled and

scrambled their way to Jenny's side. The tracker had shuffled through heaped sand, dirt and rocks to the bottom of the steep slope by that time.

"Over that rise," she whispered, her red hair now matted and yellow with sand. "I'm pretty sure it's what you're looking for."

Drake stared at her. Despite his willingness and tenacity to explore he was surprised to find he had believed this entire quest would be nothing but a wild goose chase. Even when the mercenaries attacked he assumed it had to be some kind of trap.

"A ship?" He all but goggled at her. "Up there?"

"Take a look." Jenny shrugged. "Over the rise."

Racked by mixed emotions of awe and trepidation, incredulity and astonishment, the Yorkshireman crept steadily up the sandy slope. Smyth wasted no time dropping to his side and Jenny crawled behind them to take another look. Drake stopped twice to listen and to examine their surroundings with a detailed eye. As the crest approached he slowed even further, sinking as low as the hard earth would allow.

At last, he peered over the edge.

CHAPTER THIRTY ONE

Drake felt his face go slack as a lost wonder from a bygone age filled his field of vision.

Beyond the crest of the slope lay a deep valley. About a third of the way down the opposite slope, half buried into its vertical side, its deck even now being exposed by a bevy of mercenary workers, was a perilously perched, ancient pirate galleon.

Men slipped and skidded downhill about twenty feet to reach the excavation around its deck, taking their lives into their own hands. They worked very slowly, fearfully. No wonder this was taking some time. The great bulge that constituted the galleon's side jutted out from the slope's face, an enormous stepping stone. Drake saw several rivers of sand falling away from the unseen base of the ship and winced.

That thing could go at any moment.

Or it could last an eternity.

Maybe it had. Maybe sometimes the valley filled up and allowed men to walk across. Maybe the other side emptied of sand and allowed men a glimpse of what lay beneath. But none of that mattered now. What mattered was the ship was real and the Pythians were here.

"It's . . . staggering," Jenny whispered, the first time Drake had seen her anything other than entirely self-assured.

"It's cool," Smyth agreed. "Sorta cool enough to strip even *my* coolness away."

Drake gave him a look, followed by Jenny. Smyth motioned ahead. "Stop staring at me, guys. There's a friggin' *ship* stuck to the side of that sand dune."

"I did notice," Drake said. "And the boatful of mercenaries

attached to it. I wonder where Bell is at?"

Jenny motioned briefly toward the top of the sand hill and away to the right. Drake tore his gaze away from the galleon. There, arrayed a short distance from the edge of the drop, were a muddled arrangement of camouflaged tents, covered by wire netting. He fished a pair of binoculars out of his pack.

"Jackpot. I see Bell and Bay-Dale just lounging over there. Deck chair, I think. Bay-Dale has a glass of red."

Smyth flushed with anger. "Figures. Let the commoners do the work and take the risk whilst the management sit back and laugh."

"It could be worse," Karin offered. "In ancient times, in Europe and Egypt, the Kings and Queens would have roped their own people into this undertaking. Literally."

"There's a waiter over there too." Drake rubbed his eyes tiredly, just happy that the endless drudgery of the search was over. "Lauren, you keep saying Bell's a potential ally in the enemy camp. I must admit, I really don't see that."

Lauren exhaled. "After everything I witnessed in that hotel room with General Stone, I'd like a chance to try."

Drake lowered the binoculars. "He's over there hobnobbing with Bay-Dale, whom we know to be less than sea scum. The guy's an ass."

"Maybe they're drawing Bell in. The more time you spend in someone's company the more you accept their failings. I know people, Drake. I read people. If I wasn't good at it I'd be long dead by now."

Drake hesitated. Lauren was correct, of course. Her job—essentially her *old* job—challenged her with that very decision every day. He looked away to the east where the galleon's narrow valley ended and the desert became a flat surface again. The way across was easy—a fifteen minute walk—so he couldn't even dissuade her with that excuse.

"I don't like it," he said.

Lauren glanced at Smyth. "Should I even ask what you think?"

"They're both arrogant pricks. I favor burying them up to their necks in sand and leaving 'em both with their wine glasses balanced on their fucking condescending heads."

Drake laughed. "Now *there's* a plan."

"Bell . . ." Lauren paused, thinking hard, "is a good man at heart. I know he is. I *liked* him, despite what happened in that hotel room. He was nice. I can make him help us."

Now Smyth looked over. "What? You wanna date?"

"Stop being an ass. I want what we—"

Drake's cell vibrating interrupted them. "This isn't good," he said and slithered further back down the slope until he was clear of the ridge. "Yeah?"

A deep voice explained the situation at the electrical substation where all contact with Agent Jaye and the SPEAR team had been lost just ten minutes ago. An assault team had been readied but the man had initially been ordered to inform Drake of any unexpected incidents. Drake listened with features as hard as a rough-cut diamond, then thanked the man and hung up.

He relayed the conversation to the others as they lay on their sides halfway down the dusty slope.

"Even more important now," Lauren said.

"What *was* your other job?" Jenny abruptly wondered.

Drake put his phone away. "Why is it more important, Lauren?"

"We need to know what the Pythians are planning. Now and next week and next month. Where the hell is Webb and what's he doing? The ghost ships are all about money, yes? Well, *why?* They already have a ton of the stuff."

Drake looked bleak. "And that's not even half the problem. Saint Germain, I believe, is paramount. Then we have Beauregard and the Pythians' endgame, which is already afoot." He regarded Lauren with a rueful smile.

"Now you want me to go in?"

"Bloody hell, no. I trust the bastard less than I would trust Alicia with a male stripper at a bachelorette party, but I'm not sure we have a choice."

"I can't imagine Alicia at a bachelorette party," Lauren said. "But the rest is accurate enough. I truly believe I can turn Nicholas Bell."

Smyth sat up. "I'll cover for her. All the way." He patted her shoulder. "As usual."

Drake saw the care and concern in the soldier's face. Lauren was not a woman who easily accepted help—or needed it in fact—but she gave him a grateful smile.

"So what are we waiting for?"

"I can't believe I'm saying this," he said. "But let's go talk to our friendly Pythian."

"He ain't friendly yet," Smyth growled low in his throat like a dog would.

"True. But it's either friendly or dead," Drake said. "We'll see how he wants to play it."

CHAPTER THIRTY TWO

Hayden winced as one of the twenty surviving mercenaries struck Kinimaka across the back of the neck, sending the large Hawaiian to his knees. Whilst he was down there two more mercs strapped his hands behind his back with plastic ties. Dahl was shoved into a corner and similarly secured. The majority of enemy weapons, she noticed, were the MP5SDs, a variant of the venerable MP5 Heckler and Koch MP series. It featured an aluminum suppressor integrated into the muzzle. Hayden refocused when the leader of the ragtag group approached her.

"Your cop friends have arrived outside and are preparing an assault. It won't work. We need about five minutes to get what we came for. You killed six of my men but I'll still let you live if you promise to cause us no more trouble."

Hayden stared and said sarcastically, "Oh, I promise."

"Can't even lie without mockery." The leader kicked out at her. "Must be a fuckin' fed."

"And you can't lie at all," Hayden spat. "No way are you lazy fucks going to let us live."

The leader grunted at her fearless obstinacy and tried again. "First your gun, then your badge. Then we secure you. It's my way or *their* way." He pointed to his men. "And believe me now, my way's easier for you."

Hayden didn't take her eyes off the leader. He was a bearded individual with long sideburns and straggly hair all the way down to his shoulders. He was talking nice to avoid more aggro and save time, of course, not for her benefit, but he did have a point.

Hayden dropped her gun to the floor along with her badge, then got to her knees. A man tied her hands behind her back and shepherded the three together so that they knelt under the long row of windows that looked into the office.

"Get in there," the leader told two of his men. "Secure the transmission lines with the grid links. Then we're done. And check these badges." He kicked the pile over to another minion.

Hayden listened intently, and eyed the badges dubiously. One merc might not recognize the SPEAR logo, nor even the leader, but if he reported it back to the Pythians . . . tied hands would be the least of their problems. *But hey,* she thought, *if it draws Tyler Webb out from his filthy burrow . . .*

Two men started toward the office with laptop bags tucked under their arms. Hayden eyed the leader. "Transmission lines?" she asked. "Grid links?"

He looked surprised. "You don't know? All this, and you're just swimming blindly uphill against the current." He seemed to weigh his next words, then said, "You ever hear of Path 26?"

Hayden shook her head. At that moment another man approached, this one with a ghastly snarl to his bearing and bright red scars up and down his bulging arms. "We should be torturing these fuckers, not shooting the shit with 'em."

The leader shrugged. "You think you can get anything worthwhile out of them, Hunt?"

"Who gives a fuck? Be good to practice on at least."

"They look pretty tough."

Hunt puffed his chest out. "Even better."

"You have five minutes, max."

The leader stalked away, casting an eye toward his dead men. Hayden wondered how a man who showed remorse for dead colleagues might then exhibit such a lack of consideration for captives. This was war, after all, not terrorism. The rules should be different.

But Hunt couldn't keep the spiteful grin from twisting his

face. With a leap he was upon her, forcing her over backwards so that her ankles bent and her tied wrists ground on the floor—both their combined weight pushing them down. The pain made her grimace.

"You're going to die for that." Dahl's voice drifted across, and the tone was unquestionable.

Hunt met the Swede's eyes, then pressed some more. Hayden bit her lip hard to stop from crying out as her bones grated together. Blood ran from the wound. Hunt snarled at the sight. "Don't ya worry, Englisher. I'll be at you next."

"You should have been 'at me' first. Any real man would."

Hunt stared at Hayden's lips, seemingly transfixed at the trickle of blood. "So you'd rather bleed than scream," he noted. "But you will soon do both," he promised. "First I gotta teach this foreigner some manners."

Hayden stared up at him, waiting for an opportunity. As his head lifted she saw it—and smashed her forehead against the bridge of his nose. "You bleed first," she said. Her legs weren't tied, so she twisted hard to wrap her thighs about his neck. Hunt saw her and rotated out of reach.

Several mercs laughed at him. "Run away and hide," one of them muttered. "Hunt's goddamn motto."

Hunt was furious. Jumping up, he stalked back to Hayden's feet, blowing strings of blood from his nose.

"Untie me," Hayden snapped. "Then we'll see how you do."

"Yeah, untie her!" a merc shouted. "See if you can take her down, ya fuckin' psychopath."

The mercs were all becoming unruly as they waited for the others to finish. The leader came back, looking angry, but Hunt pushed him aside.

"Fuck off."

Then he attacked Hayden for all that he was worth. Arms bulging, he punched at the side of her head, rammed another into her gut. Hayden rolled with it, but the punches still hurt.

She caught a third blow on her arm, saw an ounce of leeway, and flung her body backward whilst kicking upward.

The kick smashed Hunt across the cheek, snapping his head sideways and eliciting a cheer from the other mercs. Hayden rolled with the momentum, three hundred and sixty degrees, and then kicked again. This time Hunt was ready, catching her ankle in mid-air. Dahl and Kinimaka moved toward her, but the sudden appearance of handguns stopped them in their tracks. The mercs were okay for a tied woman to fight back, it seemed, but unhappy with her tied male colleagues trying to help her. Hunt jerked Hayden's ankle, dragging her body toward him, then twisted it so that she flipped onto her stomach. Helpless now, she could only stare into Kinimaka's eyes.

Hunt sat heavily on the backs of her knees. The leader told him to hurry up. The seconds were ticking by. Hayden faced the office wall with the wider facility behind her, listening to the jeers of men. Hunt ignored it all and punched into the back of her right thigh.

"Tell me what you know. Tell me about SPEAR. Tell me who you answer to."

The pain was excruciating but if that was the worse Hunt could do in the next minute or two then Hayden could easily take it. Concentrating on Mano and Dahl, she shut the pain away and concentrated on the best of what was to come.

It was a truly surreal moment that caused her more disquiet than Hunt's continual punching. A voice floated out of nowhere. A voice she knew couldn't possibly be here. A voice she would now love forever.

"You'd get a lot more out of her if you tanned that ass real slow, not punched so frantically below it."

Instantly Hunt drew away and Hayden rolled, just in time to see a blond blur, dressed in black, leap from a gantry above to land among the hooting, dissatisfied mercs. Two chops and two were disarmed. An arm around a throat and she had a shield. Her left hand held a compact machine pistol which she fired without mercy or pause into the group to her left. They screamed and pinwheeled, and bled and died. Once her shield was thoroughly ventilated she spun and grabbed another, still shooting. Those mercs who were close found their knees broken, their ankles twisted, and their groins jabbed. Some barely blinked before they hit the floor, gut-shot.

Seconds had passed and Alicia Myles had decimated half the mercenary force.

Hayden shuffled closer, as did Kinimaka and Dahl. The merc leader was roaring orders.

"Protect the package and get her!"

Alicia hurled her second shield straight at two more opponents, shouting "*Strike!*" as might anyone playing human ten-pin bowling. Her pistol took out two more. The leader ran past his dwindling men, wrenched open the office door, and screamed at both laptop carriers.

"Are you done? *Then get the fuck outta there!*"

Spinning, he fired, hitting his own man as Alicia employed a third shield. Then he sent a boot smashing across Dahl's face as the Swede tried to entangle him. The two men carrying laptops charged through. Alicia ignored them, intent only on saving her friends. Four more mercs now faced her.

Only four.

Alicia ran hard at them, propelling her four-limbed shield at breakneck pace. Two of the mercs peeled off and chased their leader, clearly having had enough. Alicia poked her pistol under the arm of her shield and fired, taking one remaining merc down. The other bounded aside, but Alicia dropped the shield and dived right into him, striking him hard on the breastbone with her shoulder. As they landed she punched and thrust and dug hard. The man was unconscious before he could even move.

She whirled to face Hunt, who had just watched the decimation.

"I know, I know," she said. "You wanna date me. You wanna love me. Kiss me all over. Let's both check our diaries first, huh?"

Faster than a turbocharged viper she struck with stiffened fingers. Blows to the sternum, cheekbone and pit of the stomach brought an even more abhorrent smile to Hunt's face. He moved in whilst grunting in pain, landing a blow on Alicia's ribcage. A knife then appeared in his left hand. Alicia, visibly tired after taking out so many men, backed off.

"So now you respect me?" Hunt sneered. "Wait till I jab you with this."

"Dude, that's not even six inches. Don't make me laugh."

Hunt looked enraged and then lunged, Alicia's words having had their effect on his pumped-up machismo. It was an easy task to sidestep and then break Hunt's wrist. The blade rattled to the floor.

"What the—"

Alicia incapacitated him with a crunching kick to the knee. The sound of the bone breaking made even Hayden wince and the man's scream brought both laptop men to a halt.

"Keep going!" the leader wailed. "Out!"

Alicia made sure Hunt was relieved of all weapons before bouncing over to Hayden. With a sassy smile she eyed the American's bonds. "Ah, a dream come true."

"Stop showboating and cut me the hell free."

"Bitch, at least give me a kiss. I just saved your ass."

Alicia drew a superfluous knife and quickly sawed through all three of her comrades' bonds. After much credit was accrued to the blonde, Dahl ventured the question all of them were dying to ask.

"How on earth did you get here?"

"Drake called and suggested I use your GPS. Whilst en

route I caught up on events, and then heard about the third and last facility being hit and your dilemma seemed to be worse than his. Once I arrived I saw the standard assault team being formed outside and decided to handle it myself."

"Guys," Kinimaka cut in and gestured to the rear exit door. "Shall we?"

"They're long gone," Hayden said. "Beat us here. Arranged the exit before we even showed up, I'll warrant. But be my guest."

The team jogged to the door, wary of booby traps, and opened it. Outside, dark was falling and nothing stirred, not even the branches or leaves on the stunted trees.

"Y'see?" Hayden drawled. "Long gone. Question is—what the hell comes next? And I mean *hell* in a literal sense."

"They have everything they need," Dahl said quietly. "To do as they promised and take America back to the dark ages."

"The leader spoke about Path 26," Kinimaka remembered.

"Their plan was laid long ago," Dahl went on. "So . . . if they have everything they need, what are they waiting for?"

Alicia squinted through the descending dark. "Actually, I do see something beyond the fence there. A . . . a van? See the shape? It's—"

And then it happened. Something terrible, something ruinous. The low hum that accompanied all the equipment around them and the facility itself suddenly died away. Lights flickered. Hayden was in a position to see downhill to where the lights of a distant town glowed softly.

And then the night went totally pitch black.

"Oh no," Hayden whispered. "They've done it."

"Blackout." Dahl's voice was intensely soft. "Those mad tyrannical bastards."

"They've taken out California," Hayden guessed as she began to receive and flick through her cellphone's messages. "As a statement. Remember? To prove to the government what they could do. At the expense of all those people. The risk of all those lives."

"Riots," Kinimaka said. "Robberies. Murder. Kidnapping. The list is terrifying."

Hayden knew only the innocent would truly suffer. She tapped at her Android, seeking any new leaked information and quieter sources of her own as Alicia brought Dahl's attention back full circle to the van.

"Shall we?"

"Do you think they're in that van?"

"I think there's a very good chance, my fine Swedish hunk of manliness. The only question is—do you wanna crush them as much as I do? Do you wanna teach them that it is really, really wrong to mess with good people's lives?"

"Too bloody right I do."

Hayden squinted at the far-off shadow, noting where it was parked in deepest darkness. How it almost seemed planned. "All right. There's a good chance they're working out of there, but be careful. The Pythians won't be silly enough to leave that truck without a heavy guard even if the mercs are. I'll coordinate our forces from here, call Drake, and get an update for California and its surrounds. Contact me before you act, okay?"

Alicia clasped her hands behind her back and pouted. "Okay, Mommmmy."

"Shit, just go." Hayden waved them away and then regarded the absolute darkness that had almost certainly befallen the state.

Kinimaka, always at her side, spoke the words. "God help the people."

Hayden could only imagine the terror as homes were plunged into total night all over Los Angeles and San Diego; mothers rushing upstairs to their crying babies; fathers digging out flashlights and candles and double-checking all the locks. The drapes and blinds twitched aside as people assessed the neighborhood, the folks next door, and prayed. Those who reached automatically to check their TVs and then found out the truth on the Internet. But would they? What misinformation would the government feed the masses, if any?

Then there would be cars and buses driving down cavern-dark streets, lingering overlong at inoperative stop lights, caught in fender-benders not of their own making. The disruption, the chaos; it would live in memories forever. She thought of the cops fielding hysterical call after call, the bedlam they would be forced to attend. Madness would affect even those who normally kept a low profile, and they would pay for their mistakes for years to come. Darkness was a chilling race memory, the intimidating equalizer, the haunt of all that is evil. A candle could not save you. The good people were even now sat in their mortgaged homes, willing the light to return, keeping their children calm and putting their trust in the authorities.

Indirectly, in Hayden. In Drake and Alicia and Torsten Dahl.

And, for the people *they* cared about, they would deliver at any cost.

CHAPTER THIRTY THREE

Alicia embraced the darkness like a close friend, inviting it inside as well as all around her. Her life had led up to this. The recent quest where she and her second team discovered hidden Crusader's gold had led to this. The time was at hand.

No more running. No more avoiding.

Life would always pursue her and now that it had caught up she was ready to accept the explosion. Who would suffer? Only those closest to her, who would say that it was a long time coming and would take everything that she gave.

So . . . soon. Today. Tomorrow. When events dictated.

God help whoever got caught inside her blast zone. And she meant that, truly, in a religious way.

For now though, it was Dahl who had her back, and there was only one other whom she would prefer. The Swede crept beside her like a capable hound, eyes spotting traces even she might miss. The ground underfoot was gravel-strewn, and not even they could stop the occasional crunch. At the perimeter of the property, however, soil and earth returned. Dahl fell to his knees.

"Thirty meters," he said. "Ready?"

Alicia didn't need to check. "Do you recall a time when I wasn't? For anything?"

Dahl crawled off. Alicia dropped behind him. They crept under an overhanging tree, stroked by the long branches, pausing in the deepest shadow near its trunk. Dahl then scooted to the bottom of a shallow ditch and crabbed along its bottom. As they neared the truck they paused to listen.

Alicia heard the faintest scuffling sound and then footfalls coming from the back of the truck. Somebody was definitely moving around inside there. Dahl waited patiently, scanning the almost impenetrable surroundings.

Can't see fuck all, he mouthed back at her eventually.

She strained to read his lips, then shrugged and indicated the tomb of darkness all around. *Neither can California.*

Dahl nodded. Decision made, they moved rapidly. Dahl ran up to the rear of the truck and flattened his back against one of the doors. Alicia reached for the handle. A booming sound erupted and for half a second Alicia thought a bomb might have gone off, but then enormous round lights fixed to the back and sides of the truck's roof illuminated, bathing the whole area in brightness.

"Now that's a major clusterfuck," a voice said—the mercenary leader's. "You really think we wouldn't have backup?"

Alicia stared away from the blinding truck, into the overhanging forest at its side and the thick brush at its back. Groups of men were emerging, all carrying rifles and machine pistols, and with faces painted black, wearing bulletproof vests and combat boots and backpacks full of spare ammo. The leader's next comment gave her a flash of hope though.

"Kill them quiet. Lights have been illuminated all around the substation so the cops won't figure this out too quick, but the sound of gunfire might help them."

Alicia reached for her gun, but the mercs charged in a tight cluster. Knives appeared in their hands, wide military knives with serrated edges. *Just one shot . . .*

But they were too close. Dahl readied his hands and diverted two knife thrusts simultaneously. Alicia turned one lunge against another, making one man stab his partner through the wrist. Their entanglement stalled those coming behind.

Dahl barged another attacker to one side and then grabbed

one of the truck's vertical rear bars, heaving himself up and above the heads of the mercs. First, he kicked out, dropping another man. As more congregated though he launched himself with a great yell, slamming down on top of them. Bodies tumbled and sprawled. Legs and arms jerked and broke. Dahl twisted instantly upon landing, allowing no easy target, but causing maximum chaos.

Alicia parried and dodged, her vision a blur of knives and fists. The entire scene reflected in her eyes with a vivid intensity. It grew clear in her mind that this was everything the Pythians had been driving for—thwart this attack and their plan was in tatters. And maybe the entire organization along with it.

The downside was they were but a few soldiers, the very same problem that had been frustrating the team all along. The upside was that they were two of the best soldiers in the world.

Alicia caused chaos with every blink of an eye, every slight move. Legs and arms, even the bump of her hips, sent an unwary mercenary off balance. She plucked blade after blade from her opponents' hands, depositing them in the next attacker. Fingers were broken and wrists fractured. She slipped past the side of the truck, then realized there was empty space at her back.

Bad move.

Dahl smashed heads left and right. Like Alicia he too wore a stab vest. Without it he would have been brought down four times already. The mercs were becoming more and more desperate as they saw the caliber of their adversaries. They stumbled, they dropped weapons, and Dahl maneuvered his way over to Alicia.

"Get behind me."

Another wave of mercs struck. Alicia approved of Dahl's quick thinking and positioned herself so that they stood back to back with the truck at one side. Again the wave broke over them, flooding past, bleeding and gashed and dying, yet leaving nothing but bruises on the rocks that it hit. For a moment Alicia saw nothing but snarling faces and shaven skulls; not the sky, not the mountains, not the enormous facility all around them. Life was made up of sweat and screaming and blood, and she felt that it always had been. A knife thrust against her vest, bouncing to the side even as the bruise it formed screamed at her. A punch connected solidly with her forehead, shaking her brain, but she did not flinch. Fingernails scraped at her cheek. A knee rose into her abdomen. Her response was elbows and knees, boots, fists and forehead all flashing back and forth faster than a Ferrari paddle-shifted, faster than anything these mercenaries had ever seen. As more fell the rest found it harder to get close. Alicia saw an opportunity to draw her gun.

She slipped it free. A merc dived on it, desperate to keep the noise down. She relinquished her grip rather than pull free of Dahl. And so the two gladiators stood, back to back, jabbing and punching left and right, fencing with knives, as bloody as any two warriors who ever lived. When Alicia stumbled, Dahl sensed it as it happened and caught her under the arm. When the Swede took a mighty blow and staggered, Alicia performed a vicious, spinning elbow, devastating his opponent and barely taking her eyes off her own. Terrified yells could already be heard from inside the van. Alicia pressed hard against Dahl's spine and stood her ground. Both used the van's side to crack heads with. The intensity of the battle was so strong Alicia couldn't even find a second to pose a wisecrack. Her arms were on fire, her muscles screaming. Even her reserves were beginning to dwindle.

Dahl breathed hard at her back. With a destructive effort he smashed three men against each other, cracking skulls, and stomped another. It was the last merc and a warning shout went up. Immediately, the back doors of the van swung open, but both Dahl and Alicia knew what to expect. Without pause they rolled and drew weapons, firing the instant they caught sight of a body. Their bullets struck legs. A man fell out face-first, his machine pistol hitting the grass at his side. A second went the same way, squirming as he dropped hard. Dahl rolled underneath the swinging doors, gun up, trigger finger at three-quarter pull weight.

Alicia shot at the last few mercs, winging them, and ran over to disarm them. Dahl watched the back of the truck. Lights blazed from inside but he was at too low an angle to get any kind of reasonable view.

Several hundred yards away, both Hayden and Kinimaka were sprinting to join the fight. Alicia made a huge deal of checking her watch.

Hayden held up a hand, forestalling the comment. "Did you guys do all *this?*"

Alicia blinked and surveyed the scene. Bodies writhed and struggled everywhere, some in piles, others squirming away. She shrugged, the small movement causing a lance of pain.

"Seemed like the right thing to do."

Kinimaka joined Dahl, indicating that the Swede should rise to his feet. "Get a look at that, bro."

The rear of the truck was set out like a computer station. Each side held two terminals, desks and chairs. Three scruffily dressed men and one woman sat inside, mouths open, hands in the air.

"Please," one of them mouthed.

Hayden took control. She jumped into the back of the truck, Glock very much in evidence. "Show me the fucking Z-box *now!* Do it as if your lives depended on it."

A gangly older man moved away from his console, revealing the small black box that had been positioned next to his elbow. Alicia had jumped in after Hayden and recognized the

Chinese-manufactured device.

"Gives the words 'Made in China' a whole new meaning," she muttered.

Hayden aimed the barrel of the gun at the man's throat. "If I destroy that box will the blackout end?"

"It . . . it's the master code box, the hub of the blackout program we designed, so yes . . . yes it should."

Hayden fired a shot into the truck's bulkhead. "Should?"

"Will! It will, it will!"

The next bullet wrecked the little box. Hayden looked over her shoulder at Dahl, who remained outside.

"Nothing happening," he said. "Maybe something needs to reboot."

"Call it in," Hayden said. "We have rows of geeks sitting around waiting to take care of this."

Alicia picked up the Z-box, placed it on the floor and crushed it beneath her boot heel. "Just to be sure," she said with a wink and a grin. In truth, her body was crying for a break and to start healing but she knew any respite would only stiffen up her joints. There would be time to mend later.

Hayden jammed her Glock under the tall man's throat. "Tell me all about Path 26," she said. "And how it caused this blackout."

Terrified eyes blinked rapidly. "Yes, yeah. Well . . . Path 26 is a set of three power lines that form the main link for Southern California's electrical power grid. There are other hubs at San Jose and Silicon Valley. To get into the Path you need access to all three hubs, and you can't remote it. It has to be done on site. That's why we needed the three backdoors."

As the geek explained his work he began to relax, warm up even. "Path 26 can transmit 3700MW to Southern California which only needs 3000 at full capacity. Accessing Path 26 was the key to causing the blackout—turning off the power. It gave us access to the whole system. The Z-box made it all easier, cracking that system's codes within seconds and allowing us free reign. That . . ." he started to stammer again, realizing he was out of words. "That's it."

Hayden didn't take her eyes off the geek. "Dahl?"

"They're working on it. Looks good, though."

"Stand up and put your hands behind your backs. All of you. Alicia, tie these men up."

"Ah, words I love to hear."

Hayden faced the woman. "You. Stay handy. We might need you." In another second she turned toward Kinimaka.

"And Mano?"

"Uh huh?"

"Give Drake a call. Tell him we're on our way. The gang's getting back together."

"Fucking A."

CHAPTER THIRTY FOUR

Lauren Fox felt rather like a fish out of water. The deserts of Arizona and California were a far cry from the penthouses and luxury suites of thousand-dollar-an-hour clients. This new job—hazardous though it may be—was sure granting her some crazy opportunities. *A breath of fresh air?* Well, maybe, but the danger involved made it an unlikely outlook as well as being intoxicating. Go figure.

Now, as the team led her in the direction of the Pythian camp, she again turned her mind to infiltrating it on her own little lonesome. Back into the jaws of extreme jeopardy. Yes, Smyth would shadow her as far as he was able, but not even the super soldier could save her if Nicholas Bell proved to be a devil. Add to that the presence of Clifford Bay-Dale—the other Pythian present on this escapade—and the odds weren't really stacked in her favor. But then she was a New York girl, through and through. She was used to bad odds.

Now, as darkness started to creep across her peripheral vision, the team halted and Drake confronted her once more.

This time, his words were silent, unnecessary. *You don't have to do this, love.* She added the "love" part because she figured he'd be ramping up the Yorkshire accent a little bit.

Her gaze never wavered, her eyes pure steel. She even laid a hand on Smyth's shoulder. "We'll make this work."

Drake studied the sky. "Ten more minutes. We're gonna position so we're minutes away. If you're in there for more than ten—we're coming in to get you, like it or not."

It sounded good to her.

"And I'll be listening in," Smyth said.

She knew all this. She was ready. With a last glance toward Karin and Jenny she straightened out her clothes as best she could, ran a finger-comb through her hair and took a deep breath.

Time to earn your keep.

Lauren followed Smyth's lead, creeping around the dunes toward the camp and staying low. They stuck to the lees and valleys, courting every shadow. No words were needed. Smyth crouched until a disinterested guard walked past, giving him time to reach the top corner of the camp. With a wave he urged Lauren along, boots crunching a little as they struck sand raised along the bottom edge of a large tent. Now he knelt, listening.

Lauren already had a hand on her small pistol, but nothing happened. The sky above had turned black, the clouds scudding across the moon. A moaning breeze put her in mind of an old loyal john she used to service maybe once a week—the young guy moaned like a banshee throughout the entire hour-long session, making her seriously consider the implementation of noise-suppressant earphones. Smyth caught her attention, pointing to the third tent along—Bell's tent—and she nodded.

Softly, they slipped around the canvas side, pausing once more before reaching Bell's tent. Lauren tried to penetrate the shadows behind her where Drake and the others were waiting, but saw only a thick slab of darkness. It made her feel isolated.

Smyth indicated this was as far as he could go. Lauren nodded and crept to the front of the tent. There was a small gap between the front flaps. She steadied her heart and peeked inside.

Nicholas Bell hadn't changed a bit. He sat at a makeshift desk, writing in a notepad, head down. He wore a dirty T-shirt, brown jacket and cargo shorts. Boots were unlaced but covering his feet. Within reach of his right hand was a small tumbler filled with a golden liquid and an oversized cellphone.

Lauren gave Smyth a final thumbs-up and slipped inside. It was now or never, and she didn't like to show a moment's weakness. As she moved inside the tent Bell looked up, the expression on his face changing from questioning to shock and then to outright fear. Lauren moved closer.

Bell stammered. "Wha . . . what are you . . . shit."

Lauren put a finger to her lips. "Shhhh."

"Are you here to . . . kill me?"

"No, you dope. I'm here to help you."

Now Bell looked utterly confused, shaking his head slowly. "What? How?" His hand inched closer his cellphone.

"My friends want to kill you," Lauren whispered, moving over to the table and within grabbing distance of the cellphone if required. "I told them you were a good man. I told them you're trapped inside an organization where you don't really want to be. Was I wrong?"

Bell stared for a moment, brain working. "Go," he said then. "Just get out while you can."

Lauren liked that comment. "You see? You are good. Any other Pythian would be shouting for the guards right now but you just want to help me escape."

"I don't know who or what you are. A hooker? A government agent? Is your name actually really your name?"

"Well, it's not Nightshade if that's what you're asking."

"You certainly wield a whip well." Bell smiled in fond recognition.

"Okaaaay. Well, there's *something* on the table, Nicholas, but it's not my body this time. It's an offer. Are you listening?"

"You're in incredible danger," Bell hissed. "Go. Just go."

"Do you want out?"

"It's *complicated*. The things I have been a party to . . ." Bell drank deeply of the amber liquid. "I never imagined. But once you're in—"

"Like I said. There's now a way out. Total immunity."

"Is that a joke?"

"No, it's a promise. But you have to tell us everything. If your information helps takes Webb and the rest of the Pythians down you get your deal."

Bell drained the last of the liquid, then reached under the desk. Lauren couldn't stop a flinch when he moved; her left hand questing for the hidden weapon. Bell frowned, but came up with a bottle of Jack Daniels Firewater.

"And if I say no?" he said, pouring the drink and watching her face. "Do you shoot me?"

Shit! Why are men always so fucking dumb?

"I'm offering you a deal," she said. "If your answer is 'no', then I walk away. But it won't ever come around again, Nicholas, I can promise you that. I mean, shit, it's surely a no-brainer, ain't it?"

Bell closed the notebook he had been writing in and sat back. "Tyler Webb is more than a megalomaniac. He's unhinged. No way in hell do I want to show up on his radar, and even I dread to think what might happen if he's successful at Ramses' last bazaar."

"Okay. We'll talk about that later. First—we have to get you out of here."

Bell exhaled fast and hard, then finally managed a small smile. "If I say yes do I get to date you?"

Lauren winced as she heard a growling cough from outside the tent. That would be Smyth, already prepping his weapon. "Let's talk about that later," she said, oddly flattered. Despite his mistakes, Bell was at heart a nice man. His only problem was the lack of courage to do the right thing.

"You coming?"

"They will shoot you. Shoot me. Perhaps it's best staying put."

"Never good advice," Lauren said. "You should move with life and life never stops."

"But, the consequences of leaving . . ."

Lauren watched him drain the tumbler again and knew she was in trouble.

Smyth bounced quietly on the balls of his feet, ear to the canvas, listening to Lauren's coaxing and Bell's whining. Smyth had known some pussies in his time—some of them in the military—but Bell was starting to rank with the weakest of them. Shit, if Lauren Fox walked toward him *anytime* he'd follow her into hell itself and without a fucking excuse.

Four minutes passed and then the guard came past, staring mostly at the ground in front of his size-ten clown feet. Smyth could have taken him with a noisy suppressor, a knife or even a rock, but the mission was all about stealth. Realistically, they should escape without leaving a single mark of their presence, and that was something he had been well-trained to do.

As Lauren continued to persuade her mark, Smyth became aware of another presence stalking toward the front of the tent. He recognized Clifford Bay-Dale, the jumped-up, arrogant Pythian, the energy boss.

Fuckboy!

Smyth crept low, a slinking shadow. He saw Bay-Dale pause and then lean forward as if listening. Yes, the reptile had heard Bell and Lauren talking and was now eavesdropping on their conversation. There was no doubt in Smyth's mind what Bay-Dale would do with the new information.

He slid as close as he dared, right to the front edge of the tent's side, then rose silently. Bay-Dale was three feet away. Smyth prayed that the guard's rounds wouldn't send him past now and ruin everything. He could hear Lauren's voice enticing Bell over to the noble side, but the effort was taking valuable time. Bay-Dale grunted as he listened, the sound outraged and disgusted. Destiny and fate suddenly hung in the balance.

It all hung on Smyth's next decision. Wait too long and Bay-Dale could sink them all. Let the energy boss inside the tent and his inevitable demise might then put Bell off. Trying to turn him was out of the question. In the end, there was only one course of action.

Smyth pounced like a desert phantom, as black as night and deadly as original sin. Bay-Dale cringed on sensing the shadow, perhaps already weirded out by the desert and its ghost stories of ships, bottomless sand pits and enormous worms. His mouth froze in a rictus. By then, Smyth was on him, cupping his mouth and throat, and dragging him deeper into shadow, a lethal spider hauling its victim back to its den. Bay-Dale started to struggle. Smyth couldn't let go of his mouth or vocal chords. His hands were fully occupied. Bay-Dale kicked, feet striking the side of the tent and sending up a flurry of sand. Smyth bore down.

"Naaagh."

It was all Bay-Dale could manage and it was at a very low pitch. It wasn't enough. Smyth held on and played the only move he had—he pushed Bay-Dale's face into the sand; nose, mouth, cheeks and all. Grimacing himself, he strained hard, feeling no sympathy for the immoral, murderous Pythian but experiencing some distress for the plight of his fellow man. Being smothered by sand couldn't be an easy death. Nonetheless, Smyth knew his mission and leaned on Bay-Dale's head until all movement stopped. Then, he rolled the lifeless body into deeper shadow.

Where the hell is Lauren?

Time flew inside the tent and Bells' little standoff was proving costly. Lauren had heard a small struggle and could only guess what was going on outside, mere feet away. Bell was now swigging from the bottle.

"I can't . . . can't go with you. Too . . . too dangerous."

"Fuck me!" Lauren finally exploded. "I thought you were a

harassed, bullied *good* man, not a whimpering bitch. Get out of that chair and stop drinking reality away. Take a look at what's right in front of you!"

Bell focused, abruptly and scarily sober. Lauren's words had struck the right chord in him. "You're saying . . ."

"I'm saying let's go and live for tonight. We can work everything out later." She extended a hand. "Come on, Nicholas."

The wealthy builder rose, bottle in hand. "I sure hope that I can help you."

"Put the whisky down. I like my men sober, fully functioning and not at all premature."

The bottle bumped to the sandy ground.

"Yes, Miss."

Lauren almost laughed. If she'd known it would be that easy she'd have adopted the Nightshade persona straight away. Smyth popped his head into the tent, ruining the ambience of the moment.

"We ready?"

Bell flinched. "Who is that?"

"My bodyguard." Lauren enfolded Bell's hand in her own. "Follow me, tiger."

Smyth couldn't stop blinking. "Bodyguard?" He sounded hurt. "Tiger? What the hell have you two been doing in here?"

"Nothing beyond what I was asked to do," Lauren said. "And Nicholas is now on our side."

"We'll see about that." Smyth pulled them put of the tent and into the shadows. "Stay close, both of you. The Pythians will know we're here very soon."

"What? Why?"

"Tell you later. But we need to know more about that friggin' ship first. And then the rest. Got it?"

Bell nodded. "Sure."

"Then let's go before all hell breaks loose. 'Cause it's gonna."

CHAPTER THIRTY FIVE

Drake watched proceedings aboard the galleon with fascination, actually impressed with how someone had molded the motley mercenary force into a relatively competent work crew. His other thought—not so impressive—was of the sheer number that made up the mercenary army. It had been hard to make out in the gloom last night but the tent-filled camp stretched way back from the ridge and well into the desert. He counted hundreds. Dawn had risen an hour ago and, so far, nobody had discovered Bay-Dale's body or noticed that Bell was missing. Business as usual then, over at the ghost ship. Now that he had a better chance to study it, Drake drank in the entire spectacle—the wonder of the ship in the sand, the rarity of such a find, the convergence of so many random events that must have transpired to send a galleon this far inland.

As the broad side jutted out so did part of the stern. Drake studied two tiers of shattered windows, the ruined remains of a balcony, and what appeared to be prancing lions near the top. The side that faced him bristled with cannon or at least damaged portholes that once held cannon.

"Here be demons," said a voice at his side. Yorgi.

"Aye, maybe, lad. Maybe. But the demons are all living and ransacking that bloody ship. Hundreds of 'em."

"Are they inside now?"

Drake studied what had been revealed of the deck. "Not far off."

Karin joined them, having crabbed her way along the sand dune. "You see the front? The ship's name is visible. We were right. This is Cavendish's *Content*. The ship, loaded with stolen treasure, then a pirate galleon that was never seen again."

Drake whistled softly. "Hard to imagine."

"A forty-ton gold ship, blown off course, drifting around the desert for years, scaring the locals and then found by the Pythians. What's wrong with that?"

"Well, since you put it that way."

"Don't kid yourself. The US government established a military base not far from here. You think they didn't perform GPR scans first? You think they didn't know about this ship and probably more? These governments know much more than they will ever tell or care to spend money locating, because they have most of it tied up elsewhere."

"Back pockets? Election victories? Presidential campaigns? Smart motorways touted to ease congestion that suddenly sprout more cameras and recognition programs than a Hollywood whorehouse?"

Karin nodded. "That's about it."

Drake turned away from the ship and lay on his back, staring down their dune to the very bottom where Smyth, Lauren and Bell waited and talked. He hoped Bell was giving them something juicy to work with because he doubted even the whole SPEAR team could cope with this size of enemy force.

"Activity's certainly ramping up today," he said.

"And that's why," Yorgi said. "Men just broke through deck of ship. It is not a good day, friends. We are but a few against . . ." He tailed off, daunted.

"We need a plan," Drake said. "To stop or stall them."

"Quickly," Karin said. "And then I can get to Fort Bragg."

"If you still want to go."

"It's all I want, Matt."

Drake watched clouds drift through blue skies. "I'll call Hayden. See how long they're going to be."

He made the call and connected within seconds. Hayden

had been about to call. She and the rest of the SPEAR team were only hours away. Attack choppers loaded with soldiers had left minutes before them, tasked with helping SPEAR take down the huge mercenary force and end the Pythian presence. Robert Price again had shown his worth, at least Drake assumed the order had come from his office. Drake told her that two more Pythians were now out of the picture and that one of them might even prove the undoing of Webb himself. That thread, that terrible, evil thread, was about to be snipped in half, or *circumcised,* as Alicia so delicately phrased it.

"The Pythians' shelf life is up," Drake said. "But will they go out with a whimper or a bang? I'm fearing the latter."

Hayden mentioned that a desert storm was coming. A weather center said that it was due to hit quickly and with deadly force, one of the biggest the region had ever seen. This was how ghost ships disappeared, Hayden guessed.

"Hey ho," Drake said. "Nobody ever expected this to be as easy as finding a fish and chip shop in Sheffield."

"Hey ho?" A sarcastic voice came through the speakerphone. "Who's that? What have you done to Drakey?"

"Crap," Drake moaned. "Alicia's back. This battle just got way more dangerous."

"Yeah," Dahl drawled. "We've been looking out for her for about a day now."

"Piss off, Torsty. And I just *know* ya missed me."

Drake found his thoughts wandering to Mai. "Don't be long," he said.

"Eh?" Alicia sounded surprised.

"Just hurry." Drake turned it into a command. "The mercs have broken into the bloody pirate galleon and we're badly outnumbered."

Hayden came back on the line. "We're coming in hot. Hold on, guys, those mercs will be occupied by the fight of their lives before that storm hits and we'll be home in time for Mano's barbecue ribs."

Drake tried to laugh in agreement but somehow didn't quite share her optimism. Now that he studied them the vast skies were already tinged with red. The desert broiled beneath them. A storm of storms was coming. *And here we are again, stuck right in the middle.*

He took another glance over the sand dune. The ghost ship loomed before him, as creepy and chilling and eternal as any nightmare vision. Suddenly all the stories made sense.

Many would die here today and this would be the last thing they would ever see.

CHAPTER THIRTY SIX

The next few hours passed slowly and excruciatingly. If anyone aboard the galleon noticed that their Pythian bosses were missing they gave no sign. Perhaps their leader took his orders from Webb himself. From what Bell told them the excavation job was relatively straightforward, just hazardous. They didn't need much in the way of supervision.

Drake, then Yorgi and then Smyth watched as mercs disappeared into the ship's innards, warily at first. For a long time nobody came out. Bell seemed genuinely interested at this point, begging Drake to let him know what happened next.

"Of course, this was your idea," Drake recalled.

"Yes, away from all civilian life and casualty free," Bell pointed out.

The Yorkshireman left him with Lauren, telling everything he knew. As he re-climbed the tall sand dune, heading back to where he had left Yorgi, Karin and Jenny, he realized for the first time that the hairs all along his arm were standing up. The air possessed a close sense of electricity, as if it were being charged by an incomprehensible current.

The storm was gathering.

And judging by the way it was marshaling its forces it would take no prisoners. Drake crawled up to the others.

"These next few hours, guys. They ain't gonna exactly be peaches and cream. Stay safe."

Yorgi merely pointed at the force assembling along the opposite ridge, above the ship. "Duh," he said, then: "Is that right? Duh?"

Jenny nodded. "You got it, dude. And he deserved it."

Drake wondered how Jenny and Alicia might relate to one another. *I bet they'd gel extremely quickly.*

Karin watched the skies. "You can feel it in the air."

"Storm. Rage. Battle," Drake said. "Alicia's coming."

"That's how I feel inside," Karin said.

"Keep your heads down," Drake reiterated. "Battle is not your area of expertise. Not yet, at least."

Then Karin pointed. "It's beginning."

From out of the east, far away, rose a red-tinged cloud, seemingly miles high and with a roiling curl along its top edge. A surfer's wave, but higher and deadlier than any that had ever stalked even the wildest seas. Blasting through that oncoming storm sped dozens of black shapes, their rotors spinning hard, fighting to stay together. As they blasted closer they filled the skies and the shouts went up from the army of mercenaries.

"Heads up!"

"We got company!"

"Time to earn your bread, boys!"

Drake gathered his crew, standing atop the dune now that it didn't matter. The gap to the top of the ridge beneath which the half-buried ship lay was only ten meters, but that was no longer an issue. Drake especially kept an eye on the hole into which several mercenaries had disappeared into the galleon's guts. Still no one had reappeared.

He turned. "Bell, are you with us? Totally with us?"

"Yes. What do you want me to do?"

"Nothing. Stay here and stay alive. Lauren, Jenny and Karin will stay with you. This is soldier's work. Yorgi, we might be able to use your skills over there. Especially inside that vessel."

"That is good. I am ready."

Drake prepared. A smile lit his face as a chopper hovered overhead, then settled near the base of the dune. "Good timing."

The rest of the SPEAR team jumped out, stretching his grin even further. Reunited at last. Hayden, Kinimaka and Dahl, all grim-faced and prepared for action. But a crinkle had formed at the edges of their eyes—they were just as happy to see him. Kinimaka waved even as he stumbled through piled sand.

Then that other force of nature appeared—Alicia Myles. Blond hair unfettered for now, and looking decidedly tanned and fit, the personal mega-storm that roiled above her own head was in clear evidence, at least to Drake. He knew her better than anyone on the planet and feared for what was soon to come.

"Drakester," she cried. "How's that little fucker hanging?"

Drake nodded once, including them all in the greeting. By his calculations the attack choppers were no more than five minutes away. "It's about to get real noisy here, guys."

"In more ways than one," Hayden told him. "Storm's a beauty. Miles wide and as strong as a Titan. We should take cover."

Alicia gave a strangled gulp. "You mean under the dead bodies of mercenaries, of course?"

"Oh, of course. I thought that was obvious."

Drake introduced Jenny and then Nicholas Bell. The reactions were pretty much as expected, especially between Alicia and Jenny who weighed each other with a calculating eye. Bell found himself studying sand patterns on the floor, unwilling to lift his eyes. Dahl strode to the top of the dune.

"Plans?"

Drake shrugged. "Take the bloody ship. What else?"

"Good to see we're still on the same wavelength."

"Shit, I hope not."

Dahl shielded his eyes. "A lot of mercs between us and that ship."

"Gone soft over the last few days?"

Dahl looked like he was considering a recent battle. "Not exactly."

"Good. 'Cause I've seen things out here would turn your

hair a funny color, if it wasn't already."

Dahl mock laughed. "Sand worms the size of sewer tunnels?"

At that moment Alicia joined them. "Sand worms? Don't like the sound of those any more than sand spiders. Unless they have a young Kevin Bacon attached to them. Then I could deal."

Dahl seemed perplexed. "Kevin . . . who? I don't—"

"It doesn't matter," Drake said. "It's an old movie, but a good one." He noted the attack choppers massing as they came within firing distance. "Shall we?"

"Has anyone told them to watch out for that friggin' ship?" Smyth barked.

"Of course," Kinimaka said. "We just hope they listened."

"Yeah, since we're gonna be *on* it in about ten minutes."

"That long?" Jenny Rathe spoke up from behind them. "I thought you guys were supposed to be as good as me?"

To a person, every soldier turned and eyed the redhead narrowly. "That's some claim, Miss," Kinimaka said.

Alicia wasn't so gracious. "Another redhead who's all mouth. You wanna prove that claim, lover?"

Jenny rose at Alicia's words, all heckles. "Whenever you want, blondie. An' I got better taste than the likes of you."

"Really? You don't even know me."

"I know your sort."

Alicia took a step in Jenny's direction. "My *sort?* What the fu—"

Drake decided to step in. They could barely hear over the sounds of the chopper's engines and the downdraught was starting to whip up tornadoes of sand. "Stop," he said, putting both hands on Alicia's shoulders and locking in her gaze. "Please, stop."

"A line was crossed."

"Come on, the same line you cross every day. We have work to do."

Alicia locked her jaw. "Bitch is gonna regret her words when I get back." She turned away from the group. "So let's go."

Drake waved Jenny back down the slope and fell in alongside Alicia. "I'm here," he said softly. "Use me."

Alicia didn't move. "I know and I will. Let's get through this first."

The storm loomed in the skies now, dark and shot through with reds and golds, sand spiraling inside and all around it. A brisk wind brought it straight at them and the sun's bright orb would soon be blocked out. Alicia stared right into the heart of it.

"It's time," she said.

"Then let's end this for good."

All at once, the SPEAR team charged, the choppers swooped forward, weapons noisily opening fire, and the Pythians' army of mercenaries produced countless submachine guns, rocket launchers and at least one vehicle-mounted Gatling gun.

A man-made inferno and Mother Nature's hell rained down across the desert.

CHAPTER THIRTY SEVEN

Drake raced around the edge of the valley, sand trickling away from his boot heels, the wind whipping at his clothes. To all sides ran his comrades, his team, each a hero in their own right, and prepared again to lay it all down for the sake of peace and wellbeing.

Behind them a bank of helicopter gunships rose like a swarm of insects, Sikorsky Blackhawks all, cannons, rocket pods, anti-tank missiles and short-range air-to-air missiles, locked on targets. The rim around which Drake ran was short but still the major battle engaged before he got even halfway. The mercs fired first, RPGs shooting off like wayward fireworks and leaving trails of smoke in the air. The choppers deployed evasion tactics, ducking and diving this way and that. Several opened fire, the thick *clunk clunk* of their guns assaulting the air. Sand chopped up like mini-tornadoes wherever the shells struck; men twisted and fell, some firing off RPGs as they collapsed which flew like misbehaving rockets at the ever-lowering skies.

Drake completed the circuit at last, Alicia on his heels. Gun raised, he approached the dune above the galleon. Faces turned toward him. Cries went up.

"At your backs!"

Drake zig-zagged. Alicia ran headlong into a merc, taking him to the ground. Dahl and Kinimaka replicated her, barging opponents aside. Smyth dropped to one knee and picked off all who drew beads on his friends. Hayden swept around the sides, Glock in hand, surveying the terrain and the enemy's formations.

Beyond the ledge the choppers flew and fired hard, loosing as much firepower as possible before the storm came in and forced them to the ground. Drake guessed they were clearing an area on this side of the valley to land. A bullet flashed past his right shoulder. Perfect aim in the midst of real battle was impossible, but that went both ways. He fired back and succeeded only in making his opponent flinch. They came together hard, both men flexing muscles and slamming foreheads, locking together and rolling to the ground, sand erupting all around them. The team ran hard, skirmishing among the dunes, falling down shallow valleys and then scrambling back to the top. Dips and mounds characterized the ground between them and the valley's rim. A crazy merc let loose an RPG in their direction. The rocket flew between Dahl and Kinimaka, its vapor trail singeing their clothing. Dahl laughed but Kinimaka blanched.

"Come on, man," Dahl said. "That wasn't even close."

"Too close for me. Men weren't meant to ride rockets."

"Not even you?"

"Especially not me."

Dahl bounded up to the individual, separated him from his rocket launcher and then slapped him across the face with one of its grenades. A satisfying crunch signified that the threat was ended. Dahl knew this battle covered too small an area to make RPGs effective so hurled a remaining grenade at his next opponent, causing as much shock as pain. When two more mercs came at him he swung the rocket launcher like a baseball bat at both of them, cracking heads.

Smyth had taken a bullet to the vest, nothing major. Yorgi helped to cover for him until he could focus again. Hayden saw it all, ranging around the periphery. She saw the overall battle—Drake, Alicia, Dahl and Kinimaka cutting through their quarry like a wedge; Smyth and Yorgi picking off stragglers and back-stabbing cowards; the Blackhawks pounding shell after shell into the sand like five hammers of God; the storm now looming only a mile away and growing bigger and bigger, a tornado of sand and debris, stealing the light from the sky like an irresistible thief. The sound of its coming was starting to overpower even the clatter made by the choppers. To her right ran the crumbling ridge and below it the trapped galleon. Mercs even stood atop the wooden deck, firing, probably guessing correctly they would not be fired upon.

Drake used Alicia's bent back to gain momentum for a flying kick, dislocating a merc's jaw. The man collapsed. A boot to the back of the neck ensured he would stay that way. Dahl stumbled down one side of a dune—almost comically at first—but then Drake topped the same rise and saw half a dozen mercs waiting below. Calling Alicia he dived after Dahl, backing up the Swede and crashing into their enemies all at the same time. The tangle fooled him for a split-second—he ended up grabbing Alicia's thigh to the sight of a highly arched eyebrow, then thrust it away and punched a merc right on the nose.

"Get down."

They rolled, they snared other arms and legs. Bullets flew through short spaces. Alicia grunted as one took her in the gut. Its firer jumped on her, expecting an easy finish, but was amazed to find his teeth showering down onto the sand, and then his face planted in the desert up to his ears like a new conifer. Alicia hadn't let the bullet slow her down.

Dahl kicked and Drake fought. With their adversaries finished they tramped back up the slope. Darkness, it seemed, had fallen.

"Shit, this is gonna be bad."

Drake's words were lost as the storm hit. In truth, it didn't fall fully dark. The whirling sand was shot through regularly by patches of sunlight, and the heavy breeze blew it all away. Around them, the general area was still visible. Together they struggled toward the valley's edge.

Hayden watched the choppers come down. Four drifted over the valley with its incredible trapped galleon, firing as they came, soldiers crowded at the doors, preparing rappel lines. Mercs lined up at the valley edge and fired back, bullets flashing and clanging off black metalwork and bulletproof cockpits. Bullets then tore among them - their bodies tumbling down the side of the valley, some smashing into the ship's deck. Sand and blood pursued them in steady streams, some flows staining the whole side of the valley.

All four choppers cleared the mercs and spun to set down in an area at their backs just as the storm swept in. The fifth chopper dived to avoid a missile but not fast enough. The grenade detonated on impact, fire bloomed around the fuselage, and the entire craft bucked. Men leapt free, hitting the sand and rolling. One soldier slipped halfway down the side of the valley, one gloved hand arresting his fall after a hundred feet. Hayden imagined he'd spend the remainder of the battle climbing back to the top. The chopper wasn't so lucky, crashing down in a fireball and tumbling down the cliff, chunks of metal and smoldering ruin bouncing in its wake. The four intact choppers disgorged their occupants, eight fully armed men from each. Gunfire shattered the roar of the oncoming storm.

"Go for the boat!" Hayden heard Drake's voice.

Drake angled toward the barely visible valley edge. Several rolling dunes lay before him. Sand propelled by wind tore at his face, pushing him back. Head down, he almost missed the attack of a merc, but heard the loud panting and twisted his shoulders at just the right time. The merc flew off and tumbled away, hopefully lost underneath the piling sand. His inner radar warned him that he'd been turned around. *Shit, which way is bloody up?* Alicia loomed at his side and took his arm, but Dahl was nowhere to be seen.

Stick with the agreed course.

Drake saw another figure, unmistakably a mercenary dressed in combat fatigues, and fired two head shots. The guy went down. Multiple bursts of gunfire could be heard as the pitch of the storm waxed and waned, the wind blasting and receding and spiraling into the upper skies. Ahead, a huge mass became evident and so did their intentions.

"It's the mercs," came Dahl's calm voice from Drake's side, almost making him cry out in shock. "They're massing."

"What? And for fuck's sake, Dahl, make your presence known next time. I coulda hit you."

The Swede smiled tolerantly. "No," he said. "You couldn't."

"Forget that," Alicia said. "Where's the bloody army?"

"Do I look like a friggin' sand monkey?" Dahl spluttered. "How the hell do I know?"

"Shit, I thought you were better than that, Dahl."

Ignoring the Swede's shocked and unhappy expression, Alicia smirked to herself and moved away. Drake followed her, grinning. The land sloped sharply downhill and then rose back up. The trio moved carefully, eyes slitted, guns at the ready and fully loaded. By Drake's calculations the valley edge could only be forty feet ahead but then he could be wrong. He wondered briefly what had happened to Kinimaka and the others, but knew they had to take care of themselves. The mass ahead solidified and, as the swirling sands briefly parted, revealed dozens of tightly packed mercenaries, all with guns at the ready.

Oh fuck.

Most of them saw the trio and instantly opened fire, raking the air with death. Dahl flung himself headlong, hitting a slope and rolling out of sight. Drake flung himself at Alicia, grabbing her around the waist and registering two bullets slamming into her before they were landing hard and then rolling, rolling, rolling far too fast and for far too long.

It couldn't be the cliff edge. But Alicia was screaming, and it was impossible to stop.

CHAPTER THIRTY EIGHT

Amidst the great storm, Alicia shrieked, a sound most unbefitting of her. Drake held her tightly as they tumbled, refusing to let go and quite possibly lose her forever. End over end, side over side they fell, sand erupting from their every revolution. His embrace was unbreakable and he could feel her cheek pressed tightly to his own. Just as he imagined they might roll that way for eternity they struck bottom and rolled level for a few more revolutions. The world still spun, rotating around and around inside his head. Alicia panted against his cheek. Down here, the fury of the storm had abated somewhat.

Drake rose to his knees, still holding Alicia, and opened his eyes. They had stumbled down the side of a valley, now completely cut off from the fight and faced with a hard slog back to the top. Luckily, he couldn't feel any breakages or even bruising. Some people would pay good money for a trip like that.

The thought reminded him of Alicia. It wasn't like the blond woman to just lie in his arms. Gently, he cupped her face and pushed her head back until he could focus. Alicia's eyes were closed.

"Hey," he said. "You okay?"

He wiped a smudge from her forehead. Alicia's eyes fluttered open. "Matt?"

"Aye love. It's me."

"Are we . . . alive?"

"I bloody hope so. I'd hate for this to be the afterlife."

She pulled away and checked her body. Drake remembered two bullets striking her almost simultaneously and felt his heart suddenly take a great lurch. *Oh no* . . .

Two tattered holes gaped in Alicia's clothing over her new body armor. The blonde grimaced at the sight and then stared at Drake.

"I should be dead."

"I guess we all should be. Ten times over. Maybe someone somewhere just *likes* us."

"Matt." Alicia again used his first name, something unheard of, and more than unnerving. "I should be dead. Long before now. I shouldn't be here."

Drake began to worry that she might have banged her head. "Lean over," he said, struggling to his knees. "Let's take a look."

"What?"

"At your head. I'm not sure your brain's intact."

"All my life I've been running. All my life I've been barely surviving."

Drake met those blinding blue eyes and felt a deep shiver of fear. This wasn't at all right. *Ghosts,* he thought. *Ghosts do exist out here in the desert and they've made her . . . take stock. Pause.*

The world was about to explode.

Alicia struck at him, the punch glancing off his chin. Drake saw stars. "I shouldn't be alive!" she cried. "Don't you see? I *don't want* to be alive!"

Drake threw himself into the very core of it. "Of course you do. You're a good person. You save lives and deserve to live yours. Properly!"

"Fuck you!" Alicia swung at him, two blows, the first a diversion and the second feeling like it took a chunk from his ribs. Drake gasped for air and folded. "No . . ."

Alicia leapt on top of him, her hands around his throat. Instantly she began to squeeze. "You think it's fun being me? Do you? Every decision a bad one. Every new move questionable and tainted."

Drake knew she would kill him. Alicia was imploding and exploding at the same time, running on destructive auto-pilot, and facing the crisis of her life. This was all-out war, the fury of the storm above reflected in the storm exploding within Alicia Myles.

"Move on. Move ahead. Never stop . . . never stop running. That's my creed. That's my motto."

"No," Drake managed to gasp. "Alicia Myles is 'One Life, Live It'. That's you."

"What I pretend it to be! You think I'm living my life or running from it? Don't be a fucking bell end."

Alicia bore down on his throat and Drake saw a deeper, more alarming blackness. His only thought was that she would not stop. She would kick and pound his dead corpse if it came to that until something got worked out. Slamming his hands up he connected with her face and managed to loosen the grip, then inserted a hand beneath hers. He rolled, pressing hard on her body, then rolled back. He squirmed, bent her fingers as hard as he could. Alicia yelped and jumped back. Drake hung his head, panting, barely surviving.

"None of this is your fault, Alicia. Don't you remember? Your dad was a drunk, a fucking weakling who shrank rather than stepping up and taking responsibility for his kids. Your mother didn't fight him. They both failed you. The Army took you away but then it failed you too. Made you keep on running. It's been coming a long time—this reckoning."

"But the memories." For a moment Alicia crouched there like a starving predator, eyes wild. "Nothing calms them, soothes them except the next experience. Nothing keeps them at bay. Moving on is all I have."

"But then they return even worse. You must face them and fight them and then kill them. Like you would any adversary."

Drake threw his body to the side as Alicia pounced again.

His right hand jabbed at her ribs to give her something to think about, maybe to take some of the violent ardor out of her. She sucked it up and gave only a feral grin in return.

"Give me some more of that."

He should have known better.

Alicia kicked sand at him, then flung herself into a flying head-butt straight at his solar-plexus. Drake collapsed again, feeling the energy drain away. Next, a punch drew blood from his gums and snapped his head sideways.

"Stop. Not like this," he gasped.

"What? You want me on top?"

Alicia jumped onto his lap, grabbed both his ears and wrenched them hard. Drake squealed and then threw both of them to the side; the battling duo tumbled together along the bottom of the narrow valley, spitting curses into each other's faces.

Drake couldn't help but think: *It was always going to come to this.*

Alicia halted their tumble, dragged him up by the vest, and threw him past her. Drake yelled in alarm as he smashed into what felt like a solid brick wall.

"Moving on is what it is," Alicia shouted in his face. "But I never move on. Not in here." She jabbed at his forehead. "In here I'm still fifteen and having the shit scared out of me every day. In here I'm always facing a drunk with quick fists and trying to prove that I'm not scared. That's how I am. That's me. How do I get past that?"

She threw a clenched fist at him. Drake dodged and her knuckles struck brick.

"Ow!"

Drake ducked around her, gaining a little space. As he moved he took stock of their surroundings. Above, a small V of sunlight revealed how far away the top of this narrow valley was, before it vanished in the face of the ongoing storm. Sand rained down onto his face, hair and shoulders in a constant shower. All around stood what remained of a small, tumbledown structure, an old gray, brick-built shelter, its walls short and stubby and its roof all but caved in. Drake darted into the ruins, happy to have a wall at his back.

Alicia stalked him, her face twisted with memories, her eyes wild and crazy. Drake was under no illusions that survival meant weathering this particular personal storm.

"Come home, Alicia." He simply spoke the words in his heart. "Stop running."

His words stopped her, brought a smoothness to her features. But terrible memories are like deep wounds, deep loss, they never truly repair, and they struck back now, sending Alicia into even deeper despair. She punched and kicked Drake, exploring his defenses and then getting around them, injuring his knee and smashing a tooth so hard that it fell to the sand—more blood staining the ground. Alicia stared at it as though she were staring her dead father right in the eyes once more—something she had never managed to do.

"This is all we should be," she said in a damaged voice. "Blood and bone, teeth and flesh. Not memory and feeling and opinion. I don't want that."

"Then accept it," Drake said harshly. "You lived it. You lived *through* it. Accept that one of the worst enemies you have ever discovered was your own father. It's better to mold that memory into fire and grist and desire and purpose than to try to ignore it. Better to accept and *live*. Every day."

Alicia looked spent, consumed, but that didn't stop her unleashing a violent attack. She slammed his shoulder against the brick wall at his back. The wall wavered and then collapsed, sending up a plume of mortar. Alicia was on him, bearing down hard amidst the tumbling bricks. They rolled, striking another wall, which also crumpled under their combined weight. They bowled through the rubble. Drake regained his footing, grabbed Alicia and threw her against an outer wall. The entire structure wobbled. Drake then tried to pull her to safety, but she pushed him away.

"C'mon, tough guy," she said harshly. "Fight me if you can."

And then he saw it. Finally, he saw it. Crap, he was slow but she was projecting the memory of her father onto him for the duration of this fight, this explosion, and he was fighting back. Not good. Against all of his instincts he realized he had to let her win.

"You think you're good enough," he said. "Prove it."

She came like a devil, a whirlwind. Fists struck him left and right and on top of the head, jarring his skull bones and bruising his cheeks no end. A knee caught him in the stomach and he was down on his knees. Gripping his shoulders she threw him against the outer wall and it disintegrated all around him, bricks and mortar raining down and bouncing off his shoulders. Still, he knelt there, moaning. Alicia boxed the side of his head, and he collapsed. She stomped at his ribs, making him wheeze. A hand was the only thing holding him up and then she stepped hard on the fingers.

Drake was down among the sand and rubble of the collapsed shelter. Alicia grasped the edges of the last remaining wall, heaved, and pulled it so that it fell on top of him. Blood splashed across his vision. Stars shone like a frenetic Milky Way. Blackness enshrouded all that he knew and saw.

"Die." He heard the familiar voice only a millimeter from his face. "I never got to see you die and I've been running ever since. Are you still in there?"

Drake remained silent and swam with the darkness. Then he felt Alicia pulling him out from under the wreckage.

"You don't die that easily, bastard."

A boot to the groin sent him backward against the sharp slope of the valley where he stayed, barely able to stand.

"Open your eyes."

He felt no surprise to see the pistol leveled at his throat.

"Say your last prayer."

"In the end . . ." he managed to croak. "I want you to take your future by the fucking balls and live it, Alicia. Live it while you still have time."

Her eyes widened, the tangle of lines across her forehead eased. He knew that he had gotten through, but only as the figure of her nightmare vision. He also knew that it wouldn't save his life.

The gunshot filled his brain.

CHAPTER THIRTY NINE

Drake felt blood on his cheek, across his chin. The impact had been close enough to his right ear to render a temporary deafness. As he opened his eyes he saw that Alicia had averted the barrel beyond the very last instant, unable to move it more than a few millimeters. The slug had seared his temple.

"Fuck me."

"Stay there. I'm not done with you yet." Alicia's voice was as hard and lethal as the weapon she held. Drake experienced a sudden bone-deep fear. *Did she just miss?*

He had more work to do. "Inside, you know it's over. Done. You know now that there *is* a way to move on."

That stopped her cold. "There is?" He could see the conflict within her. "Well, maybe. What do you mean?"

"Drake," he said, holding out his arms as best he could. "Matt Drake."

"Wha . . . ?" Alicia focused for the very first time, eyes upon the present rather than encrusted with the past. "What are you saying?"

"You want me to spell it out? Then fight me first."

He took the gamble of his life and came at her slowly, swatting the pistol aside and then ducking so that he could lift her free of the ground. She struggled, but only lightly. The raw fury, along with much of her energy, had been depleted. Drake hefted her, dropped a shoulder and deposited her as gently as possible onto her back, amongst the sand and rubble. Alicia could certainly take it.

"It's time to move on for good. And by that I mean *stop*. No more running, no more looking for the next adventure. It's time to live in the present and embrace all it has to offer."

Alicia sighed, struggling now but barely able to move. Drake sank down onto her legs as she managed to flip over onto her stomach, and a smile broke free through the blood and grime that coated his face.

"Now we live our lives," he said. "We live them together. You don't forget your past, Alicia, you accept that it happened and build a better future."

Alicia struggled, but gently. Drake finally laughed and reached forward. He tapped out a rock tune on her ass and thighs to help lighten the mood. Alicia managed to lift her head.

"Quit that."

"Why? It is turning you on?"

"No. I can't guess the bloody tune."

Drake enjoyed himself some more. "*Smoke on the Water*, silly."

"I think I'd prefer *Paranoid*. More rhythm."

"Oh? Well, we'll try that later." Drake turned serious and climbed off, careful to completely ignore all the hurts that ransacked his body. Still wary, he eyed his oldest friend.

"Still wanna kill me?"

Alicia too pulled herself up, breathing carefully to restore strength and equilibrium. "Maybe later."

"Have we resolved anything here?"

Alicia allowed herself a smile. "Obviously, it's not quite that easy. It's gonna be a long hard road. But I had to do this, Drake. I *had* to. It's a start. Do you understand?"

He did. "Been a long time coming," he said. "But it's pure Alicia Myles. You were self-destructing the other way and you knew it. I'm happy you chose me to . . . help."

"Who else could it be?"

"Russo?" he said. "Beauregard?"

"Russo's a good man," she admitted. "A solid man. I could

have chosen him and, if he survived, we'd be better than ever. But Beau? Nah, he's just a goal. Every woman deserves twelve inches at least once in her life."

Drake winced. "Please don't ever say that again. It hurts more than the broken tooth."

"You know something." Alicia cocked her head. "I know we have a battle to get back to. A tough motherfucker, if I'm being totally honest, but for the first time in almost twenty years I feel like I'm not going to die soon."

Drake eyed the slope that would take them back to harm's way and hoped she hadn't just jinxed their future. "First of all," he said. "Let's see if we can get outta this hole. Here . . ." He held out a blood-streaked hand.

Alicia Myles took it.

CHAPTER FORTY

Lauren Fox watched the battle unfold from atop a small sand dune to the east of the valley that held the long lost galleon. She used field-glasses to keep up with the action, saw the onslaught of the helicopters and the SPEAR team's breakneck run around the valley's crumbling ridge. She saw the fifth chopper come down, the fireballs that surrounded it, and the pitched battle between army, marines and mercs. The point where Drake joined.

And then the sand hit. The storm swirled all around and consumed her entire world.

Jenny lay at her side. "Now that's a bitch."

Lauren stared. "Who's watching Bell?"

"Karin. Why? Don't you trust her?"

"Karin's . . . delicate." Lauren hated herself for the choice of words. If anyone referred to *her* as delicate she'd do a great job of making them eat their teeth. "We shouldn't leave her alone."

"Well, that dude, Bell, he's no threat. A fried chicken could take him out."

Lauren took a last look around, then dipped her eyes against a flurry of sand particles. Quickly, she slithered back down the slope, a matter of only six feet. The Pythian, Nicholas Bell, sat with his head in his hands, obviously wishing he were anyplace but here. Lauren, still harboring a soft spot for the wealthy builder, walked over to him.

"You did the right thing," she said. "Trust me. It will work out."

Bell regarded her with a strained smile. "Just stay with me," he said. "Without you, I'm not sure I can do this."

Lauren hid a grimace, worried now what Smyth would

think. The soldier had been wonderful to her, everything a real man should be. Maybe they would even try dating when they found a little downtime. But Smyth—like any man—was a fragile piece of kit and prone to jealousy. Smyth also knew that Bell had bedded Lauren as Nightshade not so long ago.

Shit. What a mess.

She walked over to Karin. "The world's a mess up there, a battleground. I don't see what else we can do."

Karin managed a weak smile. "We wait. Our friends will come back. Don't they always?"

Lauren heard the bitter tones inherent in Karin's words. She walked away, unsure how she could help. As she approached Jenny she saw the other woman stiffen.

"Behind you."

Then a deep voice: "Don't fucking move a muscle."

Lauren turned anyway, inbuilt instinct always defiant. Two mercenaries stood facing them, wearing black and toting the usual machine pistols. Both men looked tired.

"That Bell?" one of them asked the other.

"Yeah." The other consulted a tattered photograph. "Thank fuck. We've been searching for your ass for twenty hours, dude."

Nicholas Bell looked like a rabbit caught in the spotlight. "Searching? What do you mean?"

Lauren realized that these men hadn't been sent out recently and might not know about the huge extent of the battle above. They had been out searching for the lost Pythian, it seemed.

The second mercenary waved his weapon at Bell. "We're here to rescue you, dumbass. They kidnapped you, right? Well, they sent the best out to save you."

His partner tapped him on the shoulder. "Probably not wise to call one of the bosses a dumbass, dumbass."

The first merc shrugged. "Sorry, boss."

Bell gaped between them. "You're the best? And how . . . how did you find me?"

"What, ya think the big boss don't have a tracker on you? Ha! And when I say *on* you I do mean *in* you. Get it? Probably artificially extended your sleep one night and made a doc perform a small op. Ever wake up feeling extra sluggish? No reason why? Maybe feel hungover even though you only had one glass of wine? The government does it all the time, so they say. Happens regular."

"Shit," Bell, Karin and Jenny said together.

"Yeah." The man shrugged. "Every time I wake with a weird feeling I hop on over to the bathroom and check every inch of my body. Just in case." He grinned.

Jenny shared a look with Lauren. "Yuck."

The man hardened. "Well, Bell? Get over here then, or do ya like hangin' with the dead girlies?"

"Dead girlies?" the other asked.

Girlies? Lauren bristled and she knew Jenny felt the same.

"Shoot 'em, bud. And, Troy, follow fucking orders like yer s'posed to."

Isolated, unguarded, Karin, Lauren and Jenny all knew they were fending for themselves. They were not soldiers, or warriors. They weren't even trained. But they had certainly seen action and could guess how the next few minutes would play out.

Karin acted first, perhaps thinking about her future at Fort Bragg. She darted from a sitting position, surprising Troy and making him stagger away. Lauren came next, stiff-arming Troy as she came across him, jerking his head sideways. Jenny was closest to the leader and jumped behind Bell for a split second before ducking around his other side. The leader tried to track her with his gun but the weapon was too large. Jenny was on him in a second, grappling, gritting her teeth and panting hard.

Lauren kicked at knee, groin and stomach, remembering her civilian martial arts training. The soldier looked surprised, even staggered a little when she blasted his knee. Karin tried the same from the other side, giving him an awful lot to think about. His weapon wavered between them.

Lauren picked up a rock and slammed it across his temple, wincing as she did so. Troy stumbled, his gun discharging. He threw all his weight onto her but she smashed the rock down again. Karin punched his arm until the gun clattered away, then gave him multiple blows to the face. Troy spat blood and punched blindly, trying to regain the advantage. A fist connected with Lauren's nose, making her eyes water. She gasped, trying to fend even more blows away. Karin caught one of Troy's wrists in her hand, held it, and then slammed a rock straight down onto the knuckles. A sickening crack resounded around the clearing.

Troy screamed. Karin brought the rock down again even harder. "You were going to shoot us," she said. "This is what you deserve."

Lauren knelt with her knee across the man's throat until he passed out, then they scrambled back.

Three feet away, the leader held onto his gun as Jenny tried to twist it away. She held her feet, stood her ground, but needed both hands to counter his strength. He wrenched viciously once, twice, and she staggered away, tripping as her right heel smacked against a hidden rock. Shocked at herself, she tumbled headlong to the ground, ending up on her front and then frantically twisting her body sideways.

The leader smiled. He took a moment to check his weapon and then point the short barrel at her, catching her gaze as he did so.

"Not quite up to it, hey girly. Now lie there for a minute. Perfect."

Jenny threw the heavy rock she had tumbled over and

watched it fly straight and true, striking him a glancing blow on the forehead. The leader cursed and wiped away blood. Jenny was up on her feet, head down; the knowledge that this was a fight to the death written clearly all over her face. She ran hard, legs pumping.

She was always going to be too late, but that didn't dampen her willpower.

The leader brought his gun up once more, finger itching on the trigger. He squeezed.

Then Bell slammed into him, crying out, bearing him to the ground. The shot flew high into the air. Jenny bounded after them, slipping around Bell and elbowing the leader so hard his eyes rolled. Twice more, and he was finished.

Jenny took his rifle. Lauren stood a few feet away with the other. They both looked at Bell.

"Any ideas where this tracker is hidden?" Jenny asked. "I mean, thanks for the help and all, but we really should cut that bad boy out."

Bell stared at Lauren. "There was one day," he said. "No, two days. Oh, shit, it's either in my shoulder or my upper front thigh or my back. They all hurt now and again. Your choice."

Jenny smiled with grim determination. "Don't you worry," she said with a lilt to her voice. "We'll find that sucker if it kill us."

The knives came out.

CHAPTER FORTY ONE

Drake and Alicia finally gained the top of the slope to find themselves inside a churning world of spitting sand and debris. As one they knelt and surveyed what they could of the nightmare scene.

From here, the gaggle of mercenaries could be seen still guarding the area around the cliff edge where the galleon sat below. Together, they huddled, rifles pointed from their dark bulk, a deadly final stand. Bodies littered the area all around them.

Drake saw many prone soldiers, some not moving, others just biding their time. The battle had hit a stalemate, it seemed, as mercenaries blindly carried out their orders to protect the galleon at all costs. Drake and Alicia crawled through the eddying sand dunes until they saw a bulk they recognized.

"Dahl."

The big Swede turned his head. "Where the hell have you two been?"

"Shagging," Drake said bluntly. "Why are you pinned down like this?"

"Oh, because we sent out for pizza and it's bloody late. Why the hell do you think?"

Drake studied the land ahead. It was almost completely flat. "This as close as you can get?"

"Yup."

Kinimaka shuffled over. "Man, I think there's a way over to the side. You see the ridge—" he pointed east, where the edge ran away. "We could hug the underside."

Hayden nodded. "Yorgi agrees. It's possible."

Drake allowed the smile to sweep across his face. The team was back. "Then what are we waiting for? Let's do it."

Careful not to bring attention to his aches and pains and the blood that coated his face, he crabbed away from the area and into the sand wall. Dahl was already regarding him weirdly, but that wasn't exactly unusual. Alicia stayed close. Once the team had moved far enough east they headed back toward the ridge, out of sight of the mercenaries. Yorgi stepped ahead and paused at the brink of the valley.

They came up to stand all around him, gazing down. "That's a bitch of a long way down," Smyth growled softly. "One misstep and you're rolling forever."

"Not forever," Alicia said. "Believe me."

Drake sent his questing gaze to the right where the galleon still jutted from the cliff face. The deck was dusted now with several deposits of sand and the mercenaries defending it all looked bored. Most of them weren't even staring up anymore, for their own good, they simply sat on the deck. The fury of the storm could not reach them but flurries of sand still rained down.

Yorgi indicated the bit of ridge that curled underneath the top part, a narrow horizontal mound, incomplete in three areas. It had been formed by piles of sand drifting over the top and collecting underneath, dangerous but for the most part offering some nice concealment.

Kinimaka grunted. "Not as big as it looks."

Hayden nudged him. "You can always stay behind."

"Mahalo, but that ain't happening and you know it."

Drake watched Yorgi fall to his knees and curl into the narrow channel before following suit. Alicia and then the others dropped inside. Slowly, the team crawled under the ridge toward the band of mercenaries, sheltered from the storm and prying eyes, clinging to the malleable side wall and hoping the sand didn't collapse beneath them.

"Well, if we go," Hayden said. "We all go together."

"I can live with that," Dahl said.

"Depends on who lands on top of you," Alicia shot back. "I'm baggsying Yorgi—the boy/girl/man."

"It is disrespectful." Yorgi stopped, turned and faced her. "To call me such."

"And *baggsying?*" Dahl asked. "What is that?"

"Keep going," Drake said. "Alicia's sorry, Yorgi. She can't help herself and thinks you can easily pass for all three. Dahl, baggsying means to unofficially reserve something for yourself."

In short order the crowd of mercenaries became visible and all talk ceased. Pot shots were being taken by the military but the stalemate was still in force. Walls of sand still howled from horizon to horizon. Yorgi slowed to less than a crawl.

Close enough, Drake signaled. *Ready?*

They were and action was called for. Drake and Alicia rose as one, hulking ghosts in the center of the storm, surrounded by roiling sand spouts, and threw grenades into the mercenary mass. Men reared away from the apparition, shocked into self-preservation. Dahl towered behind them and Kinimaka behind him, and more grenades were tossed.

Then the ghosts threw themselves flat on the floor.

Explosions louder than the blasting storm rocked the area, making the ground shake beneath their bodies. Screams started up a split second later. Drake was up and running from a standing start like a sprinter, hitting two surviving mercs before they knew what was happening. One fell with a broken neck, the other struggled and then went down with a shot to the face. Dahl passed him and then the others, all engaging the mercenary mass in close combat battle. Alicia grappled with one man on the very edge of the cliff, the pair locking fingers and swaying from side to side. Both tried to use the other's weight against them, both tried judo throws, but to no avail. Drake saw Alicia wilt a little—the battles today had taken so much out of her—and ran over to help, but by the time he arrived Alicia had broken her opponent's grip and booted him down the slope. They watched as he bounced twice and then struck the deck of the ship, splintering wooden planks.

"Shiver me timbers," Drake said.

"Don't be a knob." Alicia shook her head, spun and engaged the next opponent.

Another grenade went off toward the back of the group. Bodies spun and flew away, some disappearing down the slope, others falling to the piled sand. Even rocks flew through the air, and the remains of stunted trees, the debris striking indiscriminately. Kinimaka lurched as he was hit by the remains of a bush, the prickly stalk latching onto the side of his head.

"Shit!"

Hayden pulled it away, wincing. Blood leaked from half a dozen small wounds. The Hawaiian forgot about it and returned to battle. Hayden emptied her Glock and then reloaded, happy to see their own soldiers joining the fray. Flurries of sand sprayed her face. Indeterminate piles made a hazard of her footing, and even they remained in motion, always drifting. Sunshine pierced the murk intermittently and often—a startling kaleidoscope of color that confused the brain. Hayden saw a soldier go down, and moved on the merc who'd clashed with him. He batted her away with a metal plated arm which she felt all the way to her toes. Both the fallen soldier and Hayden fired on the guy at the same time, sending him spinning off the cliff, then helped each other up.

They nodded, comrades in arms.

Drake faced a huge brute with a loaded RPG resting across one shoulder. In the blink of an eye he tackled the man around the waist, but the grenade went off as they fell, shooting straight up into the sky. Drake panicked. *Straight up, straight down!* He rolled off, ready to shout a warning, but the rocket fell and detonated off to the south, a conflagration that sent flames, sand and chunks of bark and rock flashing around the battleground. More than one man went down. Drake's own world was then blotted out by the panoramic vision that rose before it.

That's gonna hurt. Again.

The massive merc dropped down onto his chest, knees first, clearly enjoying himself by the split-lipped grin that marred his otherwise ugly face. Drake bore it, experiencing hurt upon hurt and bruise upon bruise and wondering just how many weeks or months it might take him to recover. The merc enjoyed himself too much, grinding with his knees and leaving the rest of his body wide open. Drake sat straight up, chopped to the throat, nose and eye sockets, leaving him choking and blinded. A hammer-like fist swung at Drake's head, which he caught between his thighs as he rose, twisted and broke. The merc groaned into the sand.

All around the enemy was devastated, giving up. Dahl stood at the edge of the valley as, quite suddenly, the storm began to abate. Sunlight shone through the sand and the wind levels took a slight drop. The Swede stared down at the waiting galleon with hungry eyes—an alpha predator eyeing up its next happy meal.

Drake joined him. "The count?"

"On deck? No more than eight. Below deck—no idea."

"So what the hell are we waiting for?"

Drake played to the Swede's mad side even as Hayden shouted at them to wait, to be prudent.

"Oh, I see." Dahl's grin was infectious as he understood. "It's that time again."

"Be careful!" Hayden cried. "No!"

Dahl threw himself over the edge feet first, Drake a split

225

second after. Alicia shouted, *"For Kevin Bacon!"* and launched herself after them. Kinimaka stepped up eagerly but Hayden whacked him back. Smyth would have none of it, ignoring her frown and leaping into mid-air, his face breaking out into a rare grin.

Drake and Dahl raced down the sandy slope, picking up speed as they went. Sand furrowed from either side of their boots as they slid. The slope was sharp enough so that they caught air-time, bouncing back to earth with groans. The landscape flashed past at inconceivable speed. Drake concentrated as much on edging out Dahl as where he was going. The galleon's deck grew large beneath them, a wide, unstable landing pad. An overhang sent them several feet into the air, eliciting cheers and allowing Dahl an extra moment to calmly extract his handgun from its holster. They crashed back down and were then hitting the ship's deck and its pliant timbers, rolling to lose momentum. Drake slammed right into the ship's far railing, heart stuck firmly in mouth. Dahl snagged a mercenary and used him as a piton. Alicia bowled them both over.

Smyth landed perfectly, feet first, and shot two mercs on impact. Another drew a bead on him. There was no time, not even to duck. Then the merc shot backward, hit by a bullet fired from above and Smyth thanked his lucky stars for the unknown backup.

Alicia hammered at the merc Dahl had used to stay his fall, but in the end Dahl simply rose, picked him up and threw him over the rail. Drake fired at the four remaining mercs, forcing them into hiding. One of them came sprinting around a bulkhead and launched his body straight at Alicia. She held the force of his momentum though, fighting back. Together, atop the ship's deck and close to the rails they traded blows, two warriors battling over a drop that could send them two hundred feet straight down. On the edge they punched and blocked and stepped. Alicia caught a kick on her thigh, deflected a heavy blow, and stepped inside. Her opponent stumbled, swung again. She evaded it and then hit as hard as she could, his solar plexus taking the brunt. Her blows were so hard, so packed with force and power that he flew straight against the rails and then crashed right through, screaming as he tumbled to his death.

Beneath them the ship's deck groaned, the entire side trembling. It was entirely possible that this buried ship could split in half and take them all with it. But this was no time to dwell on the mind-blowing discovery they had made nor its final incredible location. Drake saw a head pop up from below and gave it a side-vent. There were other routes down to the lower decks. Dahl crept around a bulkhead whilst Smyth stole in the other direction. Bullets slammed off molded woodwork close to their heads.

"Careful!" Drake shouted. "Don't want to upset the ghosts now, do we?"

A man rose, bellowing back. Alicia's bullet took him down. Drake kept a careful eye, but then it happened. The moment that beggared belief.

Looping up from the galleon's stern, high and proud, came a black hand grenade, its thrower chuckling even as he lobbed it. A true madman then, a courter of death. Drake dropped his gun as the grenade came down, trusting Alicia to cover his sudden desperate sprint out into the open, then flung himself headlong, hand outstretched in imitation of a fielder trying to catch a ball. The grenade came down, spinning, about to strike deck when Drake's hand slid underneath it, closed around it and then flung it over the nearest rail. Even then it exploded almost immediately, the force of its blast taking a chunk out of the cliff side and sending shattered wood spinning around like spears. Dahl and Smyth stormed the stern as Drake lay breathing hard, his energy spent for a moment.

Alicia crawled over. "You okay? Nice fielding, Ian."

"Ian?"

"Botham."

"Ian Botham was a bowler and a batter." Drake knew little about the game of cricket. "I think a goalkeeping reference would be more appropriate."

"Bollocks to your sports and, for that matter, your cars. I have no time for either of them."

"Yeah, and that's gonna have to change too."

Alicia's eyebrows shot up. "Oh, is it?"

"Yep. Taking you and Dahl on a track day as soon as we've brushed this bloody battle off and showered."

Alicia looked prepared to argue, but Dahl and Smyth came rushing up. "Job done," Smyth said. "What's next?"

Drake gazed around. "Below decks," he said. "Where the real ghosts of this entire adventure lie."

"Gold," Smyth said. "You mean gold."

"Do I?"

Smyth and Dahl watched two entrances to the galleon's innards as Drake and Alicia searched for another. The obvious ones were probably on the side buried into the cliff wall, but Alicia soon found a third. By that time those above had unfurled a rope ladder that almost touched the deck. Soon, Kinimaka stepped gingerly down as if expecting his clumsiness to fatally dislodge the ship from its ancient resting place.

Dahl grunted. "Careful there," he said. "Might have to jump the last two feet."

"I did try to follow you guys," Kinimaka moaned.

"You four!" Hayden's voice rasped through the quieting day. "Did you really think sliding down the hillside on top of your enemies was a great idea?"

Dahl blinked. "I didn't really think. Besides, Drake made me do it."

Hayden huffed in exasperation, before getting over it and

reviewing the ship's deck. "And the best way in is . . . ?"

Alicia pointed toward the stern. "There's a ladder. It's one person at a time but the mercs haven't found it."

"Good. They clearly located this one first and decided to blast it open." Hayden seemed pleased.

Smyth kept his gun leveled at the shattered trapdoor until more soldiers joined him. Then a deal was offered to those mercenaries still inside. Drake thought it was a pretty sweet deal; after all most of their buddies were already roasting in Hades by now and their boss had betrayed them. Who even knew where Tyler Webb was? To a man, the mercenaries climbed out of the hole, hands above their heads, and cowed. Soldiers rounded them up. Even then, Hayden reminded the team that booby traps and even snipers could have been left behind. The next few minutes weren't going to be easy.

"Let me go first." Kinimaka headed for the hole. "You guys did it last time."

Hayden backed him up, then Drake and Dahl, Alicia and Smyth. Yorgi stayed on the ship's deck, eyeing the slope above as though he wished he'd ridden it as hard as the SPEAR team rebels.

Drake kept his handgun handy as the team slipped through the hole in the galleon's deck. As far as he could make out—and exhausting his limited knowledge of old galleons—they were somewhere around where the mizzenmast would have been, in front of the captain's cabin and officer's quarters. Most of the stern was still buried in the steep dune's sandy face and below him he assumed would be the gun deck, supplies and stores and the ballast deck. The opening that he lowered himself through was tight though he heard no complaint from the big Hawaiian, probably because Hayden followed so close. The wooden steps descended at a thirty degree angle and were quite sturdy, though treacherous with sand. Alicia slipped behind him and grabbed his jacket for support, cursing.

"Steady," Drake said. "I already lost a tooth today."

"You did? Oh, sweetie. I hope you properly punished the nasty person who did it."

"Later," Drake promised. "Later."

Wide wooden planks formed the floor of the gun deck. Kinimaka and Hayden were the first to break out flashlights, swinging the beams around. Progress was slow due to them having to constantly check for traps, but Drake soon found himself immersed in this lost, long-buried world. Here was a dusty cannon with dull scrapes along its sides and runnels beneath its wheeled undercarriage, sand-filled now but once in deadly, perfect order. Rectangular crates stood in several corners, some destroyed but others intact and awaiting discovery. Drake spied some wooden slats running across a far wall that reminded him of bars and imagined that might be the ship's brig. Absolute silence filled the area like a spectral shroud as the group stopped and took stock.

"One more level," Kinimaka said. "Down to the hold, I think. That's where all the stores are, the biscuit and salted meat, the water, beer, gunpowder, cannonballs and spare sails. It's also where pirates kept their treasure during a voyage."

Drake urged him ahead, spinning as a slight sigh reached his ears. Alicia was nowhere near him but he was sure it had been a woman's sigh. Dahl shot him a testy look.

"What now? Hearing things? One too many knocks on the head?"

Drake frowned. "Just thought I—"

His flashlight beam illuminated a bleached skull that lay on the floor. Eyeless sockets stared back at him. So the dead were watching after all. He shivered. "C'mon."

Dahl grunted. Alicia moved past both of them. Smyth, bringing up the rear, swore as he stepped on a pile of bones. "Sorry," he said quietly. "I *do* have respect for the dead."

Drake stepped after Hayden, then abruptly ran into her

back. Kinimaka's voice drifted from several steps ahead. "Um, guys. There's a funny noise down here."

Drake listened. The Hawaiian stood poised to descend another set of steps down to the next level. With no noise either above or to their sides, the team couldn't shake a feeling of isolation, of otherworldliness, but set their senses to listen. For a long moment there was nothing.

"You imagined it," Hayden said.

Then a low whine broke the silence, ascending to a wail as it rose up the stairs. The pitch of the cry set Drake's nerves on edge and made the hairs on the backs of his arms rise.

"What the hell *is* that?" Smyth asked.

"Dunno," Alicia said. "But I ain't wearing the right kinda protective vest for it."

"The wind," Hayden said. "It's just the wind."

"Are you sure?" Drake asked. "There are no windows down there."

"Well what else could it be? You believe in ghosts now?"

"Only when I'm investigating a ghost ship that's been lost for hundreds of years and still holds the bones of its crew below deck. Maybe the galleon wants a new crew."

Hayden nodded to the bulging wall that ran to their right. "And see there? Gun ports and countless imperfections in the ship, all leading to the two-hundred-foot deep valley."

Drake shrugged. "Mano," he said. "After you."

The Hawaiian gulped a little, but to his credit barely hesitated. The rest of the new ship's crew filed after. Slowly, they descended into a deeper darkness. Drake felt the breeze immediately blowing in from the right. The wail became a shriek for several seconds before dying away to a desperate moan. Something tapped him on the shoulder.

"Fuck!" he yelled, making Kinimaka jump in the process.

Dahl coughed innocently. "You okay?"

Smyth also coughed, but in an intentionally grumpy

manner. "Hurry it up down there. We just fought and beat hundreds of stone-cold killers and you pussies are scared of a couple of ghosts. Ain't this the hold?"

Drake swung his flashlight around, seeing that it was. Toward the far end the team's joined beams illuminated eight sturdy crates, all banded around with heavy metal and constructed of thick planks of wood.

"The treasure of Santa Ana." Hayden sighed. "We found it. We stopped Webb and hindered the Pythians again. It will be the end for them."

"Don't bet on it," Dahl said.

"Oh, I will," Hayden returned. "Because now we have Nicholas Bell too and I'm so fucking sick of being stalked and watched in my own bedroom that I'm gonna spend however long it takes to bring Webb to heel. My heel. That's what I'm gonna do."

"I'm not even sure they have any members left," Drake said lightly as they strolled toward the treasure chests. "Maybe Beauregard would know."

Alicia stopped in her tracks. "Good point. We don't even know where he is."

"Don't worry, we'll find him," Hayden managed a smile. "Missing anything in particular?"

Alicia tried desperately not to throw a guilty look toward Drake and succeeded . . . mostly. "Umm, nah. I'm over that stage now."

Hayden regarded her closely. "You do look a little different."

"I do?"

"Maybe. Lighter somehow. Maybe it's the gloom."

"Why, thanks."

Before the eight chests they stopped, questers eyeing well-earned prizes. More skulls and other bone fragments lay scattered about between the chests and Drake even saw what looked like the head of a tomahawk.

"From one battle to another," he said. "It never ends."

Kinimaka sat cross-legged before one of the chests. "Well, they ain't going anywhere," he said. "And we can't open them easily. I think it's time to take a break."

The team sat around him, flashlights illuminating each other and the darker spaces. Down here, among the riches and the ghosts and the sand they all felt a sense of peace. Only the outside world brought danger.

"From Odin to the ghost ships," Drake remarked. "It's been a helluva rough ride."

"But not without some merriment," Dahl said.

"And the best camaraderie," Hayden added.

"The making of the best team in the world," Smyth said. "And more than a few hard farewells."

"A new family," Kinimaka began. "Who—"

"For fuck's sake," Alicia hissed. "Are we all gonna kiss now? I'll tell you one thing that's gonna be changed tomorrow—me."

"I knew it." Hayden smiled.

"But not too much." Alicia winked. "Still gotta keep you wankers in line."

"Are we done here?" Smyth asked.

Drake unhooked his backpack and pulled out a bottle of rum. "Y'know," he said. "The world can wait. I think we're just getting started."

CHAPTER FORTY TWO

Drake passed around the rum, smiling as the whole team swigged it straight from the bottle. The pirate ship with its vast treasure groaned and moaned around them, its timbers expanding, its decks scoured by desert squalls. When his turn came the liquid burned a fiery path to his stomach and instantly put the world in better perspective.

"To fallen comrades," he said and passed it around again.

Whilst he waited, Dahl turned toward him. "Have you heard anything from Mai?"

"As much as I expected to," Drake murmured, but shook his head at the same time. "Grace is in hospital, fighting hard. She's a battler that one and she will survive."

"I have faith in Mai as much as anyone I have ever met," the Swede said. "She will return."

"I don't doubt it." Drake swigged again as the rum returned, now half empty. Sighing, he rested his weary back against a treasure chest. The bruises that marred his torso would be turning purple by now. The empty tooth socket ached. But none of that mattered.

"To the future," he said. "To beating Webb and any other idiot daft enough to take us on."

Hayden accepted the bottle with a bow of her head. "Speaking of that," she drank deeply before continuing. "The latest intel on Ramses and that terrorist arms bazaar is quite promising. It's imminent. Any day now. The NSA are working on a location."

Smyth cleared his throat. "At least give us chance to wash the desert's dust off."

"Webb will be there," Hayden responded. "Beauregard said so. And if that pans out, I don't care if it's tomorrow morning, we will be there too."

Alicia took a double swig. "Shit, woman, chill out."

"You ever wake up with a stranger staring down at you in bed?" Hayden flung back, but then—at the look that crossed Alicia's face—had to laugh. "No, no, don't answer that."

"It will never happen to you again," Drake said as Kinimaka laid a huge hand over his girlfriend's. "No more splitting up for this team. From here on in, what we do we do together."

"As good as that sounds," Hayden smiled, "it might not be entirely practical."

"Clearly." Dahl huffed slightly. "Nobody shares my bed except my wife, pal."

Drake looked exasperated. "Oh aye! That's *clearly* what I meant—"

"I did promise Crouch one more treasure hunt," Alicia said, handing the bottle to Yorgi. "But if this arms bazaar is as big as you say—we could gain an awful lot of scalps there."

"Exactly."

"You and your treasure hunts." It was Dahl's turn to take a sip of the rapidly dwindling liquid. "Always running."

Alicia plucked the bottle from his hands before his lips reached the neck and finished it off. "Not anymore," she said simply. "I'm not saying the road ahead isn't going to be hard—more like hell with me—but I'm going nowhere fast anymore."

"I hope so." Dahl nodded and looked at Drake. "Got any more o' that good grog, matey?"

Drake laughed, shaking his head. "Next time you try fighting whilst protecting a liter plastic bottle of rum in your backpack."

Hayden held up a hand. "To craziness." She held up an imaginary glass. "And all the things we have done."

Drake saluted, his mind flicking back past the Odin and

Blood King escapades to Babylon and the madness in DC. He lingered over the Pandora event where they had teamed up with a talented trio of ex-CIA agents called the Disavowed—Trent, Silk, Radford and now Collins were a force to be reckoned with and no less zany than Drake's own team. He hoped one day to team up again.

Quickly, he told them all about Karin and her request. The words were met with solemn appraisal and a blanket acceptance. Fort Bragg certainly wouldn't damage Karin and, chances were, it could help. The conversation reminded them all that Karin, Lauren, Jenny and Nicholas Bell were still out there.

Drake shifted, groaning. "I guess we should be heading out."

"One more minute," Alicia said softly. "I like this."

The team settled again, wounds and bruises aching, but even behind the grimaces hidden smiles formed. There was no greater team than the one that fought for each other, played for each other and died for each other.

"Whilst we're talking," Hayden then said, "and nicely isolated here—" the old galleon moaned and grunted around them, scoured by sudden breezes, eddies of sand blasting through the deck in mini-tornadoes; the great, heavy treasure chests complaining with age and the surrounding timbers belligerent and burdened, "—I believe we need to investigate Robert Price."

Dahl shifted uncomfortably. "The Secretary of Defense. You mentioned something like this before. Has he disobeyed one of your orders?"

"Very funny. No, I first heard it from General Stone. Remember him? He alluded to Price being dirty when he had no reason to. I just think . . . there's something off about him, and we should be careful. We have too much at risk."

Drake didn't need to question her. "Whatever you say."

"We ain't sending Lauren in this time," Smyth barked. "Not after the last shitstorm."

Drake cocked his head. "Is that the real reason?"

"Sure it is!"

"I heard she was sweet over Nicholas Bell."

"Fuck Bell. He's going to jail."

Drake refrained from ribbing the snappish soldier beyond his limits. Bell might actually be set loose if he could help them arrest Webb. He studied Alicia who sat relaxed at his side. Her blond hair had fallen across an eye and one cheek was all squashed up as she rested her head against a crate.

"You ready?"

Alicia considered the team sat around her. "One extra minute," she said. "Just one. There's no rush."

THE END

Please read on for more information on the future of the Matt Drake world

Here ends the current adventure but fear not! There's much more to come. I'm often asked/told never to end the Matt Drake series and always reply the same way—no end in sight yet! Plans are already afoot for the next three adventures, The Last Bazaar, The Edge of Armageddon, and one more, which will follow a very different style, and all *hopefully* be released in 2016, along with Alicia 3, again heading in a different direction. One of the Drakes might slip to 2017, we'll see. I even have a fresh idea for a stand-alone Torsten Dahl novel! Out of interest I am also toying with the idea of a Drake/Myles origin novel (set in the nineties it would begin their story within a larger adventure). Good idea or not? Let me know. Beyond that look out for regular signed paperback giveaways on my Facebook page.

As always, e-mails are welcomed and replied to within a few days. If you have any questions please drop me a line.

Join my Facebook page to take part in giveaways and see regular updates

https://www.facebook.com/davidleadbeaternovels

Check my website for all the latest news and updates—

www.davidleadbeater.com

And remember:
Reviews are everything to an author and essential to the future of the Matt Drake, Alicia Myles and other series. Please consider leaving even a few lines at Amazon, it will make all the difference.

Printed in Great Britain
by Amazon